MYRIAD

A collection of Stories and Poems

By

Ernest Barrett

ISBN-13: 978-1507650066
ISBN-10: 150765006X

To the African children who are starving and in need of help.

My poem 'Help Africa' says it all.

E Barrett

CONTENTS

ACKNOWLEDGMENTS

To Pilgrim Hospital for the sterling work they do in the face of reducing funds.

Deadly Vacation

1

The sun was just hoisting itself above the hills that surrounded the quiet, sleepy village of Old Bolingbroke as Inspector Robert Laxton carried his heavy suitcase to his car. Placing it on the ground, he took out his key and opened the boot lid, then, exerting himself, he hoisted the suitcase up and dropped it in the boot. He gave a loud 'whew' from the effort, as he banged the boot lid down. Horatio, his cat was meowing and circling round his feet as he turned to get into the car. Laxton had a smile on his face as he bent down and stroked him. Annie, his cleaner and general dogsbody was also fussing around him, making sure he hadn't forgotten anything.

'Come on in Horatio. We don't want you to get

run over,' she said with a chuckle as she bent down, picked the cat up and took him into the cottage. He meowed in protest as she closed the door on him, then she turned and looked up at the six-foot-three detective. 'I think that's just about everything now Mr Laxton,' she assured him smilingly.

'Thank you Annie,' he rejoined. In a soft voice, he told her, 'Keep your eye on the cottage for me while I'm gone.'

She nodded her head, her slightly greying hair falling over her round face as she reached for her bicycle which was leaning on the cottage wall. 'Don't you worry Mr Laxton, I'll watch over things here,' she assured him. As she leaned on the handlebars, she added, 'You just relax and enjoy your holiday.'

Reaching up, she pushed her hair back from over her eyes before giving him a farewell wave; climbing on her bike, she pedalled out of the driveway and on to the lane, her somewhat generous rump going up and down as she stood on the pedals. Laxton smiled inwardly as he watched her disappear from sight. He gave a deep sigh. 'What would I do without her?' he muttered to himself for the umpteenth time, shaking his head slowly from side to side as he reached out and opened the car door.

After a quick, last glance around the property, as if to assure himself that everything was in order, he climbed into his car and slowly drove out of the driveway and on to the narrow lane that ran through the village of Old Bolingbroke. Douglas, one of his neighbours, had his back to him as he walked his dog, a black Labrador, down the centre of the lane. Laxton tooted him. He stopped, looked over his shoulder and pulled the dog to the side of the lane as the car went slowly by. Douglas, a big, well-built seventy-year-old who lived in a cottage on the other side of the small village, had a broad smile on his face, as he raised his hand in acknowledgment. Laxton returned his wave, before putting his foot down on the accelerator.

The car picked up speed as he passed the ruins of Bolingbroke Castle and climbed the tree-lined steep hill on his way to the main road. A few minutes later, a contented smile on his face, he was wending his way through the beautiful Wold countryside that surrounded the picturesque village, on his way to Lincoln, where he was to catch the train at Lincoln railway station. Raising his wrist, he gave a quick glance at his watch, the car swerving slightly as he did so. It was nine fifteen a.m. His train left at around ten forty-five. He gave an almost imperceptible grunt of satisfaction, as he told himself that would give him plenty of time to drop his car off at the police headquarters car park and make the fifteen minute walk to the railway station. He had decided that he would leave his car behind and take the train to Scotland, where he had booked a two-week holiday. After driving the car every day for the rest of the year, he thought the train would make a welcome change to his usual mode of travel.

Around a quarter of an hour of steady driving had gone by, when he reached out and switched the radio on. The haunting song 'Some Enchanted Evening, sung by Dean Martin, emanated from the radio and drifted round the car. He could feel the warmth of the rising sun as it climbed over the tree tops. He felt at peace with the world as he hummed along with the popular song.

The cows in the fields on both sides of the winding lane looked up as the noise of the car engine broke into their silent world as it sped past. Giving the vehicle a seemingly perfunctory glance, they went back to chewing the lush grass, as he continued on his way through the open countryside and on to the main highway. After negotiating a busy Horncastle, Laxton settled down to concentrate on his driving. Another half an hour went by and the traffic was beginning to build up. The 'Three Sisters' of Lincoln Cathedral could be seen in the distance, just coming into view, as they jutted up into the clear blue morning sky. The road was becoming quite busy as he entered the outskirts of the city. The ten o'clock news was just coming on; he reached out and switched off the radio so that he could keep his mind on driving amidst the heavy traffic. Ten minutes later he slowed down as he carefully manoeuvred the vehicle into the headquarters car park. After stopping the car, he checked his watch; it was almost quarter past ten. Giving a nod of satisfaction, he switched off the ignition and climbed out of the car. W.P.C. Hyam, a wide smile on her face, waved to him through the office window as he opened the boot and took out his case, he grinned and waved back. After lowering the boot lid, he walked over to the office window and handed the car keys to the attractive young policewoman, requesting her, 'Keep your eye on the old girl while I'm gone Jane.'

'Don't worry, it will be safe there,' she assured him with nod of her head. Smiling his thanks, he turned away, heavy case in his hand as he strode out of the car park and made his way to Lincoln railway station. On arrival, he approached a porter and told him his destination; he was directed to the appropriate platform and told to change at Grantham. There were just four others waiting as he placed his case on the floor and stood watching as the train approached in the distance. A few minutes later it drew into the platform amid a cloud of steam and diesel fumes, then with a judder and a grind of brakes, it stopped. Laxton, reaching out, opened the carriage door and climbed on to the train. After walking the length of the carriage he came across what he was looking for, an empty compartment. Giving an inward smile of satisfaction, he slid the compartment door back and stepped inside; with some effort, he heaved his case up on to the luggage rack. After unbuttoning his jacket, he sat down.

Taking a deep breath, he stretched his long legs out in front of him and relaxed, leaning back on the comfortable seat of the Lincoln to Grantham train. There was a loud grinding noise as it pulled slowly out of the station, gradually picking up speed as it made its way through the built up area and out into the open countryside. Laxton looked out over the panoramic view of the fields through half-closed eyes, as the sound of the train's wheels shattered the silence of the Lincolnshire Wolds with a 'rat-a-tat-tat', as it monotonously wended its way through the rolling countryside, swaying from side to side almost rocking him to sleep, like a baby in a cradle. An hour or so later it pulled in at Grantham, where he was to change trains. Reluctantly, he got to his feet and yawned out loud, as he stretched his arms out wide before reaching up and taking his case down from the rack.

Sliding open the compartment door, he disembarked to the sound of a monotone voice making an announcement over the loud speaker, informing the commuters which trains were due and of the platforms that they would be arriving on. After making a few enquiries Laxton was directed by a porter to the appropriate platform, where, some twenty minutes later, among a considerable number of other like-minded commuters, he boarded the busy Kings Cross to Edinburgh train.

Detective Inspector Robert Laxton was on a two-week holiday, his police work forgotten. He had made his mind up that he was going to relax and enjoy, what was to be, his first holiday in Scotland. Checking the compartments, he came across one with an elderly couple in it. They were sitting by the window. They glanced up at him as he struggled through the door with his case; hoisting it on to the rack, he sat down and made himself comfortable on the seat just inside the door. Running his fingers through his wiry iron-grey hair, he gave a deep sigh as he rested the back of his head in the palms of his hands and leaned back as the train drew out of the station and gathered speed. The grey-haired elderly couple, who were sat on the opposite side of the compartment, nodded their heads and smiled politely, before going back to reading their morning newspapers. Laxton glanced across the compartment and looked out of the window, over the open countryside as it flashed by. He had a contented expression on his lean face as he closed his eyes, crossed his legs and stretched his long frame out across the compartment and dozed off. Suddenly the peaceful spell was rudely interrupted as a loud voice called out, 'Nottingham.'

The elderly couple, who had put away their newspapers, were on their feet in readiness to leave the train. After a farewell nod to Laxton from the old man and a smile from his lady, they squeezed past his legs in readiness to disembark.

Laxton returned the nod with a slight smile on his face as the couple went out of the compartment, sliding the door shut behind them, leaving him alone. He settled back in his seat as the train drew into the station. Glancing out of the window, he could see that there were crowds of commuters standing around, waiting to board the train as it drew into the station platform. There was a loud screech of metal on metal as the brakes were applied and it ground to a halt. Doors banged open as the commuters climbed noisily on to the train. It was just beginning to pull out of the station, when the well-worn compartment door noisily slid open, interrupting his reverie.

'Excuse me,' a female voice snapped impatiently.

Laxton looked up. An attractive blonde woman pushed her shapely legs against his bony knees as she struggled to get by him to take a seat on the opposite side of the compartment. Her hands were full as she backed into the compartment carrying a large case in one hand and two smaller bags in the other, one of the bags falling out of her hand on to the floor as she squeezed past.

Wiping the disappointed look from his face, he quickly withdrew his outstretched legs, making room for her to get past him. He gave her a somewhat stilted apology as he sat back in his seat.

'I hope you didn't expect to have the compartment

to yourself did you?' the woman remarked, a look of annoyance on her face as she noticed his expression.

'Err no,' replied the tall man as he leaned over and picked up the bag from the floor that she had dropped, adding lamely with a shrug of his shoulders, 'I was just relaxing.'

Suddenly the train jerked forward as it started to move off, causing her to momentarily lose her balance and fall against him, almost sitting on his knees as she struggled to lift her large case onto the rack above her head. She let go of it as she attempted to stay on her feet. The case fell onto the seat opposite them as she sprawled across him, trying, in vain, to prevent her skirt riding up and displaying her stocking tops and shapely legs.

Laxton reached out and grabbed her shoulders, steadying the somewhat red-faced woman, with his big hands, before quickly jumping to his feet. 'Let me help you?' he offered, as he leaned over and took hold of the large case. Hoisting it up, he placed it on the rack above her seat.

She turned towards him and looked up into his eyes, her rather attractive features losing their sternness, as they softened visibly. 'Thank you,' she gushed, a pleasant smile on her face, adding to her attractiveness, as she pushed back a few fronds of blonde hair that had fallen over her face and sat down in the seat on the opposite side to him. Laxton gave a smile and nodded his head as he opened his newspaper that he had bought whilst on the station platform.

A few seconds later a man followed her into the compartment, swaying perceptibly from side to side, as he slid the door shut behind him, before sitting down clumsily beside her. He looked to be in his thirties.

'I'm shorry my dear!' he exclaimed drunkenly, as he bumped into her.

He's obviously had one or two drinks too many, Laxton thought to himself, as he weighed up the heavily built, bleary-eyed, younger man, who had flopped down in the seat beside the woman, his thick mop of black hair falling over his forehead.

The woman wrinkled her nose in distaste at the strong smell of stale whisky emanating from the man. She shuffled along the seat away from him, giving him a sidelong glance as she did so, her blue eyes icy.

'Where are you going hen?' the man asked her in a strong Scottish accent, as he shuffled a little closer to her.

'I don't know as it's any of your business, but I'm going to Edinburgh,' she answered tartly, with a toss of her blonde hair.

'Don't be like that my dear, I'm only trying to be friendly,' the man, his tanned face wreathed in a broad drunken smile, told her as he placed his hand on her arm and moved closer, his voice a little slurred.

Laxton, who had been taking this all in, leaned over towards the man and tapped him on the knee with his finger. 'You heard the lady, leave her alone,' he snapped, his eyes narrowing as he folded his newspaper.

'You keep your nose out,' growled the six-foot Scot, as he stood up menacingly, swaying from side to side, his chin stuck out belligerently. 'It's got nothing to do with you.'

'I said *leave her alone*,' repeated Laxton, a steely tone in his voice as he looked up from his seated position at the big man.

The Scot, who by this time was losing control of his temper, reached out for Laxton who was still seated. Swaying to one side, he avoided the strong hands that attempted to grab his lapels. Simultaneously the Scot's head went back, intending to butt the seated man in the face with his forehead. But Laxton was ready for him, delivering a short jab with the tightly folded newspaper to the drunken man's solar plexus, a trick he'd learned during his time in the police force, as a constable, when he was on the beat. His adversary stopped as if paralysed, grabbing his midriff, his brown eyes widening as he fell to the floor gasping for air, then he passed out.

Laxton got to his feet, then, grunting with the effort, he lifted the big man back on to his seat; after undoing his collar, he made him comfortable. The woman held out her hand and thanked him.

'My name is Lila, er, Lila Blankly,' she told him, holding out a well-manicured hand. There was a concerned expression on her face as she looked at the heavily breathing Scot, who was beginning to fall over. 'Will he be all right?' she asked anxiously.

'I'm Robert Laxton,' he answered, shaking the small hand. Then reaching over to the younger man, he moved him along the seat and leaned him against the window to steady him, before assuring her, 'Yes he'll be okay although he may have a bit of a headache when he wakes up.'

The compartment went quiet, except for the snoring Scot and the rat-a-tat of the train as it ate up the miles. Laxton turned his attention to the open countryside as it flashed by.

Lila Blankly raised an eyebrow as she looked across the compartment at the casually dressed, tall man. She took in his strong jaw line and his greying wiry hair, giving him a distinguished look. *Quite handsome in a mature way*, she thought to herself. 'Are you visiting Scotland on business?' she asked him conversationally, as he relaxed back into his seat and continued looking out of the window.

Laxton, a smile on his face, turned and looked across at her, shaking his head. He didn't want to disclose the fact that he was in the police force. 'No I'm on vacation,' he told her in a quiet voice. 'I'm staying at the Mactavish Hotel in Dalmally. It's a small village in Strathorchy, a bus is picking passengers up at Edinburgh.'

'Well, what a coincidence, so am I,' remarked the blonde-haired woman. She had a pleased expression on her face as she pushed her blonde hair back from over her forehead and looked into his eyes.

Lila, a thirty-two-year-old attractive woman, looked across at the man opposite her with interest, again taking in his ruggedly handsome features. She'd decided to take a holiday in Scotland following traumatic divorce proceedings, after living apart from her ex-husband for over two years. She'd moved in with her mother who lived in a council house in Beeston, Nottingham. She and her former husband had been buying a semi-detached house in Gedling, a suburb of Nottingham, until she'd found out that he had been having an affair with another woman. There was a blazing row.

'Get out!' she'd screamed at him. 'And don't come back.'

He stormed out of the house, telling her she wouldn't be seeing him again. After he'd gone she discovered that he'd spent all their savings. 'Obviously on women and gambling,' she told herself. The amazing thing was, she'd had no knowledge of his activities, until a neighbour informed her of his infidelity. Thankfully they didn't have any children.

She sold the house and settled up with him, although, as the judge presiding over the court proceedings had said, 'He doesn't deserve a penny.'

After moving in with her mother (her father had passed away three years earlier after a massive heart attack), she got herself a job at the local supermarket and settled down, promising herself that there wouldn't be another man in her life.

'Lila,' her mother had told her, after she hadn't been out of the house for nearly six months, 'you carried a torch for that no-good husband of yours for too long. It's time you started to enjoy your life.'

That was when she had decided to take a holiday in Scotland.

In the meantime the Scotsman, who had been reclining in the corner seat where Laxton had placed him, was beginning to come round. His eyes were closed as he shook his head slowly from side to side and massaged his solar plexus. He didn't look well as he ran his fingers through his black unruly hair, then, without a word, he got to his feet and staggered towards the compartment door, sliding it open he made his way along the passageway. He didn't return, leaving Robert Laxton alone with the blonde woman. After a pleasant few hours' chit-chat, in which she told him she was a divorcee and that she came from Gedling near Nottingham, the train arrived in Edinburgh. Laxton reached up and took his and Lila's cases down from the rack before following her out of the compartment and on to the platform. A coach, parked outside the station, was waiting to take them to Dalmally.

'Are you married?' she asked him as they disembarked from the train and headed for the coach. Laxton, carrying Lila's case, shook his head, but said nothing. She thanked him as he handed the driver the cases to store in the luggage compartment, then they climbed aboard and took their allotted seats. He frowned as he saw the big Scot climbing on to the coach just as it was about to leave. It looked as though he was going to the same destination.

On arrival at the hotel, which was situated in a picturesque position by the side of Loch Awe, they were all shown to their respective rooms. Laxton locked the door of the comfortable well-furnished room behind him, before throwing his case on to the large double bed. A few minutes later he undressed and took a shower. He felt good as he vigorously rubbed himself down with the towel. Fastening the towel round his waist, he walked over to the window and looked out over the open countryside in front of the Loch to the distant mountains on the far side; he gave a deep sigh at the majestic sight in front of him. 'I'm really going to enjoy this holiday,' he murmured to himself, with some conviction.

After getting dressed, he went down to the large dining room for the evening meal, where he was directed to a table. He was just running his eyes over the menu that the waiter had handed to him, when a delighted Lila was shown to the seat on the opposite side of the table. 'I feel fate is taking a hand,' she gushed, as she settled herself down and looked across at him, her blue eyes sparkling.

Robert Laxton raised his eyebrows as he looked up from the menu that he was reading and smiled at her in return, his eyes taking in the good-looking, shapely woman in front of him. He dragged his eyes away from the low-cut dress, that didn't look adequate enough to contain her shapely breasts, as he reached across the table and poured out a glass of dinner wine from the bottle that he had ordered. 'Would you like a glass of wine?' he asked her, still holding the bottle out as the waiter arrived with the starter.

She nodded her head in reply. He poured the drink for her then raised his glass. 'To an enjoyable holiday,' he pronounced as their glasses clinked together.

After finishing his meal, he excused himself and made his way out of the dining room to the long bar where he ordered a whisky and soda. Leaning his elbow on the bar, he cast his eyes around the large room and dance floor. A stage had been set up at one end of the hall for the band who were just beginning to settle themselves in. A sign over the bar indicated that the star turn was to be a comedian. Half an hour went by and the tables around the dance floor filled; the band struck up with a lively quick step.

'A pint of bitter please?' The deep voice with a strong Scottish accent echoed along the bar above the sound of the music.

Laxton turned his head, the voice sounded familiar. Looking sideways, over his shoulder, he saw that it belonged to the man he'd had trouble with on the train. The big Scot, his black, tousled hair hanging over his brow, returned the look, paid for his beer and approached him. Laxton braced himself. The man held out his hand, it was as steady as a rock; it was obvious that he was sober.

'I'd like to tell you that I'm sorry for the way I behaved on the train. It was totally oot of order!' he exclaimed apologetically in a pronounced Scottish accent. 'I'm afraid I'd had too much to drink on an empty stomach.'

Laxton reached out and shook the proffered hand, nodding approvingly as he saw the look of sincerity in the younger man's brown eyes. 'That's okay,' he told him, accepting his apology. 'I hope I wasn't too rough on you.'

The younger man shuffled his feet embarrassingly, as he looked down at the floor. 'I got what I deserved,' he grunted, rubbing his still tender stomach. 'My name is James Mc'Linney. Will ye have a drink with me?'

Three drinks later the Scot had told Laxton all about himself. He told him that he came from Edinburgh where he lived with his parents, and had been visiting relatives in Nottingham. At the moment he was nearing the end of one month's leave from his job.

'I work on the oil rigs. I often stay here at the

weekends when I'm working,' he declared, raising his voice a little, over the loud music that was coming from the band.

Laxton, his head back, was just tipping his glass to empty it, when, from behind him a female voice whispered in his ear. 'Aren't you going to ask me to dance Robert?'

He turned round, a surprised look on his face. It was Lila, a little worse for drink. He looked into her big blue eyes for a few seconds, then with a smile breaking out on his face he slid off the high stool. 'May I have this dance?' he requested, with an over-emphasised bow.

She giggled and moved into his arms, to be swept away, a little clumsily, onto the dance floor. After a couple of dances he returned to his preferred position at the bar; dancing wasn't his forte. Lila went laughingly on her way. After they had played a few more dances, the band retired and a comedian took over the stage, dressed in a kilt and sporting a long ginger beard, which was obviously false. After a half an hour or so of listening to a few corny jokes had gone by, Laxton finished his drink and yawned loudly, as he stretched his arms out wide. He turned to Mc'Linney.

'I'm tired,' he muttered, rubbing his eyes. 'I think I'll call it a night,' he told him, as he moved away from the bar to leave. He paused for a moment as Lila, on the arm of a heavily built man, unsteadily made her way towards him, and introduced her companion.

'Robert, this is William,' she slurred.

The man half smiled and proffered his hand.

Laxton looked the man in the eyes as he reached out and grasped the hand. He didn't like the limp grip and the way the man shiftily looked away. He turned to Lila Blankly. 'I'm off to bed, it's been a tiring day,' remarked Laxton, looking at her as he spoke, 'and if I were you I'd do the same,' he advised her.

'It's such a lovely night, I think I'll take a breath of fresh air before I turn in,' she told him. There was an enticing look in her eyes as she spoke. 'I don't suppose you'd like to join me?'

He raised his lip in a lopsided grin as he shook his head, refusing her obvious advances.

The man who had been dancing with Lila excused himself, stating that he was going to the toilet. Laxton followed her out of the room. She stopped for a moment before turning to leave him to go outside the hotel. 'Goodnight Robert,' she whispered seductively as he turned to go to his room.

He paused for a few seconds and looked over his shoulder at her, giving her a sideways glance. Then, after bidding her, 'Goodnight,' he carried on walking, smiling to himself as he left the bar and made his way to his room. 'She's quite a woman, is Lila,' he muttered to himself, as he put the key in the lock and opened his apartment door.

Lila Blankly walked out of the hotel and stood on the top step for a moment as she took a deep breath of the night air. It was a really balmy evening. The full moon lit up the lake and the surrounding mountains. Making her way carefully down the steps that were situated outside the entrance to the hotel, she walked languidly across the spacious car park, that was bordered by a colourful array of flowers, the air was scented by the flowering gorse bushes as she exited the car park and walked on to the road that ran along the front of the hotel. Strolling across the road she stepped on to the narrow footpath that was bordered by a low stone wall, she looked out over the fields, to where she could see the moonlight glistening on the river that ran into Loch Awe. What she didn't see was the shadowy figure that silently crept up behind her. She gave a stifled scream as a hand covered her mouth, lifting her bodily over the low stone wall. There was a five-foot drop on the other side of the wall. He threw her on to the grass below. Her attacker, who was wearing an improvised balaclava, leaned over her. She clawed at him with her long fingernails as she felt his hand reaching under her dress.

'Take your hands off me you filthy beast,' she gasped as she struggled against the strength of her attacker.

Kicking out with her feet and clawing at him, she made a desperate attempt to free herself; he drew back suddenly, his hand on the open neck of his shirt.

'You bitch!' he snarled, blood running down his chest from a deep scratch.

'Keep away from me, don't touch me!' Lila shrieked as she attempted to get to her feet; her scream was cut short by a savage blow to her head which knocked her unconscious.

Her assailant, overcome by lust, looked down at the helpless woman. Unfastening his belt he lowered himself down on to the prostrate body. A few minutes later he rolled off, breathing heavily. The balaclava he wore for disguise was soaked in sweat as he pulled it back to cool off, uncovering the bottom half of his face.

'I know who you are,' a voice blurted out. 'You're…'

The man looked down at her. She had regained consciousness. He grabbed her by the throat and squeezed hard, choking off the remainder of the sentence. 'You'll tell no one,' he hissed in a strong Scottish accent. 'Do you hear me?'

There was no reply as he eased his grip. The stricken woman's face was blue, her eyes staring lifelessly into the night. Suddenly the enormity of his cruel act came home to him.

'What have I done?' he asked himself as he got to his feet and ran his fingers through his thick black hair. 'It had all been so easy before.'

He straightened up, breathing heavily as he looked over the wall and glanced along the road. In the suffused street lights he could just make out, in the distance, a young couple with their arms around each other, who were strolling down the footpath towards him, oblivious to anything but each other. Swiftly, he dragged the body of the woman out of sight under the edge of the wall, then, crouching down in the dark shadows, he waited until the couple had walked past. After a few minutes had gone by he looked over the wall and checked the road again, seeing that it was clear, he clambered over the wall and quickly made his way back to the hotel.

2

Elsie and Norman Balton were up early; they had decided they would take a walk after breakfast. After a good wash and shave, Norman looked in the mirror and ran his hand over his almost bald head (a few well-groomed hairs were plastered to his scalp).

'Ee lass, just come and look at the beautiful view from here,' said Norman in a broad Yorkshire accent, as he walked out of the bathroom and stood in front of the wide window, lifting his thick leather belt over his paunch and fastening it.

Elsie, who had just finished running a comb through her greying hair and putting a little make-up on her face, joined her husband at the window, and looked out over the calm waters of Loch Awe; the reflections off the water of the sun just peeping over the mountains were really something to behold. 'It's lovely Norm,' she agreed as she took in the restful panoramic view, a happy smile on her face as she pulled at his arm, telling him, 'come on dear, we'll be late for breakfast if we don't get a move on, we've got plenty of time to admire the scenery while we are out walking.'

'Okay lass,' replied Norman as he turned away from the window. Taking his jacket from out of the wardrobe, he put it on. He stopped for a moment and took in the luxurious furnishings of their holiday flat.

'A bit different from what we've got at home in our Barnsley terraced house,' he told himself, as he energetically gave his arthritic knee a good rub, before following his wife Elsie out of the door.

Taking the lift down to the ground floor, the elderly couple made their way to the dining room. As they were about to go in Norman glanced out of the large glass double entrance doors that were situated at the end of the spacious entrance hall, at the distant mountains.

'Do you know what Elsie? I just fancy a drop of fresh air before we go in for breakfast.'

Elsie shrugged her shoulders resignedly. 'All right Norman,' she told him, adding, 'just for a few minutes then.'

With this, they walked to the hotel entrance and stepped outside; they stood for a moment and took a deep breath of the cool, fresh, Highland air.

The seventy-two-year-old couple were on two weeks holiday, it was their fiftieth wedding anniversary. Their son Raymond had handed them an envelope containing two tickets, a couple of weeks earlier when he had come to visit them, telling them, 'Mum and Dad I want you to have a nice holiday in Scotland, to celebrate your golden wedding. I've booked you in at the Mactavish Hotel in Dalmally for two weeks. Now go and enjoy yourselves.'

Walking out of the pleasant grounds of the hotel, they crossed the road to the footpath. Norman looked out over the low wall that lined the path, to Loch Awe and the distant mountains. The sun was just beginning to break through the mist that hung over the vast stretch of water. He took a deep breath and drank in the tranquil scene.

'It fair takes yer breath away,' he told her, lifting his cap and running the palm of his hand over his bald head.

'Oh my god,' gasped Elsie. She grasped her husband's arm, her other hand to her mouth as she looked down at the field below the wall.

Norman turned to her as he put his cap back on, a frown wrinkling his forehead when he saw the look of horror on her face. 'What's up lass?' he enquired.

'Look,' she gasped her eyes wide as she pointed below the wall. 'Down there on the grass.'

Her husband's eyes followed the direction of her finger. He leaned over and looked down at the base of the wall. His brow furrowed as he spotted the object of her curiosity. 'Good grief,' he uttered as he saw the crumpled body of a woman lying there.

'Do you think she's all right?' asked Elsie, a note of concern in her voice.

Norman, who'd seen many a dead body during his time as a fireman in the Barnsley Fire Service, didn't answer. But he feared the worst as he lowered himself down the wall with some difficulty towards the grass below.

'Be careful Norman,' advised Elsie worriedly, knowing how unsteady he was on his feet.

Norman ignored her and jumped the last eighteen inches, stumbled and landed on his backside on the wet grass, his cap landing beside him. Getting unsteadily to his feet, he placed his cap back on his head and glanced up at her sheepishly as he brushed the dew from his trousers. Bending over the prostrate body of the woman, he reached down and checked her pulse. Shaking his head from side to side, he looked up at his wife, a sombre expression on his round face. 'You'd better get across to the hotel straight away Elsie, and call the police,' he called up to her, adding almost as an afterthought, 'I reckon she's dead.'

His wife ran across the road as fast as her rheumy hips would carry her. Half an hour later the area was swarming with police, paramedics and forensics. Norman was questioned by the police. After giving them his name and telling them as much as he could, he was told, 'Leave it with us now sir we may want to have a word with you later.'

With this he joined his wife and went back into the hotel for breakfast.

The sun was already streaming through the window as Laxton finished dressing. He opened the window wide and looked out over the Loch, to where the sun had risen over the mountain tops, and was reflecting off the placid water. Breathing deeply, he filled his lungs with the fresh country air.

'It's going to be a fine day,' he told himself as he turned to go down for breakfast. Taking his seat at one of the tables in the large dining room, he ordered his breakfast. After fifteen minutes had gone by he checked his watch. He had almost finished his meal and Lila hadn't come down. 'She must have made quite a night of it,' he smilingly told himself as he finished his coffee. He was just about to get to his feet, when two policemen approached him.

'Mr Robert Laxton?' one of the men enquired.

'Yes,' he replied, an inquisitive expression in his eyes. 'What can I do for you?'

'We've been informed that you are acquainted with a woman named Lila Blankly.'

'Yes I am slightly acquainted, why do you ask?' countered Laxton, questioningly.

The two men told him that they had been told to contact him.

'What's the problem?' he asked them concernedly. 'Has Miss Blankly been hurt?'

'Were you with her last night?' one of the officers enquired, there was a serious look on his face as he ignored Laxton's question.

'Yes I was,' he answered. 'Has she been hurt?' he repeated, a worried tone to his voice.

'Can you accompany us to the police station sir? You'll find out when we get there,' was the sharp reply.

There was a puzzled expression on Laxton's face, as he took in the presence of the ambulance, police and paramedics that were gathered on the opposite side of the road.

'What's going on?' he enquired as he followed them out of the hotel to a parked police car.

The twenty mile journey through the rugged countryside was completed in unbroken silence. On arrival at the police station in Callander, he was taken to an office where he was asked to take a seat; a police sergeant named Macullock sporting a thick mop of unruly black hair and a droopy moustache came into the office, took a seat behind a desk and prepared to question him. Before he could speak, Laxton butted in and revealed to him that he was a member of the police force in Lincoln and that he was an inspector.

'Have you any identification on you?' asked the sergeant, plucking at his moustache for a few seconds as he looked across the desk at him.

Laxton shrugged his shoulders. 'No I'm afraid not,' he replied a little apologetically with a shake of his head, before going on to tell him, 'You can give my boss a ring, he'll soon verify it.'

'We'll look into that,' Macullock told him after being given the phone number of the Lincoln office by Laxton. Turning to one of his subordinates, he instructed him to verify the inspector's statement, then, leaning back in his chair and clasping his big hands on his rather plump paunch, he turned his attention back to Laxton. 'First of all I'd like to ask you a few questions,' he intoned, his eyes never leaving the inspector's face.

'Fire away Sergeant, I'll help you as much as I can,' Laxton replied, his brow furrowed as he attempted to work out what was going on. By all the activity, he could see that whatever it was, it was certainly serious.

After persistent questioning the sergeant accepted his explanation of his movements the previous night. At that moment the constable returned and placed a sheet of paper on the desk. The sergeant picked it up and ran his eyes over it, then picked up the phone and dialled a number, his piercing brown eyes never leaving Laxton's face as he spoke into the receiver. 'Yes sir, no sir. Okay I'll do that sir,' he grunted, giving Laxton a long look as he put the phone down.

'That was Chief Inspector Wilberton,' he explained. 'He's verified your statement sir,' stated Macullock in a more conciliatory tone, as he leaned forward and placed his elbows on the desk in front of him. 'He says that you could be of some assistance to us.'

'Now then Sergeant, can you tell me what this is all about?' asked Laxton, leaning back in his chair and folding his arms.

There was a pause as the sergeant looked down at his interlocked fingers for a few seconds, then he raised his eyebrows and looked the inspector straight in the eyes. 'A Miss Lila Blankly has been murdered,' was his stark reply.

'Murdered?' repeated Laxton in disbelief, a shocked expression on his face as he sat bolt upright in his chair.

'As far as we know she was strangled and may have been sexually assaulted sometime last night,' rejoined the sergeant. 'Her body was discovered this morning, in a field opposite the Mactavish Hotel, by an elderly couple who are staying there. They were out for an early morning walk.' He paused for a moment before going on to tell the inspector, 'It seems as though she'd been out there all night.'

At that moment the phone rang, he turned away from Laxton and reached out for it; after a short conversation, he replaced the phone, his brow deeply furrowed; he paused for a couple of seconds, before turning his attention back to the inspector. 'The body has been taken to Stirling. The coroner is performing a post-mortem on Monday,' he informed Laxton.

Rubbing his chin with the back of his clenched fist for a few moments, deep in thought, Laxton asked him, 'Have you had any other similar incidents happen?'

'Hold on a minute, I'll check the records,' replied Macullock, as he pushed his chair back.

Reaching into a drawer in the desk in front of him, he drew out a large incident book. Laying it on the desk, he opened it and ran his finger down the pages. 'Ah!' he exclaimed after a few seconds of concentration. 'Here we are. Rape, rape, attempted rape, rape.' He paused, his eyes, following his finger, continued down the list of offences. 'Here's another rape and an attempted rape, and of course, the latest incident.'

He looked up as Laxton got out of his chair and moved round the desk, to his side, leaning over his shoulder to check the list himself. 'Four rapes and two attempted rapes in the last three months, and that's not including the one this week.' Laxton mused, as he ran his eyes down the list. 'I assume all these victims of the rapist have given detailed accounts of the attacks on them.'

Macullock nodded in assent. Reaching into the drawer again, he took out a number of signed statements and handed them to the inspector. Running his eyes over them carefully, Laxton reached into his pocket; taking out a notebook, he wrote down a few details, before he informed the sergeant that it was time for him to leave.

'I'll get Constable Maclean to take you back to your

hotel in Dalmally, Inspector,' the sergeant told him.

He shouted to a young man in uniform who was sat at a desk at the rear of the office. 'Take this gentleman back to the hotel, Hamish.'

The young man nodded his head, before getting up out of his seat and walking over to them.

Robert Laxton placed the note book back in his pocket. After thanking the sergeant for enlightening him, he followed the constable out of the police station to the car. A few minutes later he was on his way back to the hotel. He was deep in thought, as the car wended its way along the winding road on its way to the Mactavish Hotel. On arrival, he climbed out of the car, thanked the constable and went straight up to his room. Closing the door behind him, he kicked off his shoes and poured himself a shot. After tossing it straight back, he gave a shudder, as the fiery drink hit the back of his throat, then he stretched out on the bed, on his back, with his hands clasped under the back of his neck, his thoughts concentrating on Lila and her murder. Faces from the night before flashed through his mind as he attempted to match one of them to the killer. He shook his head in frustration.

'It's no good,' he muttered out loud to himself. 'The killer could be a complete stranger.'

He massaged the back of his neck to ease the tension.

'It could be anyone,' he grunted. Sitting up, he made a decision. 'Today is Sunday,' he told himself. Tomorrow he would go to Stirling and see what the post mortem turned up.

It was a solemn-looking Laxton that went into the

bar after the evening meal, when he'd sat at the dining table opposite Lila's empty chair. He hardly ate anything as he pictured her smiling across the table at him. Getting to his feet he went over to the bar and ordered a whisky. A lone pianist struck up with a catchy tune, as he leaned on the bar on one elbow and downed a couple of the strong drinks. A few minutes later Mc'Linney approached him. 'I'm sorry to hear about the young woman being attacked and killed last night,' he intoned.

Laxton looked at him over the rim of his glass, as he tossed back a third drink. 'Yeah,' he growled, with a shake of his head, as he placed the empty glass on the bar. 'It was quite a shock when I heard about it.'

'Are you having another drink with me?' Mc'Linney offered.

He smiled grimly as he shook his head. 'No Jimmy, I've had enough – thanks anyway,' he replied, holding up his hand, adding, as he turned away from the bar, 'I'm having an early night.'

With this, he walked out of the large room just as the pianist struck up with a quick step. He closed the glass door behind him, shutting out the lively tune as he went up to his room. After taking a shower, he donned his pyjamas and climbed into bed. He was out as soon as his head hit the pillow.

The next morning he was down in the dining room early. Twenty minutes later, after he finished his breakfast, he hired a car from the hotel and set off on the twenty mile or so journey along the winding road through the scenic, mountainous countryside to Stirling, the rugged beauty of it all barely registering itself with him as his mind went over the recent events. On arrival, he made his way to where the post-mortem was being performed. He introduced himself to a young nurse, who took him to the cold, uninviting room and introduced him to the pathologist who was writing at a desk. He looked up at the inspector and nodded, telling him his name was Charles Collard. He got up from behind the desk and went over to where the naked body of Lila Blankly was laid out on a large table covered by a sheet. Laxton's eyes narrowed as Collard pulled back the sheet from her face. He had a deep frown on his forehead as he looked down on her. He shook his head from side to side as he took a deep breath and exhaled slowly. It was hard to believe that the lifeless figure in front of him had been such a vibrant being only two days ago.

'Well Inspector what can I do for you?' asked the grey-haired bespectacled man who had picked up a scalpel and steadied himself in readiness to begin the examination of the body.

'When was the time of death?' enquired Laxton in a quiet tone of voice.

The pathologist paused for a moment, the scalpel hovering some two inches from the body. 'I would estimate, between ten o'clock and twelve o'clock on Saturday night,' was the reply as he made an incision. He gave a slight shrug of his shoulders. 'Give or take.'

Robert Laxton, his eyes half closed, stroked his chin slowly with the palm of his hand, as he cast his mind back to that fateful night. 'That's strange,' he muttered, his brow furrowed. 'I was with her until ten-thirty. As I left her she told me she was going outside for breath of fresh air.'

At that moment the door opened. A distinguished-looking man in uniform walked into the room, Collard introduced him with a wave of the now bloodied scalpel. 'This is Superintendent Hughes,' he muttered in a low voice, as he returned to his messy activity.

The superintendent turned to Robert Laxton. 'And you are?'

'Inspector Laxton, sir.'

After explaining that he was on vacation, he went on to tell him of his connection with the dead woman. The superintendent turned his attention to the pathologist as he was about to make another incision. 'What have we got here then Charlie?'

'Female, strangled, probably raped,' returned Charlie, looking at Hughes over the top of his thick-rimmed glasses.

'What do you mean by probably?' enquired Laxton.

'Well there are signs of sexual activity, but no evidence.'

'You mean…?' The sentence went unfinished as Hughes butted in.

'He used a condom.'

The pathologist nodded in agreement before adding, in a matter-of-fact tone of voice, 'The same as all the others.'

Taking his hat off and scratching the back of his balding head, the tall, lean superintendent turned his attention to Laxton. 'We've been having a hell of a job catching up with this serial rapist,' he admitted with a shake of his head, telling him, 'and now it looks as though he's become a murderer.'

'Are the attacks all local?' asked Laxton, dragging his eyes away from body.

'Well you could say that they are, they're all within a twenty mile radius,' returned Hughes as he placed his hat back on his head.

The inspector, deep in thought, tugged on his earlobe for a couple of seconds, then spoke up. 'From what you say, it has to be someone residing or working in the area,' he surmised.

'Ah, now what have we got here?' muttered Charlie, holding up his scalpel, which he'd just used to scrape under the deceased's fingernails. He placed it under the microscope. The two officers leaned over to get a closer look. A small piece of tissue was being magnified. 'Our killer may not have got away with it this time!' exclaimed Collard triumphantly as he placed the tissue in a plastic bag, ready for it to be sent away for analysis. 'He might have left some evidence.'

Hughes and Laxton exchanged meaningful glances.

'If that's what I think it is, we're probably looking for someone with deep scratches,' Laxton suggested. With this the two officers thanked the pathologist and turned to leave.

'I'd like to have a word with you before you return to Dalmally,' confided Hughes as they walked to the car park. Laxton followed the superintendent to his car and sat in the passenger seat beside him, listening intently as he spoke. Hughes paused for a moment before asking him, 'Have you told anyone at the hotel that you are a member of the police force?'

Laxton chewed on his bottom lip for a couple of seconds as he cast his mind back. 'No I haven't,' he replied, shaking his head.

The superintendent sat quietly for a moment, stroking his thin moustache with his forefinger and thumb, before carrying on. He looked Laxton straight in the eyes. 'When you return, I want you to keep it to yourself. I know you are on holiday, but it would be much appreciated if you could give us some assistance in apprehending this killer,' he asserted as he fastened his seat belt. As an afterthought, he told him, 'It wouldn't do to put the killer on his guard.'

Laxton nodded in agreement as he got out of the car and closed the door. He stood for a moment as Hughes put the car into gear and slowly pulled away, before going to his car and climbing in. A few minutes later he was leaving behind the town of Stirling and the forbidding sight of its ancient castle set high on its rocky base. On his journey back to the hotel where he was staying, Robert Laxton had plenty to think about as he drove through the magnificent mountain scenery. Rough-looking sheep dotted the steep slopes, negotiating the rocky terrain like mountain goats. They raised their heads inquisitively from the long, coarse grass, as the car sped noisily along the highway, breaking the tranquility of the warm summer day. On his arrival back at the hotel in Dalmally, he went up to his room and showered ready for the evening meal.

3

Relaxing soft music, emanating from speakers strategically placed around the large dining room, drifted in the air as Laxton was shown to his seat by a young woman dressed in a tartan skirt and white blouse. After sitting down, the pretty young woman placed a menu in front of him; he smiled and nodded his head in her direction, as he picked it up and took a quick glance through it, choosing the tomato soup as a starter, then indicating to her that he would like the poached salmon as the main course. A few minutes later a steaming hot bowl of the soup was placed in front of him. He had just tasted a spoonful, when he noticed a good-looking, dark-haired woman taking a seat on an adjoining table. *About thirty years old*, he thought to himself as he gave her a quick appraisal out of the corner of his eye, before lifting the spoon to his lips and swallowed another mouthful of soup.

She glanced across at him. 'Good evening,' she said politely, giving him a friendly smile as she sat down and made herself comfortable before picking up the menu that had been placed in front of her.

'Good evening,' he replied with a slight nod of his head, his face creasing into a smile as he greeted the raven-haired woman. 'Have you just arrived?'

She nodded in reply to his query, as the waiter came with her soup. In between courses she told him that her name was Marina Cortley.

'And my name is Robert Laxton,' he told her, reaching across to shake her hand. Her brown eyes widened slightly at the mention of his name. She had a smooth Scottish accent. *Definitely not Glaswegian*, he told himself as she finished her meal.

'I'll just go and powder my nose,' she declared, getting up to leave the table.

Laxton watched with an appreciative eye, as her shapely figure swayed its way towards the door. A few seconds later he was brought back to the business in hand, as the waiter brought his sweet and placed it on the table in front of him. Quickly finishing off his plate of apple pie and custard, he got to his feet and strolled out of the dining room. Going into the long bar, he ordered a pint of bitter. He ran his eyes around the almost empty room which consisted of a dance area and a few tables and chairs, as the barman handed him the foam-topped drink, he looked at it for a few seconds before taking a long satisfying swig. The resident pianist was playing a rendition of 'My Way', an old Frank Sinatra piece; a lone couple had the large dance floor to themselves as they executed, with some finesse, the well-known 'slow foxtrot'. Tipping his head back he emptied his glass, then, after placing the glass on the bar, he walked out of the room and went outside for a breath of fresh air.

The sun was just dipping below the mountains on the far side of the Loch, bathing the beautiful scene in a golden glow. A warm feeling went through him as he viewed the distant mountains through half-closed eyes. 'There's something special about the Scottish Highlands,' he told himself, as a light breeze rippled the water of the lake. Shaking his head at the wonder of it all, he was deep in thought, his brow furrowed as he walked across the road to where the murder of Lila Blankly had taken place. He looked over the low wall into the field, to the spot where the body had been discovered. The investigating team had vacated the scene of the murder, which, the day before had been swarming with men in white overalls. The area had been taped off.

'No doubt forensics have given it a good going over,' he told himself as he looked down to where the grass had been trampled down.

He cast his mind back to when he had first met Lila. His chest heaved as he shook his head and gave a deep sigh. Half closing his eyes he pictured the vibrant young woman. Suppressing his feelings with some difficulty he turned to go back into the hotel. He couldn't wait to get his hands on the swine who'd perpetrated the crime. Suddenly as he turned to walk away, he saw something glistening on the side of the granite stone wall. It was stuck in between the stone blocks. He poked it out with the biro that he always carried with him and held it in the palm of his hand. It was a cufflink. 'Forensics must have missed it,' he muttered as he turned it over and checked to see if there was a name on it. Painted on the cufflink was a tartan design. He studied it for a minute; there was a thoughtful look in his eyes, as he reached out and carefully replaced the cufflink exactly where he had found it, before returning to the hotel. Music could be heard coming from the hall as he pushed open the glass doors and entered, a young group were playing a lively tune as he made his way to the bar.

'Aren't the band on tonight?' he asked inquisitively, as he ordered a pint of bitter.

'No,' the barman replied as he carefully pulled the beer. 'They move around the hotels. They take in a different one every night, they'll be back here again on Saturday.'

He explained that there were six hotels in the area. The entertainers visited each one in turn.

'How far away do they go?'

The barman had a questioning expression on his face as he cocked his head on one side.

'How large an area do they cover?' enquired Laxton, patiently spelling it out.

'Ach!' replied the man behind the bar as he placed the frothy pint on the bar top; he had suddenly grasped what the tall man was getting at. 'I would say aboot a twenty-mile radius of this hotel,' he informed him in a rich Scottish accent.

Laxton, a thoughtful expression on his face, thanked him, as he picked up his drink and turned away. He took a seat at one of the tables near the dance floor. Marina was dancing and talking animatedly to her partner. After the dance she went to a table and sat alone. A couple of minutes later she was on the dance floor again. Laxton smiled inwardly, she was really enjoying herself. Her low-cut dress was drawing men to her like flies. She caught his eye as she swept past. At that moment Mc'Linney walked through the door and made his way to the bar. Laxton's eyes narrowed as he noticed a plaster on the Scot's neck. The music stopped and Marina came over to him.

'You're putting yourself about a bit aren't you?' he told her jokingly.

She leaned over towards him, a strange expression on her smiling face. 'I've got my reasons Inspector,' she whispered secretively in his ear as she walked past him.

'Well I'll be!' he gasped, taken aback by her statement. How did she know he was an inspector? He hadn't told anyone, except of course the superintendent and Macullock.

Laxton's eyes followed the slim, curvy figure as she went to the bar and ordered a drink. He shook his head a few minutes later when he saw her on the floor again. This time she was dancing with Mc'Linney. After a particularly energetic tango she came to his table, her face flushed.

'Right young lady,' he told her, looking up into her eyes. 'I want a word with you.'

'Okay,' she rejoined, taking a deep breath as she brushed aside a tendril of hair that was stuck to her forehead, then she sat down opposite him and placed her elbows on the table, her chin cupped in her hands. 'Fire away.'

'First of all, how did you know I was an inspector?' he demanded in a low voice.

'The super informed me when he put me on the case,' she replied. 'He told me I was to work with you. He also advised me to keep my identity secret. Incidentally I'm Detective Constable Marina Cortley.'

Laxton looked at her for a few seconds, then his face creased into a lopsided grin. 'You certainly fooled me,' he confessed, then went on. 'By the way, what do you mean you've got your reasons?'

'Well I can tell you. Except for Mc'Linney, none of the men I've danced with is the rapist,' she confided in a low voice.

'What makes you so sure?' queried Laxton.

'I've questioned them,' she replied. 'They are all here on holiday and none of them were here when the other incidents occurred.'

Robert Laxton's brow furrowed as he raised an inquisitive eyebrow. 'What about Mc'Linney, why don't you include him?'

'He was here on the weekends of the last two attacks.'

She had a thoughtful expression on her face as she added. 'And there's that patch on his neck. He says he cut himself shaving.'

Laxton stroked his chin with his thumb and forefinger for a moment before telling her about the incident on the train. 'He may be innocent. But be careful, he could be dangerous when he's had a few drinks,' he warned her.

At that moment Mc'Linney approached the table, smiled and nodded at Laxton, who returned the nod courteously. 'May I have this dance?' he asked, turning to Marina. She got up from the table and moved into his arms, to be swept away to the beat of a slow foxtrot.

4

Rebecca Nantwich stepped out of her comfortable little cottage. She took a deep breath of the warm August night air as she looked up at the stars glittering in the heavens. She'd lived alone since her ex-husband Ronald had taken off with the local barmaid over five years ago. She smiled to herself as she recalled the times he'd told her he was working late at the Fox and Hounds pub. He'd been caught out when the landlord of the pub phoned her to ask him to come in early the next day, to help with a delivery of beer barrels. She was waiting for him when he arrived home. After listening to the same old excuses, she told him of the phone call. He looked at her and laughed guiltily before confessing to her that he'd been seeing Ruth the barmaid at the pub. The next morning he moved out.

'Oxo, stop pulling,' she snapped at the energetic black Labrador as he almost dragged her over. To no avail, he was still tugging hard at the leash. She sighed and shook her head, making her slightly greying pony tail swing from side to side. 'All right then, off you go,' she laughed, as she reached out and unleashed the dog. He gave a bark of pleasure as he bounded away full of vitality.

The village of Crianlarich wasn't very well lit, the small lights that the local council provided were nothing near adequate. Looking further along the road, she could just make out the lights of the Crianlarich Hotel. She had planned to take the dog as far as the hotel (an almost daily routine), then make her way back to her cottage. Oxo had other ideas; he had decided to investigate the bushes in the grounds of the hotel. Knowing that the owner of the hotel wasn't very keen on dogs being let loose on the property, she went after him. She was unaware of the dark figure that slipped out of the shadows and approached her from the rear. The first thing she knew of anyone in the vicinity, was when an arm encircled her neck from behind. A large hand covered her mouth just as she was about to scream.

'Let me go,' she mumbled through the man's fingers. Gripping his fingers with her small hands, she tried to pull them away from her mouth, at the same time lashing out with her heels, as she struggled desperately to free herself.

Kicking and struggling, she was dragged inexorably towards the bushes. She opened her mouth wide and bit down as hard as she could on her attacker's fingers. Grunting with pain, he loosened his grip. She screamed as he lashed out at her, knocking her to the ground. The cruel eyes that glistened through the holes of the improvised black woollen helmet were cold and ruthless as he pinned her down with his body. He reached to lift her dress. Suddenly he turned, something had caught his eye. A black whirlwind smashed into him, knocking him over. It was Oxo; he had heard his mistress's scream.

'What the hell?' exploded the hooded man in a pronounced Scottish accent, as he attempted to fight off the big dog. Oxo sunk his teeth into the attacker's forearm. There was a shout of pain as the man, struggling to get to his feet, kicked out at the dog. Oxo, his hackles up and fangs bared, snarled. He was a frightening sight as he prepared to attack again. The would-be rapist scrambled to his feet and backed off as the dog advanced towards him, massaging his injured arm as he did so, whatever act he had in mind was forgotten. All he wanted now was to get away from the fearsome animal as it snapped at his ankles; a few seconds later he turned and ran, his figure fading into the darkness. Rebecca threw her arms around Oxo's neck and hugged him as the shadowy figure disappeared into the night.

'Oxo you beauty!' she exclaimed shakily, tears of gratitude in her eyes, then, with her hands shaking, she gave the dog a kiss on his snout.

Clambering to her feet, she dusted herself down to remove the grass that clung to her skirt as the dog fussed around his mistress, wagging his tail at the attention and affection he had received. Fastening the dog's lead back on, she looked nervously to her left and right, then she hurriedly made her way back along the lane to her cottage. She quickly opened the door and went inside, locking the door behind her. She leaned back on the door and took a deep breath.

After giving herself time to recover her composure, she picked up the phone and rang the police and informed them of the frightening attack on her.

Robert Laxton was just digging into a hearty

breakfast when Marina Cortley arrived at the table, a plate of cereal in her hand. She took the seat opposite him. 'You're late,' he mumbled through a mouthful of sausage.

'Yes the sergeant at the station has just been in touch,' she told him, as she sat down and carefully poured milk from a jug that had been placed on the table over her cereal. 'They informed me that another woman, a Rebecca Nantwich, had been attacked last night in Crianlarich,' she explained as she carefully lifted a spoonful of cereal to her mouth.

Laxton was deep in thought, as he pierced another portion of sausage; he looked up at her, his thick eyebrows raised. 'Is she okay?' he enquired, a concerned expression on his face, as he placed the sausage in his mouth.

'Yes,' she replied, with a nod of her head, then went on to explain. 'Her assailant wasn't successful. It seems that her dog, a black Labrador, jumped on the man and chased him off.'

Laxton paused for a few seconds, as he picked up his cup and swallowed a mouthful of coffee to clear his throat; there was a deep frown on his forehead as he asked her, 'What time did the attack occur?'

Marina placed the last spoonful of cereal in her mouth before responding, then, raising her eyes from the empty cereal dish, she cleared her throat and told him, 'It was around eleven o'clock last night.'

'Mmm…' muttered Laxton, his brow furrowed as he folded his arms and stroked his chin thoughtfully. 'If he is the person who was responsible for the other attacks, then Mc'Linney isn't our man. Crianlarich must be over fifteen miles away, and he was here at eleven fifteen.'

'And, as I've said, the woman was attacked at eleven o'clock, so that lets James, er Mc'Linney, off the hook,' she volunteered.

Laxton, a questioning look on his face, raised an eyebrow at the first name term.

'He *does* seem nice guy,' she expanded, a little guardedly, shrugging her shoulders as her face reddened slightly.

Laxton gave her a knowing smile. She swung a playful slap at him as he got up to leave the table. He swayed to one side as her small hand just missed his face.

'What are you doing today?' she asked him as he was about to go.

He paused for a moment, his hand on the back of his chair as he gave his answer. 'I've decided to go this morning to have a few words with Rebecca Nantwich and see if I can come up anything more to what we already know,' he told her as he pushed the chair back under the table, before leaving her to go up to his room.

After a quick wash he was ready for the journey to Crianlarich.

Robert Laxton's eyes were half closed against the bright sun and the strong, fresh wind that blew through the open car window, ruffling his thick iron grey hair as he drove along the winding road that cut through the mountainous terrain. Casting his mind back, he mulled over the recent events. Having already been to the scene of the attack on Lila Blankly, outside the Mactavish Hotel, he told himself that except for the finding of the cufflink, which may, or may not have some bearing on the murder, he hadn't come up with any further information. He was now on his way to call on Rebecca Nantwich to ask her a few questions about the attack on her.

Stopping the car outside the well-built stone cottage, he disembarked, opened a small wooden gate and walked up the path, which ran through the beautifully flowered garden as he approached the front door. There was a strong-scented smell emanating from the flowering sweet peas, which were growing in profusion on a cane frame that had been fastened around the doorway. Reaching out, he lifted the brass doorknocker and gave a couple of sharp knocks on the door. An attractive woman who looked to be in her late forties answered it nervously, as she peered round the partly open door a questioning expression on her face. 'Yes!' she exclaimed. 'Can I help you?'

'Mrs Rebecca Nantwich?' he enquired, a half smile on his face.

'That's me,' she replied tentatively, looking up at the tall man in front of her.

'My name is Robert Laxton, I'm a police inspector. May I have a word with you?' he asked the somewhat, apprehensive woman, in a soft voice.

'You're not from Scotland are you?' she rejoined, her pale blue eyes flashing. It was more an accusation than a greeting.

'No,' he replied with a slight shake of his head.

'I'm English.' He went on to explain that he was in Scotland on holiday and that he was assisting the local police with their enquiries.

'You'd better come in then, I don't want the whole neighbourhood to know my business,' she told him as she stuck her head out of the door and glanced up and down the lane. Then she opened the door wide and stood aside to let him in.

A black Labrador that was standing beside her growled menacingly as he passed closely by and followed her into the small, lived-in lounge, where she signalled with a wave of her hand for him to take a seat in a comfortable armchair. He gave her a half smile and nodded his head as he sat down. Leaning back, his eyes wandered around the room, taking in the numerous photographs of the dog and the large oil painting of the local church that hung over the stone fireplace. What looked to be a twenty-four inch television was positioned by the side of the fireplace. A grandfather clock stood in one corner at the rear of the room, its pendulum swinging rhythmically from side to side as it monotonously ticked away. There was a loud 'dong', as it showed twelve-thirty.

There doesn't seem to be a man in her life, he thought to himself as the dog, its hackles slightly raised, continued his deep throated growling.

'Oxo! Get in the kitchen,' she snapped, pointing with her finger; a few seconds later she placed a small coffee table in front of him.

The dog, still growling, reluctantly walked away, his head turned to keep one eye on the intruder as he slowly made his way into the kitchen. After making a pot of tea she placed a tray on the table, then sat down opposite him and carefully poured two cups, Laxton held his hand out and shook his head as she reached for the sugar dish, then waited patiently as she poured a small amount of milk in each of the cups of tea. After stirring them, she handed him one of the cups. Taking a sip, he raised his eyebrows and looked across the table at the rather stiff-backed, stern-looking woman.

'Did you notice anything special about your attacker?' he put to her in a conversational tone of voice as he placed the cup back on its saucer.

'Not really, everything happened so quickly,' she replied, in a sharp Scottish accent, as she shook her head from side to side.

'What about his features, could you make out what he looked like?' He paused for a moment and leaned forward, his elbows on his knees; he had a serious expression on his face as he told her, in a low voice, 'I want you to think carefully.'

The woman folded her arms and leaned back in her chair. She placed her forefinger and thumb on the bridge of her nose and half closed her eyes, thinking deeply for almost three minutes, as she attempted to bring back the events of the previous night.

'Well he wore a black woollen helmet, with two eyeholes cut out of it, sort of, like a balaclava,' she explained, demonstrating with her hands. She paused for a few seconds as she gathered her thoughts, before going on in a low voice. 'It was just going dark, but I'm almost certain his eyes were brown and a tuft of greasy brown hair poked out through the side of one of the eye holes in his balaclava,' she muttered.

'Could you make out how tall he was?' persisted Laxton after taking another sip of his tea. His pen was poised in readiness over a notebook that he had placed on the table in front of him, as he waited for her reply.

'Mmm, I would say he was about five-foot-ten, thickset and very strong,' she mumbled, as she tipped her cup and finished drinking her tea. 'I hope I've been of some assistance Inspector,' she announced, as she waited for the inspector to stop writing and finish his drink, before gathering the cups and placing them back on the tray with the teapot.

Laxton, who had been carefully writing down the information that she had given him, sat back, raised his eyebrows and looked up at her, as he folded the notebook and placed it in his pocket with his pen. 'Your contribution has been most helpful Mrs Nantwich!' he exclaimed dutifully. He went on to tell her, 'You seem to have been very observant.'

Rebecca Nantwich's face lit up in appreciation of the inspector's praise, as he got to his feet and prepared to leave. She felt a warm glow in her body as she looked up at the tall man standing in front of her. 'Thank you Inspector, I feel much better now. I do hope you catch the man before he commits another crime.'

'We'll catch him, you can be certain of that,' he assured her, a grim look on his face as he shook her small hand and bid her goodbye. Oxo, who had come back in from the kitchen, growled as Laxton stepped carefully around him and made his way to the door.

As he drove back to the Mactavish Hotel, along the country lane that wended its way through the rugged countryside that was dotted with sheep and highland cattle, he summed up the evidence so far. They now had some idea of what the man that they were seeking looked like. He was around five-foot-ten and thickset. He had brown eyes, dark brown hair and deep scratches. There was also the chance that he'd been injured by the dog. And of course there was the cufflink, the wearing of which would possibly place him in the middle aged bracket, say thirty-five to forty-five. That is of course, if it belonged to the killer.

On arrival back at Dalmally, he parked the car and climbed the few steps into the hotel, where he went directly to the bar and ordered a stiff drink. Marina Cortley approached him, a glass of wine in her hand as he tossed his drink back. 'Where have you been?' she enquired, her brow furrowed as she lifted her glass to her lips and took a sip of her wine. 'I've been looking for you all morning.'

Laxton placed his empty glass on the bar and ordered another whisky and soda, then told her of his visit to the home of Rebecca Nantwich in Crianlarich, and of his conclusions that they now had far more information about the man they were looking for. He reached out for his drink and raised it to his lips. Suddenly he stiffened, his brow deeply furrowed as he peered over the rim of his glass and focused his eyes on the bar behind her.

'What's the matter?' asked Cortley, turning her head and following the direction of his eyes, which led to a large poster on the wall at the back of the bar.

'Can you see the dates on that poster behind the

bar?' he asked her in a low voice.

The poster in question advertised among other things, the star turn for the evening, plus future and past events and the dates.

'What's wrong with that?' she asked, giving a slight shrug of her shoulders. 'It's indicating the star turn for the evening, a ventriloquist.'

'Look under the main event,' he insisted; there was a hint of irritation in his voice.

She looked again, this time carefully. On the bottom of the poster were the days and dates of the future and past events. She shrugged her shoulders as she turned back to him, she still couldn't see anything significant. Laxton took out his notebook and plucked at his bottom lip, his eyes half closed as he studied it for a few seconds.

'According to the information that I picked up at the police station and since, the assaults have taken place in the vicinity, and at the same time as the Highland dance band and comedian have performed,' he declared.

'It could be someone following them around,' she suggested.

'Possibly, but I doubt it. They're not that good, plus the fact that they would have to be in the same area as the band for weeks,' replied Laxton shaking his head. After finishing his drink he went to the phone and contacted police headquarters in Stirling. He was handed over to the super.

'Ah Laxton!' exclaimed the superintendent. 'Have you come up with anything?'

Laxton told him of his interview with Mrs Nantwich, and of his conclusions. There was a long pause, as Hughes thought over carefully the information that Laxton had given him.

'So you think our man could be one of the band or star turn?' he put to him.

'It looks that way to me,' answered the inspector.

There was a pause for a few seconds as the superintendent again mulled over Laxton's statement. 'That gives me an idea,' he replied, asking him, 'would you inform Sergeant Cortley that I'd like a word with her?'

Laxton slowly replaced the phone on the hook. There was a thoughtful expression on his face as he returned to the table near the bar where Marina Cortley was just finishing her drink; he leaned over her shoulder and told her in a low voice, 'The super wants a word with you.'

Finishing her drink, she went to the phone. A few minutes later she returned. She leaned across the table towards Laxton, a secretive expression on her face. 'I've been instructed to try and lure the attacker out into the open,' she whispered, throwing him a meaningful look.

Laxton's brow creased as he raised his eyes and looked up at her, shaking his head slowly from side to side. 'That's dangerous, you'll have to be careful,' he warned her, his voice dropping in volume.

'I'll be careful,' she assured him. 'But I'm going to need your help.'

'I'll do my best,' he grunted. 'Now let's see, it's

Friday today. The band and the comedian will be performing here tomorrow night.'

She nodded her head; there was a serious expression on her face as she chewed her bottom lip nervously. Robert Laxton placed a reassuring hand on her arm.

'Don't worry Marina, whatever you do I won't be far away,' he promised her, as he turned and strode out of the bar and went upstairs to his room, where he turned on the radio, flopped down on the bed and listened to a rendition of light music, which eventually lulled him to sleep.

Two hours later he woke up. He checked his wrist watch; it was five o'clock. Reluctantly climbing off the bed, he undressed and got under the shower. After drying himself and taking a shave, he swiftly dressed and went down the broad staircase to the dining room; feeling a new man, as he took his seat at his allotted table.

He was running his eyes over the menu, when Marina, looking stunning in a low-cut, pink, silk dress, arrived at his table, a broad smile on her face as she greeted him. Raising his eyebrows, he returned her smile as she took a seat opposite him. After deciding what meal he was going to have, he passed the menu to Marina.

Music from a record player filled the background as the waiter approached them, causing him to raise his voice a little as he ordered steak and chips and a bottle of wine. He leaned forward across the table. 'For both of us,' he told her in a low voice.

Marina smiled her thanks and told him that she didn't want the steak, as she ran her eyes down the menu and decided to go for the chicken salad. A few minutes later the waiter arrived with a small trolley carrying the meals and wine and placed them on the table in front of them. Laxton reached out and picked up the bottle of wine; placing his thumb under the edge of the cork, he pressed hard, compressing his lips at the effort. There was a loud 'plop', as the cork shot across the table. Marina, taking evasive action, raised her hands and ducked her head, as the missile flew over her shoulder. She burst out laughing at the sight of Laxton's red face, as he apologised profusely. Pulling himself together, he reached out and commenced pouring the wine.

'Say when?' he intoned as the clear liquid neared the top of her glass.

'When!' she exclaimed sharply, holding up her hands.

After filling both glasses, he took a long drink, then tucked into the inviting meal in front of him with some gusto. Ten minutes later he leaned back and rubbed his stomach with both hands. 'That was delicious,' he announced as he reached across the table and topped up the two glasses with the remainder of the wine.

A few minutes later, after finishing their drink, they both left the dining room and went through the glass doors into the long bar that overlooked the large dance floor. The resident pianist had taken over from the record player. He was giving a pleasant rendition of a medley of tunes. Three couples were on the dance floor as he and Marina took a seat at an empty table. Laxton signalled to the waiter and ordered a pint of bitter and a martini. After a few sips Marina leaned over and asked him, 'Aren't you going to ask me to dance Robert?'

Laxton, his pint of beer in his hand, looked across at her, took a deep breath, then, with a half smile on his face, reluctantly nodded his head and got to his feet. The pianist had just started to play a quick step, the only dance that he was what you might call 'passable' at.

'Okay!' he told her as he placed his arm around her slim waist. 'Let's go.'

With this, he swept her out on to the dance floor, executing a couple of reverse turns as he guided her round the perimeter of the dancing area.

'Mmm, not bad for an old man,' Marina whispered in his ear as his strong arms held her close. 'Not bad at all.'

Suddenly she felt his back stiffen as they glided past the pianist.

'What's the matter?' she put to him, a questioning expression on her face.

He looked down at her, his brow deeply furrowed, he was deep in thought. 'Did you see the pianist's cufflinks?' he whispered in her ear.

She shook her head and shrugged her shoulders noncommittally. 'Have a good look when we go past him again,' he confided.

A couple of minutes later, she looked carefully as they went by the pianist. She gave a quick intake of breath, as she got a clear view of his cufflinks.

'They've got a Scottish tartan on them,' she told him, lowering her voice.

Laxton nodded his head as he reminded her, 'Just like the one that I found at the scene of Lila Blankly's murder.'

'What are you going to do about it?' she asked him as the music stopped and they walked off the dance floor and took a seat at the table.

'First of all, I think I'll make a few enquiries,' he replied as he finished off his drink.

Getting to his feet, he went across to the man behind the bar, who was busy serving a customer. Leaning on the bar, he waited for a couple of minutes until the barman was free, then he called him over.

'What can I do for you sir?' the barman, a different one to who he had spoken to before, enquired in a rather polite Scottish accent.

Laxton looked across the bar at the round-faced, Oliver Hardy-like figure. 'I would like some information,' he informed him.

The fat man shrugged his shoulders and told him, 'Go ahead.'

'Could you tell me where the pianist would have been performing on Saturday night?' Laxton asked him in a serious tone of voice.

The barman scratched the back of his neck and half closed his eyes as he cast his mind back. 'Now let me see,' he muttered, almost as if to himself.

'Saturday night the band was on stage.' He paused for a moment, then carried on. 'He only plays here, when the band are away at the other hotels.'

Laxton butted in. 'Does that mean he is free for the other evenings?' he put to him.

The barman shook his head, his double chin wobbling as he did so. 'No!' he exclaimed sharply. 'He has to perform at one of the other hotels in turn,' he added.

'The barman who was on yesterday told me they were around a twenty-mile radius from here,' Laxton rejoined. Then he asked him, 'What distance would that make them from Dalmally?'

'Mmm, I would say the nearest one to here would be around ten miles,' he replied, after giving the statement a little thought.

'So he wouldn't be in this area?' Laxton put to him.

The barman shook his head from side to side. 'No,' he announced emphatically, as he picked up a towel and proceeded to wipe along the top of the bar.

Laxton, deep in thought, thanked him and turned away from the bar, then suddenly, he turned back again as an afterthought and asked the fat man. 'What time does he finish playing the piano?'

The barman chewed on his bottom lip for a few seconds, before leaning across the bar and telling him, in a low voice, 'I'm not one hundred per cent certain sir, but I would say somewhere around eleven o'clock in the evening.'

Laxton thanked him again, as he returned to the table where Marina was waiting for him.

'Did you find out anything?' she asked him as he sat down.

Laxton, a distant look in his eyes, paused for a few seconds before answering her, then leaning his elbow on the table, he nodded his head. 'Just one thing,' he told her, adding, 'the pianist isn't our man.'

'How do you come to that conclusion?' she queried.

He shrugged his shoulders as he explained to her, 'On Saturday night he would have been performing until eleven o'clock at one of the other hotels, which, according to the barman are situated at least ten miles away. He couldn't be in two places at once.'

Marina, who had been listening to him intently, glanced over his shoulder. Her eyes suddenly lighting up as her solemn face broke out in a wide smile. Laxton turned round and looked over his shoulder, to see Mc'Linney approaching; his brown eyes twinkling as he nodded his head and greeted Laxton with a friendly, 'Hello,' then he turned to a smiling Marina and asked her in a quiet voice, 'May I have this dance Marina?'

Giving a slight nod of her head, she got to her feet, to be swept out on to the dance floor, to a slow foxtrot. Laxton smiled to himself, as he observed the young couple gliding effortlessly round the floor, their eyes only for each other. After watching them for a while, he checked his watch. It showed five past nine. 'I think I'll have an early night,' he muttered to himself as he got to his feet and made his way up to his room.

5

It was just turning light as Laxton pushed back the blankets and checked his watch, it was seven-thirty a.m. Climbing out of bed he strolled over to the window and looked out at the lake and distant mountains, he stretched his arms wide, before running his fingers through his hair. Taking a deep breath, he looked to where the sun, which had just cleared the distant mountains, was reflecting from the smooth waters of the lake. The light wind causing patches of ripples as it gusted across it.

'It's going to be a lovely warm day,' he told himself with a sigh of contentment, as he made his way to the bathroom. After a shave and a shower, he towelled himself down vigorously; ten minutes later he was dressed, then, feeling ready to meet the day, he closed the apartment door behind him.

'Where has the week gone?' he muttered to himself, shaking his head in bewilderment, as he turned to go down to the dining room for breakfast. It was now Thursday; it had seemed like only yesterday that he had walked through the glass doors of the hotel at the start of his holiday.

Marina, looking fresh and really lovely was already sat at the table, tucking into a plate of cereal when he arrived. She looked up as he took a seat opposite her, and greeted him with a smile. He discussed with her the implications of the cufflink and the fact that the pianist, although he was not a suspect, had one. Pouring milk on his corn flakes, he tucked in to them.

'That doesn't prove anything,' she mumbled through a mouthful of puffed wheat. 'Lots of people wear them.'

'I agree with you, but what it does prove is the fact that the man who wore the cufflink that I found, was at the spot where the murder occurred,' he retorted, as he finished his cereal.

At that moment the waiter approached him; after a quick scan of the breakfast menu, he turned to the waiter and ordered bacon, egg, and tomatoes, his favourite breakfast. 'Oh! And a pot of tea,' he called after the waiter as he turned away.

A few minutes later the meal was placed on the table; Marina smiled inwardly, as he rubbed his hands together in anticipation, before getting stuck into the inviting meal in front of him.

Twenty minutes later, feeling fully satisfied, he finished his breakfast, and got up to leave the table. 'I'll see you later,' was his parting remark to Marina, as he turned to walk away.

Going out of the hotel, he made his way across the road and checked the wall where he had replaced the cufflink. It had gone. Continuing along the road he was deep in thought as he summed up the situation. The person who had lost the cufflink, must have gone back to where he knew it must have been dislodged. There was a good chance that he was the attacker. A quarter of an hour later he returned to the hotel. Marina was just entering the lobby. She approached him, smiling. 'Where have you been?' she asked him, a questioning expression on her face.

He told her of how he had found the cufflink and about replacing it where he had found it and that it had gone.

'Maybe we should check on everyone in the hotel,' she suggested.

'No I don't want him frightened off,' Laxton said pointedly.

'What are you two acting so secretive about?' a loud voice enquired. They looked round. It was Mc'Linney, he had just come out of the dining room. 'Come on I'll buy ye both a drink,' he offered jovially. They declined, telling him it was a bit too early in the day. Marina turned to him, 'Do you wear cufflinks Jimmy?' she asked innocently.

'Do I look that old?' he replied laughingly. 'Why do you ask?'

Marina didn't answer him as she turned to Laxton. 'Have you come to any conclusions yet?'

Laxton stroked his chin thoughtfully before answering. 'Not yet, I'm going to ask a few questions among the band and the comedian.'

'Is there anything I can do to help?' asked a puzzled Mc'Linney.

Laxton exchanged looks with Marina, before deciding to confide in him. He explained to the Scot that he was a police inspector on holiday, and that he was helping the local police to apprehend the killer and rapist that was on the loose. Mc'Linney listened intently as they carefully explained to him what they had in mind. 'Tonight the band and the comedian are performing here. If we mingle discreetly with the entertainers when they have their rest period, we may come up with something,' suggested the inspector.

'If there is any way that I can help, don't hesitate to call on me,' a serious-looking Mc'Linney told them.

With this they went to their respective rooms. Laxton spent some time looking through the local newspaper which he had picked up in the hotel foyer, checking it to see if there was any word on the recent attacks reported in it. Finding nothing, he decided to take a walk along the banks of the Loch. The sun was shining from a clear blue sky as he left the hotel and made his way through a gap in the wall that ran along the opposite side of the road. He took a deep breath as he strolled along the side of the lake, through the flowering scented heather that adorned the bank; all that could be heard was the sound of the honey bees working away and the squawking of the gulls as they swooped down for the many small fish that were foolish enough to come to the surface. After walking for what seemed hours, he checked his watch. It showed one-thirty. By the time he returned to the hotel in the late afternoon, he had the beginnings of a healthy tan, except for being almost eaten alive by the much-vaunted Scottish mosquitoes, he'd enjoyed it immensely. After wearily climbing the wide stairway he eventually arrived back in his room.

Throwing his jacket over the back of a chair, he flopped down on the bed and fell fast asleep, awaking two hours later. Stretching his arms out wide, he climbed off the bed and decided to clean himself up, then, after taking a shower, he went down to the dining room feeling completely refreshed. Marina had almost finished eating when he took his seat at the table opposite her and ordered his meal. A few minutes later the waiter was placing a plate of chicken and chips and a bottle of wine on the table in front of him.

'I think I'll go and pretty myself up,' she exclaimed to him, as she finished her meal and got to her feet in readiness to leave.

Laxton nodded his head in acknowledgement, mumbling unintelligibly through a mouthful of tender roast chicken.

After his meal he strolled into the bar in what could only be described as a *noisy* ballroom and ordered a pint of bitter. The members of the band were tuning up their instruments before starting in earnest. Mc'Linney was leaning on the far end of the long bar. He was halfway through a pint of beer, as he nodded imperceptibly at Laxton. After an introduction by the M.C. the band struck up with a lively quick step.

'Aren't you dancing Robert?' a female voice behind him enquired.

He spun round, it was Marina. His bottom jaw dropped in amazement. She was wearing a low-cut red silk dress that left nothing to the imagination. It had a slit up the left side exposing a large portion of her thigh.

'Well...' He was almost lost for words as she grabbed his hand and dragged the reluctant Laxton on to the dance floor. 'If that dress doesn't attract our man, nothing will,' he whispered in her ear as they danced. After three or four turns around the floor the music stopped. The band leader announced they were going to play some jive. Laxton heaved a sigh of relief as he revealed to her he couldn't jive. He turned to lead a disappointed Marina back to her seat, when James Mc'Linney approached them.

'May I have this dance Marina?' he enquired, a broad smile on his face.

'Yes please Jimmy,' she replied, her eyes lighting up as she moved gracefully into his arms.

The next five minutes were a revelation. The sensual gyrations by Marina would raise the blood of any man, as she flashed her shapely thighs. When the music stopped they were both breathing heavily as they came to where Laxton was sitting; James Mc'Linney was sweating profusely as he gave Marina a big kiss on her cheek.

'Well what do you think?' she gasped breathlessly, her face flushed with her exertions.

'Yeah, that should do the trick,' drawled the inspector with a nod of his head. He had a serious expression on his face as he drummed it into her. 'I want you to be extra careful. We are dealing with a very dangerous man.'

'I think I'll take a breath of fresh air,' declared Marina, a meaningful look in her eyes as she turned to leave the dance hall.

'Don't forget what I've told you,' warned Laxton as she walked away. 'Be careful.'

Laxton turned to the barman and ordered two more pints. He was just about halfway through his drink, when he stopped, the glass still at his lips. He sensed something had changed. Then it struck him. The band had left the stage and the comedian was on. He turned to Mc'Linney, who was just taking a drink of his beer. He had a questioning expression on his face. 'Where's Marina?'

'I haven't seen her since she said she was going outside to cool off,' replied the Scot as he placed his drink on the table. 'She hasn't come back yet.'

They looked at each other for few seconds before suddenly making a dash for the door, the younger man outrunning Laxton.

Marina walked out of the hotel and took a deep breath of the cool night air. Shadows from the trees appeared, then disappeared, as the moon slipped from behind the drifting clouds, then back again, bringing total darkness. She didn't see the shadowy figure close in on her. A gloved hand covered her mouth and an arm wrapped round her neck from behind, dragging her towards the bushes that lined the driveway. She gave a muted scream as she fought desperately to free herself. The attacker picked her up and threw her to the ground, knocking the wind out of her. He bent down, reached out with his hand and held her firmly, his eyes glittering cruelly through the holes in his balaclava helmet. Suddenly a figure broke out of the darkness, striding towards Marina and her assailant. He launched himself at the would-be rapist.

'Oh no you don't, you filthy swine,' spat a voice in a strong Scottish accent.

It was Mc'Linney. He jumped in, swinging his foot, catching the attacker a heavy blow in the ribs, knocking him backwards. He in turn kicked out at the Scot, hitting him with a painful blow to his kneecap. Mc'Linney lashed out with his fist as he fell to the ground, delivering a punch to the side of his adversary's jaw. The attacker, fearing that he could be on the wrong end of a good hiding, scrambled to his feet and melted into the darkness, just as Laxton arrived breathlessly on the scene. Marina told him what had happened. Sitting up, she put her arm around the young Scot and gave him a hug as she explained his part in her rescue.

'Are you okay?' enquired Laxton concernedly, as he reached out and helped her to her feet. He turned his attention to Mc'Linney who was still sat on the grass massaging his knee. 'Did you get a look at him?' he asked, a sense of urgency in his voice.

The young man shook his tousled head, a frustrated expression on his face. 'I couldn't see his face. He wore a balaclava,' he told the inspector disappointedly, 'but I did catch him with a good punch to the jaw.'

'Did you see which way he went?' asked Laxton.

'Back towards the hotel I reckon,' replied Mc'Linney, rubbing his knee vigorously, as he got up from the grass and climbed painfully to his feet.

With this the three of them went back into the bar, with D.S. Cortley arm in arm with the limping Scot.

'Has anyone come into the bar in the last few minutes?' Laxton asked the barman.

'No,' he informed him with a slight shake of his head. 'There's been no one enter that door since you went out.'

'Is there any other way in?' asked Marina, a questioning look on her face.

'Yes,' replied the barman, raising his hand and pointing through the entrance to the bar. 'Through the reception and round the back. It leads to the room where the entertainers prepare to go on stage.'

Laxton asked Mc'Linney if he would keep an eye on the people that were already there. Then he and Cortley went out of the bar and through the reception, to where the band was gathered as it prepared to take the stage. They were all busy talking to each other.

Laxton stood in the middle of the room and called out, his loud voice rising above the hubbub of the chattering members of the band. 'Can I have your attention please?'

The room went quiet as they turned to the speaker. After introducing himself and D.S. Cortley, Laxton carried on. 'Will any of you, who left the room in the last twenty minutes, raise your hand please?'

Nearly all of those present put their hands up. Impatiently he told them to lower them. At that moment the M.C. popped his head through the door, telling the band they were on, at which point they all trooped out of the room. The two detectives returned to the bar, to be met by Mc'Linney.

'Nothing untoward happened out here,' he told them, shrugging his shoulders.

Laxton nodded in acknowledgement, his eyes carefully scanning through the band. Suddenly he stopped and stared intently at the bandleader, who had his right arm, in which he held the baton, raised ready to start.

'What have you seen?' whispered Cortley, seeing the inspector's eyes concentrating on the stage where the band had congregated.

'The man who's conducting,' he answered, nodding in the direction of the band. 'He's wearing cufflinks, can you make them out?'

Marina, reaching out, grabbed Mc'Linney by the hand and dragged him onto the dance floor just as the band started up.

'What are you doing?' he asked her as he placed his arm around her waist and swept her on to the dance floor. 'We're going to get a closer look at those cufflinks,' she whispered in his ear.

The dance was a slow foxtrot. They executed a half turn, bringing them close to the band leader, giving them plenty of time to get a good look at his wrist. The cufflink was fully exposed as they drifted past. The tartan design could clearly be seen. They returned to where Laxton was waiting.

'It has a tartan design on it,' she informed him in a low voice as she and Mc'Linney swung out on to the dance floor again.

Laxton, his eyes half closed, slowly nodded his head in answer to her information. 'We'll keep an eye on him; he could be our man,' he asserted as the young couple gracefully executed a reverse turn and drifted out into the middle of the dance floor to the haunting sound of 'Strangers in the Night'.

Half an hour later the dancing session came to an

end, and the comedian took over as the members of the band trooped off the stage. The inspector beckoned to D.S. Cortley to follow him as he made his way to the back room, where the band were gathered around a small bar having a drink. They pushed their way through to where the band leader was leaning on the mini-bar, a drink in his hand.

'I'd like a word with you,' Laxton informed him in a somewhat sharp tone of voice.

The bandleader, Charles Huntley, a big, well-built man, his black hair plastered down, turned and looked at him, a quizzical look in his brown eyes. 'And who the hell are ye?' he retorted belligerently in a sharp Scottish accent. He was obviously offended by the inspector's attitude.

Robert Laxton ignored the comment from the annoyed Scot and went on to explain to him that they were police officers and would like to ask him a few questions. Huntley visibly calmed down when he learned who they were. 'Okay,' he grunted in a heavy Scottish accent, taking a long drag on the cigarette he held in his nicotine-stained fingers. 'Get on with it.'

The inspector's eyes narrowed slightly at the somewhat mocking reply, and went on to tell him that they were investigating the recent murder of Lila Blankly and the other attacks on local women that had occurred.

'What's that got to do with me?' Huntley demanded, somewhat truculently.

'I have reason to believe that the murderer and rapist may have worn cufflinks similar to the ones you're wearing.'

Huntley pulled up the sleeve of his jacket and exposed his white shirt and the cufflink. 'Do you mean these?' he asked.

Laxton eyed the tartan design on the cuff link closely. It was the same as the one that he had discovered in the wall across the road.

'Yes that's the same design,' he declared, looking the big man in the eyes.

The bandleader threw back his head and laughed. 'That's part of our dress mon. We had them specially made, they go with the dickie bow,' he confided. Indicating the tartan tie, he told him, 'All the members of the band have them.'

Laxton apologised to the big Scot. He rubbed his chin ruefully, the disappointment showing on his face, as he realised he'd made a mistake. At that moment Marina spoke up.

'As they were made especially for the band Robert, that means it is still possible that one of them could still be the person we are looking for.'

He nodded his head in agreement and continued questioning Huntley. After he'd answered all the questions satisfactorily, and the inspector was certain that he wasn't the murderer, he turned to the rest of the band, who had been listening intently. He explained to them that during their investigations they'd discovered that the man they were looking for may have deep scratches on his lower neck or chest.

Charles Huntley stepped forward. 'You can check me Inspector,' he offered, taking off his tie and opening the neck of his shirt. 'I've got nothing to hide.'

Laxton gave an appreciative nod of his head and turned his attention to the rest of the members of the band. 'Now will the rest of you follow the example of Mr Huntley, so that we can eliminate you from our enquiries?'

One after the other they complied with the request. None of them had any scars.

'Is that all of you?' enquired the inspector in a loud voice, casting his eyes around the congregated men.

They all turned and looked around. Suddenly a man from the back of the group, called out, 'Where's William?'

'He was here a few minutes ago,' declared another of the members. 'He must have left.'

'William?' queried Laxton, his brow furrowed. 'Who is William?'

'William Stockworth,' echoed Huntley, explaining, 'he's our drummer.'

The inspector rubbed his chin thoughtfully for a few seconds as he mulled over the recent happenings. Stockworth was the man Marina Cortley had introduced to him. He'd gone to the toilet just before she'd gone outside, he recalled.

At that moment Mc'Linney came into the room and told them that the receptionist had seen a man dash out of the hotel.

'Right, come on,' urged Laxton, leading the way through reception to the double doors at the entrance, followed closely by Mc'Linney and Marina. As they dashed out on to the car park, a car engine could be heard as a car raced through the hotel gates.

It was Stockworth. He turned left as he went out of the entrance gates and on to the road, heading towards Stirling. Cortley phoned the Stirling police and warned them that the suspect was headed their way. She was informed that he would be intercepted. She and Mc'Linney followed Laxton to his car. They swiftly climbed in and took off after Stockworth, the inspector driving. They had glimpses of the car's rear lights ahead as the moon disappeared behind the clouds. The inspector, his foot pressed down hard on the accelerator, sped after the fleeing man.

William Stockworth leaned forward, hunching over the steering wheel, a wild look in his eyes as he peered through the patches of mist that hung over the winding road. The tyres screeched as he rounded a sharp bend. His eyes widened in horror. 'What the hell?' he exploded.

A sheep had wandered through a gap in the stone wall that lined the highway. It was standing in the middle of the road, bleating as it looked balefully into the oncoming headlights. There was no way round it. He stood on the brakes to no avail. The car hit the unfortunate animal full on. The steering wheel spun in his hand as the car, diverted by its impact with the sheep, shot off the road and smashed head-on into the solid stone built wall. Stockworth, dazed, with blood running down his forehead from a deep gash, reached out and opened the car door. As he staggered away from the wrecked car, he saw the headlights of the pursuing vehicle in the distance. Climbing clumsily over the wall, he set off unsteadily across the rock strewn field towards the mountains in the distance.

'It looks as though he's had an accident,' declared Mc'Linney, peering ahead.

It was obvious that the white car had encountered some trouble, as their headlights lit up the scene. The car was off the road, its near side buried in the wall as steam rose from under the bonnet. A sheep was lying on the road, bleating in agony. Laxton went over to the car. It was empty. He turned and addressed his companions, 'It looks as though Stockworth's made a run for it,' he announced.

'There he is!' shouted Marina, as the moon appeared from behind a cloud, lighting up the scene. She pointed to a shadowy figure dashing across the open heath, heading towards the distant mountains.

'What is he up to?' questioned Mc'Linney, shaking his head. He could just make out the fugitive in the bright moonlight, as he reached the base of the mountain.

'He isn't going to get anywhere up there.'

At that moment two police cars arrived on the scene, from the direction of Stirling. The chief inspector approached Laxton. The inspector introduced himself.

'What's the situation?' asked the chief.

'He's making a run for it,' declared Laxton, pointing into the far distance to where Stockworth was scrambling through the rocky terrain. 'I can't make out what he's after.'

'A single rail track runs along the mountainside,' explained the chief. 'There's a train due in about ten minutes, it's the last one tonight. I reckon that's what he's making for.'

He ordered four of the policemen he'd brought with him, to go after Stockworth, who by this time had just about reached the single rail track that ran precariously along the mountainside.

Stockworth glanced over his shoulder. He could just make out the police officers that were following him. He cursed his bad luck, hitting that sheep hadn't been in his calculations.

Standing on the wooden sleepers, he looked along the metal railway lines, which were glinting in the moonlight as they twisted along the side of the mountain. He bent down and placed his ear to the rail. The vibrations could be clearly detected. The train wasn't very far away. 'I may yet avoid capture,' he told himself. 'If I could just get above the train as it goes by, I could still get away.'

The police were getting close by now. He smiled grimly to himself, as he pulled himself up the mesh that was fixed to the rocks to stabilise them. Laxton looked up as he and the others drew closer. The smoke and steam from the old engine billowed up as it made its way painstakingly along the single track, its front lights almost obscured by the hissing steam from under the steel chassis.

'The bloody fool!' Laxton exclaimed, as he observed Stockworth, a mad expression on his face, hanging on grimly to the mesh. 'He'll never make it.'

Stockworth, a wild look in his eyes, gritted his teeth as he prepared himself for the approaching train as it slowly made its way towards him.

'If I could just climb above the train and jump on

to it, I could cheat them yet,' he muttered out loud, taking a firm hold as he climbed further up the mesh.

The engine drew closer, smoke belching out of its funnel. Stockworth readied himself as it approached, he had to be careful; the mesh, which by now was taking his full weight wasn't as secure as he first thought. Suddenly it began to come away from the rocks. He changed his grip to get a better hold. It came away in his hand. The engine chugged nearer; he could smell the mixture of steam and smoke as it drifted towards him. He felt the mesh giving way. He scrabbled desperately, his fingers bleeding as he attempted to get a better hold to no avail – he was falling. A terrifying scream echoed around the valley as he landed on the rail directly in front of the train, its iron wheels rattling unfeelingly over him as it dragged his mutilated body along the line.

Laxton and the others were stopped in their tracks, overcome by the horrific incident, made more macabre by the moonlight. Marina Cortley shuddered as everything went quiet, except for the chugging of the engine and the screech of its brakes as it ground to a halt.

'I think we'd better stay back here Marina,' advised Mc'Linney, placing a comforting arm around her shoulders.

Laxton and the chief climbed up to the single railway track to where the four police officers were looking down at the mangled body of Stockworth.

'I don't think there's much we can do for him sir,' announced one of the officers. A pronouncement that Laxton considered was a bit of an understatement.

The train driver and his mate climbed out of the cab, a concerned expression on their faces as they walked back along the track to where the body lay.

'I couldnae stop in time,' asserted the shocked driver, shrugging his shoulders.

'That's okay, it wasn't any fault of yours,' grunted the chief inspector. He turned to one of his officers. 'Get on the radio Hamish and get the paramedics and forensics here,' he ordered as he stood over the body. 'So that we can get this mess cleared up.'

Turning to Laxton, he told him, 'We'll let you get on with your holiday now Inspector,' he grunted, adding, 'Oh! And thanks for your help.'

Robert Laxton nodded his head at the chief. 'Glad to be of assistance,' he rejoined with a raise of his hand as he turned away.

Then as the moon dipped behind a bank of cloud, he picked his way through the rocks that lay at the base of the mountain below the railway line, and made his way across the heath, to the car, followed by D.S. Cortley and Mc'Linney.

'Well it looks as though the women of Scotland will be a little safer now,' stated Laxton, as he changed gear to negotiate a sharp bend in the road.

'What puzzles me,' said Mc'Linney, scratching the back of his head, 'is how he thought he could keep getting away with it.'

'He probably knew it was inevitable that he would eventually be caught. The problem was, he couldn't control his sexual appetite,' rejoined Laxton.

The following morning Stockworth's room in the hotel was thoroughly searched. The balaclava was found among his belongings. An examination by the pathologist revealed the recently healed scars, on what remained of his chest. The tissue under the nails of Lila Blankly, matched samples taken from Stockworth's body. After recording the evidence the case was closed. Robert Laxton enjoyed an uneventful second week of his holiday, taking in the beautiful scenery, and exploring the mountains that looked down on the hotel.

'Goodbye Robert, I hope you'll come to Scotland again soon,' said Marina, a little tearfully, placing a kiss on his cheek as he boarded the bus that was to start him on his long journey back to his home in Lincolnshire. James Mc'Linney shook his hand warmly. The couple had their arms around each other as they waved him off.

Robert Laxton smiled to himself as he waved back to them. He gave a deep sigh as they disappeared from sight.

End

Justice Deferred

1

Martin Danister sat quietly in the driving seat of his red Consul. His eyes, wide with wonderment, reflected the leaping flames, as he lowered the side window of the car and watched the results of his handiwork. There was a sadistic smile on his face, as he surveyed the scene in front of him. This was the third house fire that he had been responsible for. The first two, he told himself, hadn't been so spectacular. But this one was really satisfying. Taking a deep breath, he reached out, started the car and prepared to pull away as the flames began to take hold.

The fire was raging in the downstairs rooms and thick smoke was belching out of one of the two upstairs windows when the fire engine, approaching from the opposite direction with sirens wailing, drove past him. He turned his attention to the rear view mirror and took one last look at the potential death trap that he had caused, before accelerating away. The driver of the fire engine, a questioning expression on his face, looked down at him as he slowly went past, giving him a hard stare as the engine drew up outside the semi-detached house, number six Mansell Road, Arnsford. Alan Parkinson, his wife, and two children were leaning out of the other upstairs window. The children were screaming with fear as the firemen jumped out of the vehicle and swiftly went into action.

'Hang on, we'll have you out in a few minutes,' called out the chief, as the extending ladder swung towards the window. One of the firemen, Ron Wendle, a big, strong, burly man, stood on the top rung.

'Pass me one of the children first!' he shouted, his brawny arms outstretched, as the ladder was placed in position. The man at the window, his eyes wide with shock, picked up the smallest child and swung her out over the top of the ladder and into the arms of the fireman, he in turn lowered her to another fireman who was further down the ladder, he swiftly carried her down and handed her to waiting arms that took her to safety. A few seconds later he was back up the ladder ready to receive the second child, a young boy. The woman, with the help of her husband and Wendle, the fireman, clambered out of the window and carefully descended the ladder to ground level. Parkinson, with some difficulty, followed her out of the window. A few seconds later as he was descending, there was a loud 'whoosh', as a sheet of flames filled the room behind him. He shook his head from side to side. He was a lucky man.

'Is there anyone else in there?' the chief, who was overseeing events, shouted to him above the din of the powerful hoses and the crackle of the flames as he reached the ground.

The shocked man, his face blackened by the smoke, nodded his head. 'My son Bobby,' he croaked, indicating with his finger as he pointed at the flaming window. 'He's in the back bedroom.'

Ron Wendle, who had just descended the ladder, jumped off the vehicle, took his helmet off and wiped the sweat from his brow with a large handkerchief as he approached the chief. He'd overheard Parkinson's comments. 'I'll go in and get him before the fire gets too far gone,' he volunteered a little breathlessly, his shaven scalp glistening as he placed his helmet back on his head.

The chief, George Hambleton, looked up at him. 'It's a bit risky Ron,' he countered, shaking his head slowly from side to side as he stroked his chin thoughtfully.

He cast his eyes at the flames that were leaping out of the windows at the front of the building, as he informed the big man in front of him, 'It looks as though the fire might have spread into the back rooms.'

'I'll have to give it a go, I can't let the other youngster die,' grunted Wendle, streams of sweat running down his face, as he pulled his collar up round his ears and adjusted his goggles for maximum protection.

Using his size eleven boot as a battering ram, he smashed open the front door and disappeared into the smoke-filled hallway of the house. He stopped for a moment as a faint smell of petrol filled his nostrils. He looked down and saw a match on the floor. He bent down and picked it up, it hadn't been used. A frown furrowed his forehead as he put it in his pocket and turned to the task in hand. Flames were beginning to take hold on the lower part of the stairway, as he climbed the stairs two at a time, he burst open the first door he came to. It was the bathroom and it was empty. He turned to another door; the smoke and heat, by now, becoming almost unbearable. Kicking it open, he crouched down and looked under the heavy blanket of smoke that hung from the ceiling. He could just make out the body of the boy stretched out on the floor of the bedroom. In two strides he was across to where the motionless boy lay. Getting a good hold he slung the limp body over his shoulders and staggered back out of the room towards the top of the stairs, where the roaring flames were beginning to envelop the stairway. Taking a deep breath of the hot air, he carefully descended the stairs with his load. It seemed an eternity before he got to the bottom step with flames licking around his feet. He was, by now, almost in a state of collapse through lack of oxygen. Making a final thrust towards the doorway he staggered out into the fresh night air, to where eager hands were waiting to help him. The boy was taken from him. A loud cheer went up from the group of neighbours that had gathered outside the house as the fireman collapsed to the ground in a heap. Ambulance men rushed to his aid, placing a mask on his face and administering much-needed oxygen as they placed the stricken boy on a stretcher and carried him to the ambulance. Wendle attempted to sit up, but fell back gasping for breath, his blue eyes half shut as his chest heaved.

'Don't move, just lie back and relax,' one of the ambulance men told him as he checked him for any injuries.

'How is he?' asked Hambleton, a look of concern on his face as he leaned over the medic who was tended the gasping man.

'Except for one or two superficial burns, he's okay,' was the reply.

'Good, although for the life of me I can't understand how he got into the building and back out again. It's nothing short of a miracle,' he said, shaking his head and scratching the back of his neck as he looked at the raging inferno that was engulfing the house. It was becoming obvious by now, that the firemen, who were working hard in their attempt to extinguish it, were fighting a losing battle.

At that moment Ron Wendle sat up and ran his big hands over his blackened face as the sound of the wailing ambulance could be heard in the distance, as it turned out of Mansell Road and sped on its way to the County Hospital in Lincoln.

'How is the boy?' he enquired as he staggered to his feet and stretched himself.

'He'll be okay,' the ambulance man assured him. 'Except for inhaling a lot of smoke, he has no other injuries.'

The ambulance man took Wendle by the arm and

attempted to lead him to the other ambulance. 'Come on we'll get you checked over,' he told him.

The burly fireman cast off the helping hand. 'I'm okay,' he rasped.

'Are you sure?' asked the man who was helping him, a worried frown on his face.

Wendle nodded his head as he waved him away. He was deep in thought as he turned and walked across to the chief.

'Well done Ron!' exclaimed Hambleton, reaching out and giving him a pat on the shoulder as he approached. 'Well done.' Then he noticed the serious expression on Wendle's face. 'Something wrong?' he queried.

The big fireman, his eyes narrowing, as he slowly wiped his sweating face with the large handkerchief in his hand, stood quiet for a moment before answering. 'Chief,' he began, a questioning expression on his face. 'There's something not quite right about this situation.'

'What do you mean '*not quite right*'?'

Wendle looked him in the eye. 'I think the fire was set deliberately.'

'What makes you come to that conclusion?' the chief put to him.

'When I went into the hallway, there was a faint whiff of petrol and I found this,' replied Wendle.

He reached into his pocket and took out the unused match. Holding out the palm of his hand he offered it to Hambleton. The chief took it from him and studied it for a few seconds. He nodded his head, telling Wendle, 'I tend to agree with you Ron. It looks as though we may be dealing with an arsonist.' He paused for a moment before going on. 'In his haste to get away, the person responsible for the fire must have dropped it.'

'There's something else bothering me,' muttered Wendle, a faraway look in his eyes as he stroked his blackened jaw.

'Oh!' exclaimed Hambleton. 'What would that be?'

Wendle went on to tell him of the man he had seen in the red Ford Consul, as the fire engine approached the scene of the fire and of the maniacal expression on the man's face.

The chief nodded his head as he took in the information. 'Okay Ron,' he told the burly fireman, giving him a pat on the back. 'You'd better be off home and get yourself cleaned up.'

Hambleton cast his eyes over the scene in front of him as Ron Wendle walked off. All that was left of the house, by now, was a smouldering ruin, which was finally being brought under control by his men, as their hoses, which were pouring water on to the flames, gradually put them out. There was a thoughtful expression on his face as he reached into his tunic pocket, pulled out a mobile phone and dialled a number.

'Is that the Arnsford police department?' he enquired. After a few seconds delay he spoke into the phone. 'I'm at the scene of a house fire,' he explained, then went on. 'I have reason to believe that it may have been started deliberately. Can you send someone down to investigate?'

He nodded his head at the phone as the person at

the other end spoke, then, after giving the address of the stricken property, he switched off the mobile, put it in his pocket and turned to Wendle, who was drinking coffee out of a large chipped mug that one of the onlookers had given him.

'Let's see if we can find out why anyone would want to hurt the people who were living in the property,' he confided, a deep frown on his forehead.

Ron Wendle, taking a drink of his coffee, looked at him over the rim of his mug and nodded his head in agreement.

Constable Garnett wrote out the message, then he put the phone down and went over to where Sergeant Gordon Buckmaster was sat at a desk, poring over a document.

'This has just come from the chief fire officer,' he explained, laying the sheet of paper on the desk in front of the heavily built Buckmaster.

He looked up at the young constable over the rim of his glasses.

'What have we got here then?' he queried in a bluff Yorkshire accent, his double chin almost covering his black tie, as he picked up the document and cast his eyes over it. 'Mmm…' he muttered, as he reached out and placed it on a small stack of papers that were on the desk. 'I'd better get down there and see what's going on.'

Getting to his feet, he gave the constable a couple of instructions, before going out of the office to where his car was parked at the front of the police station. A couple of minutes later he guided the car out of the car park and drove off, arriving at the scene of the fire fifteen minutes later. Hambleton looked up at the police car as it approached the still-smoking property and pulled up. He went over to the heavily built sergeant as he struggled to get out of his car. 'What's this all about then George?' Buckmaster enquired, a little out of breath through his exertions.

Hambleton went carefully through the details that fireman Ron Wendle had discovered and his conclusion that something untoward was going on. Wendle had also mentioned that there had been a car parked opposite the house. It was just leaving when the fire engine arrived on the scene.

'I must say. It does seem a little fishy,' the sergeant declared, plucking at his bottom lip as he mulled over what the fire officer had told him. 'Did he say what type of car it was?' asked Buckmaster.

'He said it was a red Consul,' the chief told him.

He went over to the still-smouldering remains of the house. Only the walls of the property remained intact, the roof and floors having caved in and been consumed by the fire. He was deep in thought as he surveyed the pile of ashes that were all that was left of the once comfortable family home.

'Trouble is, it's going be difficult to find anything that may be incriminating; the fire seems to have destroyed any evidence that may have been there,' he remarked with a shake of his head as he turned away from the scene of destruction.

After spending a few minutes talking to the neighbours who were still hanging about, Buckmaster discovered that the occupants of the house had only lived there for four months. After writing down a few details in his note book, he went over to the fire chief and commended him for the efficient job his men had done. Hambleton, who was in the process of wrapping everything up, nodded his head in appreciation and told him they were about to leave.

A few minutes later, with Wendle giving a farewell wave of his arm out of the cab window, the large red fire engine carrying the extending ladder pulled away, closely followed by Hambleton in his car.

Sergeant Buckmaster stroked his double chin for a few seconds as he cast his eyes over the demolition job that the fire had done. 'It's going to take extensive investigation to sort this out,' he muttered to himself, as he turned away and went to his car.

The following day on arrival at his Arnsford office, he checked all the relevant information that he had received with his superior, who in turn, ordered him to contact head office at Lincoln. He picked up the phone and dialled the appropriate number. 'Hello,' he grunted. 'This is Sergeant Buckmaster here from the Arnsford office. I'd like a word with Chief Inspector Wilberton please.'

He waited patiently for the message to be passed on; after a few seconds had gone by a voice said, 'Hello, Wilberton here.'

'Hello sir, this is Sergeant Buckmaster.'

He then went on to tell him of the fire in Arnsford and the evidence that had been discovered, indicating that the fire may have been deliberate. After spending a couple of minutes studying the information

Wilberton told him, 'Leave it with me Sergeant, I'll get somebody down there as soon as possible.'

2

Detective Inspector Robert Laxton was just about to leave his home in Old Bolingbroke to set off on his journey to Lincoln, when the phone rang. He reluctantly turned and went back into the lounge and picked it up, 'tut-tutting' as he did so.

'Hello,' he began, a little sharply, 'Laxton speaking.'

'Oh hello Robert!' exclaimed the chief. 'It's Wilberton here. There's been a house fire in Mansell Road, Arnsford. It seems there are some unusual circumstances involved. I'd like you to go there straight away and find out what it is all about.'

Laxton nodded his head at the phone as his cat Horatio meowed around his feet. 'Okay Chief. I'll get down there right away,' he replied, wincing as the cat clawed at his leg.

'Now! Now! Horatio,' he laughed, as he put the phone back on its stand. Reaching down, he gave his leg a rub as he simultaneously pushed the cat away.

'Annie!' he called out to his house keeper, who was busy in the kitchen.

The short, stocky woman left off washing the breakfast pots and stuck her head round the kitchen door. 'Yes,' she called out, a beaming smile on her round face.

'Feed Horatio will you?' he requested.

'Yes I'll do that,' she replied, as she dried her hands, laid a dish of cat food on the floor and called out to the cat. Horatio, hearing the rattle of the dish on the floor, swiftly padded down the hallway and into the kitchen, as Laxton stepped out of the door and closed it behind him.

It was a lovely, bright, sunny day. Laxton looked up at the clear blue sky as he slid open the garage door. Taking a deep breath, he climbed into his car and started the engine. He looked with some pride at his garden as he drove out of the garage and on to the driveway. The row of multi-coloured tulips that grew along the edge of his driveway was in full bloom. He frowned a little as he noticed that the grass lawn needed cutting. He resolved to get it done when he got back home; putting his foot down on the accelerator he drove carefully out on to the lane which ran between his cottage and the remains of Bolingbroke Castle. One of his neighbours, Charlotte, was walking her dog as he drove along the country lane. He gave her a wave as he carefully drove around her, to avoid the dog that was straining at the leash. Charlotte smiled and waved back in acknowledgement, as she struggled to control the lively setter. A couple of minutes later, he put his foot down and accelerated up the hill, leaving Old Bolingbroke behind him. Reaching the top of the hill, he drove out on to the main road, then, making a left turn, he made his way across country to Arnsford. He was deep in thought as he drove through the fields of grazing cattle, eventually pulling up close to the smouldering remains of the terraced house in Mansell Road. Climbing out of the car, he went over to where forensics (who had just arrived), were poking about in the pile of ashes that was once a comfortable home. Bernard Howsell, the man in charge of operations, was overseeing the search for clues as to what or who had caused the fire. Bernard greeted him with a nod of his head. He had a serious expression on his face as the inspector approached him.

'What have we got here then Bernard?' Laxton enquired as he stood beside the head of forensics and looked down at the still-smoking ruins.

'We don't quite know yet,' he rejoined. His brow furrowed as he pushed his trilby forward and scratched the back of his head, adding, 'One of the firemen has made a statement, saying that he could smell petrol when he went into the blazing building.'

One of the three men who were searching for any signs of skulduggery suddenly stepped back, a look of horror on his face. 'Over here!' he shouted, waving his arm and pointing his finger.

Howsell and Laxton moved quickly to check what the man had discovered. The inspector's eyes narrowed when he saw what the forensics officer was pointing at. A badly burned human skeleton had been uncovered by the man who had been scraping among the ashes.

'Right men!' called out Howsell. 'Concentrate around this area.'

With this the three men, wearing rubber gloves, carefully scraped away the ashes and bits of charred wood that covered the bones. Laxton and Howsell were looking on intently as they worked away.

What's that?' exclaimed Laxton, his eyes screwed up in concentration as he pointed at something poking out of the ashes that were half covering the skull.

'Stand back Jim,' snapped Howsell to one of the men, as he bent down and carefully cleared the ashes from around the skull that Laxton had indicated. It showed a rusty metal comb. He picked it up. Howsell turned and handed it to the inspector.

Laxton looked at it closely. He saw that it was curved. 'It looks the type that women use to hold their hair in place,' he said in a low voice.

Howsell gave a loud groan, as he straightened up and vigorously massaged the lower part of his aching back. 'Seeing that the skeleton was below the level of the damp proof course and that the ashes were covering the skeleton, I would say that it had been placed in the two-foot gap under the floor boards,' he offered.

The inspector bent over and picked up a sliver of charred wood that was lying on top of the skeleton; placing it in the palm of his hand he studied it for a few seconds. 'I tend to agree with you. It's pretty obvious that the body of the deceased had originally been placed under the floorboards quite some time ago,' he announced as he straightened up and addressed Hambleton. 'The biggest problem we've got,' he told him, 'is finding out how long the remains have been lying there.' He paused for a few seconds, his brow furrowed as he plucked at his bottom lip. 'And that's before we can attempt to discover how or why it happened in the first instance,' he concluded, his voice dropping in volume.

The men from forensics had, by now, carefully cleared the ashes from around the remains of what was once a human being. After making sure that there were no more in the vicinity, they stood back.

The five men looked down in silence, as if in reverence of the deceased.

'Allowing for the size of the bones, I'd say the dead person wasn't very tall,' grunted Howsell, breaking the spell.

Laxton nodded his head in agreement. 'I reckon the deceased would be around five foot,' he surmised. 'That would make it either a young male, or a female.'

'Looking at the pelvis, I would say it was female,' suggested Howsell.

Laxton studied the remains for a few seconds, then he turned his attention to the metal comb that he held in his hand. It was obviously a woman's. 'I reckon you're right,' he concurred, with a slight nod of his head.

At that moment an ambulance arrived. Before the medics could remove the skeletal remains, Laxton squatted down and checked the area around where the skull was situated.

'Ahh…' he exclaimed as he held out his hand. Between his fingers he held a tuft of long hair. He stood up and turned to Howsell. 'Red I would say.' Then after a few seconds pause, 'What do you reckon?'

The chief of forensics took the hair from him and laid it in the palm of his hand and studied it closely. 'Mmm…' he muttered. 'I would say it is more, gingery.'

Handing it to one of his men, who in turn placed it in a plastic bag as the human remains were placed on a stretcher in the same position that it had lain when found, it was then carefully carried to the ambulance. A few minutes later the ambulance drove away with its macabre passenger on its way to Lincoln.

'Well!' exclaimed Laxton. 'I'll get off back to headquarters now and check on what our next move is going to be.'

With this, he bid goodbye to Howsell and climbed into his car and drove off on his journey across the Wolds to Lincoln. His forehead was deeply furrowed as he made his way through the sunlit, picturesque countryside. At any other time he would have taken great pleasure in the journey, but the eventful happenings of the last two hours weighed heavily on his mind. Forty minutes later the cathedral hove into view. He checked his watch. It showed twelve-thirty, and around ten minutes later he pulled into the police headquarters car park. Climbing out of the car he pushed open the glass doors and entered.

'Afternoon Inspector,' a bluff voice greeted him as he entered the reception office.

Laxton, a half smile on his face, raised his hand to the heavily built Sergeant Bellows who was poring over some papers in front of him.

'Afternoon Sergeant,' he replied, emphasising the 'sergeant'. 'Is the chief in?'

Bellows looked up at him and returned the smile. They had been close friends for years, having come up from the Sheffield branch together, to join the

Lincoln Police Force.

'I'll just let him know you are here Robert,' he rejoined, asking him, 'would you like a coffee?'

Laxton nodded his head.

'William!' bawled out the sergeant, over his shoulder.

A tall, gangly constable who didn't look a day older than eighteen, jumped to his feet at the back of the office and called out, 'Yes Sarge.'

'Brew two mugs of coffee,' ordered Bellows, as he picked up the phone and contacted the chief.

The young man replied, 'Right Sarge.'

The sergeant informed the chief that the inspector was in the outer office, then after a few seconds, to the sound of rattling pots, he put the phone down and informed the inspector that he could go through.

Chief Inspector Wilberton was sitting behind his large desk. Leaning back in his comfortable swivel chair, his arms folded, he greeted Laxton as he came through the door. 'What have you got then Robert?' he enquired, eyeing the tall inspector, as he pulled out a chair from under the front of the desk and sat down, facing him.

Laxton, a serious expression on his face, leaned forward and placed his elbows on the desk in front of him, before going on to tell the chief of that morning's events and of the human remains that had been discovered. He was just about to carry on, when there was a sharp knock on the door and the young constable came in with a tray carrying two mugs of coffee. The chief thanked the young man as he carefully placed the tray on the desk and left the room.

Wilberton took a sip of his coffee and looked at the inspector over the rims of his half glasses that were perched in their usual position, on the end of his nose.

'What are your conclusions then, Robert?' he spluttered, almost spilling the hot drink as it burnt his lip.

Laxton, blowing a couple of times on his drink before tentatively taking a sip, replied, a serious expression on his face, 'I think we are looking at a murder here.'

Wilberton leaned forward over the desk, a querying expression on his face. 'Have you questioned the people who were rescued from the house yet?' he asked the tall inspector sitting opposite him.

'No not yet' replied Laxton, with a slight shake of his head. He had a sombre expression on his face as he explained. 'They were in too bad a state for questioning.'

'Well the best thing to do would be to contact them this afternoon,' the chief told him. Almost as an afterthought, he added, 'That is of course, when they've had a little time to recover from their ordeal.'

Laxton tipped his head back and finished off his coffee. Placing the empty mug on the tray, he got to his feet and addressed the chief. 'Any idea where they have taken them?' he asked as he replaced the chair under the highly polished desk.

Wilberton looked up at him and shook his head negatively; after a couple of seconds had gone by, he came to a decision. Reaching out, he picked up the telephone and dialled a number, then, tapping his finger rhythmically on the desk, he waited for an answer. Eventually the phone clicked. A young woman spoke. 'Hello! This is Lincoln Hospital, can I help you?'

'Oh hello,' he replied, somewhat officiously. 'This is Chief Inspector Wilberton here. Can you tell me if the family who were involved this morning in a house fire, in Arnsford, are still at the hospital?'

'Give me a couple of minutes while I check on them,' the young woman requested.

The chief rested the phone on his shoulder and turned to the inspector, who was patiently waiting. 'She's gone to find out,' he told him in a low voice.

Laxton, who was concentrating on the chief, nodded his head in reply.

Suddenly Wilberton straightened up. 'Yes,' he grunted into the mouthpiece. 'I've got that.'

Then, after a nod of his head at the phone, he placed it back on its cradle.

'She says that they are all okay and that they have been taken to the Arnsford Council offices to be allocated temporary accommodation, where they will be kept until they can be permanently re-housed,' he announced.

Laxton looked at his watch. It showed one-fifteen.

'I'll get a quick bite to eat then I'll get straight down there,' he informed Wilberton, as he turned to leave the office.

Giving a parting wave with his right hand to

Bellows, he walked out on to the station car park, climbed into his car and drove off. After driving for around five minutes, he pulled up at a popular restaurant in the city and ordered Haddock and chips and a large mug of tea. Fifteen minutes later he leaned back and rubbed his stomach. 'I enjoyed that,' he muttered under his breath, as he reached out and finished off his mug of tea. The waiter who had seen that he had finished his meal, came over to him.

'Will that be all sir?' he enquired, a smile on his rather boyish face.

Laxton nodded his head, telling him, 'Yes thank you.'

The young man reached into his pocket, pulled out a note book, made out the bill and placed it on the table in front of him.

Picking up the bill, he saw that it amounted to £3.50. Reaching into his pocket, he took out a fiver and handed it to him, telling him to keep the change. The young man gave a broad smile as he withdrew the chair from under the tall man as he got to his feet, thanking him as he did so. Laxton nodded his appreciation as he turned away and left the premises. The sun was high in the sky as he strode out and swiftly made his way to his car. Climbing behind the steering wheel, he carefully drove out of the car park and, after negotiating the busy streets in the centre of Lincoln, he eventually found himself driving through the open countryside on his way to Arnsford. Turning on the radio, he took a deep breath and gave a long sigh of contentment as he leaned back and enjoyed the magical voice of the old maestro, Bing Crosby, as he continued his scenic journey over the Wolds.

Thirty minutes later he pulled into the small car park by the side of the Arnsford Council offices. Climbing out of his car, he entered the outer office. A middle aged woman in her late forties, with long red hair and blue eyes greeted him, a broad smile breaking out on her freckled face, as he entered the office. 'Hello Robert,' she gushed, as he leaned on the long counter. 'What can I do for you?'

'Hi Muriel,' he countered smilingly, noting that she still was a handsome woman. He and Muriel went back quite a long time. It seemed like only yesterday that they had met at the police Christmas ball. *Was it really ten years?* he asked himself as he squeezed her small hand affectionately. He was quite struck on her at the time, but she wasn't looking for a serious relationship, having just lost her father to bronchial pneumonia. Her mother, who was broken hearted at the loss of her husband, blamed his death on the fact that he had worked down the pit all his working life. *She was probably right*, he had told himself.

'I'm here to have a word with the family that was involved in the house fire in Arnsford. I'd like to ask them a few questions,' he explained to her, as he leaned his elbows on the long counter that split the spacious office in two.

She reached under the counter and pulled out a book. After putting on her glasses and spending two or three minutes fingering through it, she stopped and leaned over it to take a close look. Then, picking the book up, she placed it in front of the inspector and pointed to an address that was written in it. 'They are being housed there temporarily,' she informed him, looking at him over the rim of her glasses.

Laxton took a pen out of his pocket as she placed a blank sheet of paper in front of him. Thanking her, he commenced to write the address down. After completing it he folded the sheet up, placed it in his pocket and turned to leave.

'I hope this isn't the last we are going to see of each other Robert,' she told him in a low, provocative voice.

He stopped in his tracks and looked at her for a few seconds before smiling broadly and telling her in a soft voice, 'We'll see, Muriel,' before going out of the door, and walking to his car.

He sat for a couple of minutes in deep thought, before starting the engine. A few seconds later he was driving out of the car park and on his way to Allington Street, it was situated at the other side of Arnsford. Children were playing in the street, as he pulled up outside a row of council properties. Reaching into his pocket, he took out the folded sheet of paper that he had written the address on. Opening it up, he glanced down and ran his eyes over it.

'Number fifteen,' he muttered to himself, as he placed the note back in his pocket, before climbing out of the car and making his way to the house number indicated.

Opening the wooden gate, he walked up the flower lined path that split the two front lawns and knocked on the door of number fifteen.

A short, rather plump woman who looked to be in her late forties, dark roots showing in her blonde hair, opened the door, a questioning expression on her worn, lived-in face, as she looked up into his eyes.

'Yes, can I help you?' she asked the tall man in front of her.

'Are you Mrs Parkinson?' he enquired in a soft voice, not wishing to make her nervous.

'Yes!' she exclaimed, nodding her head.

'I'm Inspector Laxton of the Lincoln police department,' he told her. 'I'm investigating the house fire that you and your family were involved in.'

She took a step back and called out at the top of her voice. 'Alan, there's a policeman at the door. He wants to have a word about the fire.'

'Well ask him in then!' an exasperated voice replied loudly.

She gave a shrug of her shoulders and beckoned him into the sparsely furnished flat.

He smiled his thanks, as he stepped through the doorway and followed her along a poorly lit passageway and into a small lounge, where Alan Parkinson, who had been stretched out on a threadbare settee, was just getting to his feet, as he entered the room. Laxton introduced himself to the five-foot-seven, skinny, unshaven man. Parkinson, running his fingers through his thinning, dark hair, nodded in return, offering the inspector a well-worn easy chair. It was obvious to Laxton that the furnishings had been gathered together at short notice.

'Norma,' he called out, as he sat back down on the settee. 'Make the inspector a cup of tea will you?'

Laxton held up his hand. 'No thank you!' he exclaimed adding with a shake of his head, 'I haven't really got the time.'

Alan Parkinson, a questioning expression on his face, leaned forward, his elbows resting on his knees. 'How can I help you Inspector?'

Laxton leaned back, his hands clasped in front of him, the picture of the skeleton in the back of his mind, as he chewed on his bottom lip for a couple of seconds before looking Parkinson in the eyes. 'How long have you lived at the address in Mansell Road?' he put to him.

Alan Parkinson pulled at his left ear lobe, his eyes half closed, as he thought over the inspector's question. 'I would say about fourteen months,' he grunted, adding with a shrug of his narrow shoulders, 'give or take a few days.' Then he paused for a few seconds, before asking him, a frown creasing his forehead. 'Why do you ask?'

Laxton hesitated for a moment, deep in thought, before going on, ignoring Parkinson's straight forward query. 'Have you any known enemies?' he asked pointedly, switching tack.

'We hardly know anyone around here,' replied Parkinson, somewhat irritably, shaking his head in annoyance at the same time. 'Why are you asking me all these questions?' he snapped.

The inspector leaned forward, his elbows on his knees. 'We have reason to believe that the fire was started deliberately,' he asserted.

Alan Parkinson sat bolt upright as the implication sunk in. 'Who would want to hurt me and my family?' he protested angrily, clenching his knees with his fingers.

Laxton held out his hand to calm him. 'I wouldn't

worry if I were you,' he told him. 'I don't think you were a target.'

Why would someone set fire to my home, if I wasn't a target?' Parkinson queried sharply. There was a note of disbelief in his voice.

'Yours is the third house fire in the area in the last six months. It could be that there is an arsonist on the loose and he's picking his victims at random,' Laxton explained to him, as he got to his feet in readiness to leave.

'At random?' rejoined the younger man. 'Again I ask. Why my family?'

The inspector stood for a moment and looked Parkinson in the eyes and asked him, 'Did you lock your door before going to bed?'

Parkinson, his eyes half closed, ran his fingers up and down the bridge of his rather long thin nose for a few seconds as he cast his mind back. 'I'm not sure,' he mumbled, almost under his breath as he shook his head, telling him, 'it is possible that it wasn't locked.' He went to the outer door and shouted, 'Bobby!'

A few seconds later his older son came running through the door.

'What do you want me for Dad?' he asked breathlessly.

'When you put the cat out on the night of the fire, did you lock the door?'

The young lad looked at the floor sheepishly. 'No Dad,' he mumbled. 'I…I never thought.'

Laxton reached out and patted him on the head. 'Never mind son,' he told him. Then he turned to the young boy's father. 'That was probably why he chose your property.'

'Anyway thanks for enlightening us, as to what may have happened!' exclaimed Parkinson as he got to his feet. 'I'll make sure that the door is locked in future.'

Well, I've just given you my view of what may have happened,' rejoined the inspector as he reached for outer door knob. He followed this up with, 'By the way, did you know the previous tenants of your home on Mansell Road?'

Parkinson shook his head negatively. 'No Inspector, I'm afraid I can't help you there.'

Laxton paused for a couple of seconds as he absorbed the reply before going on to tell him, 'My advice for you is to keep your wits about you and your eyes open.' As he opened the door to leave, the two youngest children rushed through, laughing and shouting as they unceremoniously squeezed past him and wrestled each other on the lawn. 'It doesn't seem to have bothered them!' he exclaimed smilingly, as he slowly closed the door behind him and walked down the path to his car.

He was deep in thought as he put the car into gear and pulled slowly away, carefully avoiding a gang of children that were kicking a ball about on the street.

The sun was high in the sky as he drove back to Lincoln to discuss the day's happenings with the chief. The journey was uneventful, as he made his way across the undulating Wold countryside. Three quarters of an hour later he was pulling into the headquarters car park.

Sergeant Bellows, who was sat at his desk going through a sheaf of notes, looked up as Laxton came through the door. 'Afternoon Robert,' he greeted him, as he approached the counter.

Laxton nodded and smiled back at him.

Bellows reached out and picked up the phone. Inspector Laxton has just arrived sir,' he grunted into the mouthpiece. He nodded his head before placing the phone back on its cradle and turning to Laxton. 'He says to go straight in.'

The inspector raised his hand in acknowledgement as he walked across the floor and entered Wilberton's office.

'Come in Robert,' intoned the chief, as he entered the office, holding out his hand and beckoning him to take a seat in front of him.

Laxton, a half smile on his face, nodded at his superior as he pulled one of the two chairs from under the large desk and sat down.

'What have we got then?' enquired Wilberton, as he leaned back and folded his arms, his chair balancing precariously on its two back legs.

The inspector went on to enlighten him of his knowledge of events so far, and his own summing up of the situation.

'Mmm,' muttered Wilberton, leaning forward; there was a sharp crack, as the legs of the chair hit the floor. 'So you think that our fire bug has been at it again.'

Laxton, sitting back in his chair, his arms folded, had a serious expression on his face. 'I'm pretty certain about that,' he told the chief. He paused for a few seconds. 'If we don't catch him soon, he's going to kill someone, then we will be looking for a murderer.'

Wilberton was deep in thought as he leaned back and formed a pyramid on his chest with his fingers. He raised his eyebrows and looked over the rims of his glasses at the inspector and informed him, 'I've been making some inquiries, regarding the remains of the woman that were discovered on the site of the fire.'

'Have they been able to ascertain how long they have been there?' queried Laxton.

The chief shook his head negatively. 'Forensics are still examining the remains. They should have some idea by tomorrow morning,' he replied.

The inspector checked his wrist watch – it was nearly five o'clock. Stretching his arms out wide, he gave a loud yawn. 'It's been a long day,' he muttered to himself, as he pushed the chair back and got to his feet.

Wilberton came from behind the desk and walked with him to the door. 'See you in the morning Robert,' he intoned, as Laxton, with a nod to Bellows, went out of the police station and on to the car park.

A few minutes later, he was driving out of the city and on his way to his cottage in Old Bolingbroke, his mind going over the day's events as he wended his way through the heavy traffic that had built up on the busy main highway. Eventually he came to the sign that indicated the turn off that led to Old Bolingbroke. He gave a sigh of relief as he left the busy road behind him and negotiated the undulating country lanes that led to the quiet, picturesque Wold village. Turning into the gates of his home, he stopped the car on the cobblestoned driveway; climbing out of the car, he stretched his arms out wide to ease his aching back before entering the cottage. Horatio, his cat, came to meet him, almost getting tangled with his feet as he opened the heavy wooden door and entered the cottage. Bending down he picked up the purring cat and stroked him for a few seconds before putting him down. Walking along the hallway, he entered the kitchen where Annie his daily help was preparing his dinner; he took a deep breath as the mouth-watering smell of braised steak greeted him.

'Annie that smells wonderful,' he sighed, as he leaned over the comfortably rounded woman and gave her an affectionate squeeze as she dished out his meal.

'Get away with you,' she laughed, wriggling her way from under his strong arm as she carried the tray into the dining room.

Sitting down at the table he rubbed his hands together in anticipation of the meal she was setting before him. After making sure that she had taken care of all his needs she put her coat on, telling him as she went to the door in readiness to leave. 'I'll be off now Mr Laxton.'

She had a wide smile on her round face, as she saw how he was tucking into the meal that she had prepared for him. He raised his hand, nodded his head in appreciation and mumbled his mouth full, 'Thank you Annie.'

There was an eerie silence as the outer door banged

shut. Halfway through his meal he checked his watch; it was almost six o'clock. Getting to his feet, he went over to the television and switched it on. The evening news was just coming on as he sat down again. The news reader went on to announce the facts about the fire and the skeleton that had been discovered.

He listened intently to the summary as he finished the remains of his dinner. Reaching out he picked up the glass of orange juice that Annie had poured out for him. After finishing it off, he got to his feet, gathered up the dirty dishes and took them into the kitchen. After placing them in the sink he poured himself a generous shot of brandy topped up with soda water and retired to the lounge. Placing a record on the player, he stretched out and relaxed on the settee to the haunting music. He leaned back and closed his eyes, as he went over in his mind, the day's events. After listening for an hour or so to his favourite rendition by Johann Strauss, which included 'Tales from the Vienna Woods', he decided to take a shower and have an early night.

3

The sun was shining through the bedroom window as Robert Laxton, who had slept like a baby, opened his eyes and stretched his arms out wide. After checking his watch (it showed seven-thirty) he jumped out of bed and went over to the window and looked out over the ruins of Bolingbroke Castle before going into the bathroom for his morning wash.

What will today bring? he asked himself as he brushed his teeth vigorously.

Half an hour later, after a bowlful of cereal, a couple of slices of toast and a pot of tea, he closed the heavy oak door behind him and made his way across the courtyard, to the large outbuilding that served as a garage which housed his car. He smiled to himself, as he glanced up at a pair of blue tits that were chirruping away as they flitted in and out of the bird box that he had fitted on to the wall of the building, completely ignoring him. *Probably feeding their young,* he told himself as he swung open the two wooden doors. The sun, which had risen over the surrounding hills, was beginning to warm up as he closed the garage doors and climbed into the driving seat of the car. After settling himself down, he switched on the ignition. Annie, a red beret holding down her long black hair, was just arriving on her bicycle, her ample buttocks rhythmically going up and down as she guided the bike into the driveway, just as the engine roared into life and he moved off. She gave a wave of her hand, her round face wreathed in a broad smile as she, a little clumsily, dismounted. Waving his hand in reply, he carefully manoeuvred the big car out of the driveway and on to the narrow road that led through the village.

A few minutes later, a smile of contentment on his ruggedly handsome face, he was drumming his fingers on the steering wheel in time with the music that was emanating from the radio as he drove steadily along the steep, undulating, narrow country lanes, as he made his way out of Old Bolingbroke, on his way to head office at Lincoln. The journey, except for the odd rabbit risking its life running across the lane in front of the car, was uneventful as, half an hour or so later, he joined the stream of traffic that was approaching the outskirts of Lincoln. Another ten minutes went by and the 'Three Sisters' of the majestic Lincoln Cathedral hove into view. After negotiating the busy city centre, he eventually pulled into the Lincoln police station car park; climbing out of the car he pushed open the glass door and entered the outer office. He gave Bellows a salutary nod and a, 'Good morning,' as he carried on past him and knocked on the chief's door.

'Come in,' a loud voice called out.

Opening the door, he walked in. Pulling a chair out from under the desk, he sat down opposite his superior, Chief Inspector Wilberton.

'Now then Robert!' exclaimed the serious-looking chief, his black hair slicked back and sporting a thin Errol Flynn style moustache, as he leaned back in his chair and folded his arms. 'I want you to go to Louth and see what you can dig up about the recent fires that have been reported in the area.'

The inspector leaned forward, his hands resting on his knees. 'Have forensics come up with anything regarding the skeleton that was discovered in the fire at Arnsford?' he asked.

Wilberton picked at a spot on his chin with his forefinger, his brow deeply furrowed, as he carefully thought over what Laxton had said. 'They haven't got back to me on that yet,' he muttered, almost to himself, as he reached out and picked up the phone. 'Give me the forensics department!' he exclaimed sharply into the mouthpiece. A few seconds went by as he rested the phone on his shoulder and tapped his finger on the desk top. Suddenly he placed it to his ear and asked them what progress had been made so far regarding the human remains that had been discovered. 'Yes… Yes, I've got that,' he muttered into the phone, nodding his head as he did so.

A few seconds went by as he absorbed the information that he had been given, then, giving a curt, 'Thank you,' he reached out and placed the phone back on its rest. He had a thoughtful expression on his face as he turned to Laxton and told him, 'It seems that there hasn't been a lot of progress up to now. Except for the fact that they have ascertained that the remains are those of a female, they are finding it difficult to determine who the victim was and how long she has been dead.'

There was a hint of disappointment in his voice, as the inspector got to his feet and went to the door. He was just about to turn the door handle when he stopped and addressed the chief. 'What about checking through records, say, over the last ten years?' he suggested.

Wilberton folded his arms as he thought over what Laxton had said. 'Mmm…' he mumbled. 'There isn't much to go on.'

'Well!' exclaimed Laxton. 'What we are certain of is the fact that the deceased was a female and that she had ginger hair. That will do for a start.'

The chief nodded his head in agreement. 'You may be right Robert. I'll see what I can dig up,' he declared.

With this Laxton pulled the door shut behind him. He smiled to himself, as he saw that Bellows was being harassed by three women, complaining about being wrongly issued a parking fine, as he exited the building.

The sun was just clearing the rooftops as Laxton walked across to where his car was parked. Taking off his jacket, he tossed it onto the passenger seat before climbing behind the wheel and starting the car; driving out of the car park he joined the heavy traffic and made his way to Louth. It had been quite some time since he had been to the elegant Lincolnshire town with its handsome church and spire. Half an hour later he negotiated the roundabout at the beginning of the bypass and made his way towards the centre of the town. The tall spire jutted above the surrounding buildings, into the distant blue sky. He shook his head in wonderment as he drew closer to the sandstone built church, which always gave the impression that it was as new-looking now, as it was when it was built all those years ago.

A few minutes later he was turning into the Louth Police headquarters car park. Switching the engine off, he climbed out of the car and after pushing open two swing doors, went into the building. A young, blonde, quite good looking police woman, who was standing behind a counter that almost ran the length of the room, addressed him as he entered the reception area. 'Yes sir,' she said politely. 'Can I help you?'

Laxton leaned both elbows on the long counter and identified himself, before telling her what he was there for. The policewoman picked up the phone and spoke into it. A couple of minutes later, he was directed to an office at the rear of the room. It had a glass door which had the words 'Information room' on it. Lifting a flap at the end of the counter, he entered what you might describe as the 'business' side of the office, tapped on the door and walked in. A sergeant, a tall, heavily built man who had been sat behind a desk, was just getting to his feet.

'Good morning sir. I'm Sergeant Moxin,' he told the inspector gruffly, as they shook hands. 'How can I help you?'

Laxton folded his arms and ran the forefinger of his right hand down the bridge of his nose for a couple of seconds, a thoughtful expression on his face, before answering. 'I'm looking for any information concerning the recent house fires,' he declared in a serious tone of voice.

The sergeant, listening intently to what the inspector had said, nodded his head understandingly before going over to one of the large metal cabinets that stood along one side of the large somewhat bare room. He pulled open a drawer. After a few seconds of foraging, he took out a sheaf of papers and handed them over to the inspector. Then he indicated a chair at the desk for the inspector to sit on. Laxton nodded his thanks as Moxin turned to leave the room. Placing the papers on the desk, he sat down.

'Would you like a coffee?' enquired the sergeant as he was opening the door.

'Yes please,' Laxton told him, with a slight nod of his head, as he put his glasses on and commenced going through the details of the three fires in question.

The documents told of the fires, but had seemingly very little information as to how or why they may have been chosen in the first place. It did mention that the smell of petrol had been detected at one of the badly damaged properties. 'That could explain how they had been started,' he told himself. He noted that the occupants of the properties had, by now, all been re-housed. Their new addresses and phone numbers were stated by the side of their names.

Laxton smiled and nodded his thanks at the young policewoman as she placed a mug of coffee on the desk in front of him. Picking up the phone that was on the desk, he dialled the first of them, a Mr Johnstone. After letting it ring for quite a while, there was no answer. He put the phone down and phoned the next one, a Mr Thomason.

The inspector studied a rather amateurish painting of Louth church that hung on the bare painted wall in front of him, as he waited for an answer. After a few seconds the call was answered. 'Yes,' snapped a man's voice on the other end.

'Oh, hello sir,' grunted the inspector into the mouth piece. 'Am I speaking to Mr Thomason?'

'Yes, speaking.' announced the voice, a little irritably.

'This is Inspector Laxton of the Lincolnshire police department,' he said officiously. 'I'm inquiring into the house fire that you were involved in a few weeks ago and I would like to ask you a couple of questions.'

'Well… I'll help you if I can Inspector,' replied Thomason, his voice softening a little. 'Fire away.'

'First of all,' started Laxton, after picking up his coffee and taking a good swallow before placing the mug down on in front of him on the desk. 'Did you leave any doors unlocked on the evening of the fire?'

There were a few seconds of silence, as Thomason cast his mind back to that eventful night. 'Come to think of it Inspector, yes I did. Er… how did you guess?'

Laxton, who had been tapping his fingers on the desk top, as he waited patiently for a reply told him, 'We have come to the conclusion that you weren't singled out and that the arsonist is picking his targets at random. If you had locked your door you probably wouldn't have been attacked.'

'Mmm…' muttered the man at the other end of the phone. 'You may be right Inspector.'

'Now I want you to think carefully,' Laxton told him in a serious tone of voice. 'Did you see anyone acting suspiciously that night?'

There was a long pause before Thomason replied, 'As I recall, I did see a car that didn't belong to any of the neighbours parked on the opposite side of the road as I came back with my wife from visiting her mother.' He paused for a second before going on. 'It was still there when I closed the curtains, before going to bed.'

'What time would that be?' enquired the inspector, after taking another long drink of his coffee.

'Mmm… I would say it was around eleven p.m.,' was the reply.

'Did you get a look at the driver?'

Thomason sucked on his bottom lip as he thought deeply, before saying, 'It was too dark to make anyone out in the car or get its number, although I did manage to see the make of it.'

'What would that be?'

'A red Ford Consul,' was the positive reply.

Laxton was deep in thought as he thanked Thomason for his help and placed the phone back on its rest. Picking up his mug, he finished his drink and got to his feet. After thanking the sergeant, he closed the door behind him. The blonde policewoman gave him a sideways glance and a smile as he lifted the flap. He nodded his head at her in acknowledgement as he dropped the flap, walked out of the police station and went to his car. He looked up at the church clock as he drove the car through the busy centre of Louth. It showed two o'clock. A few minutes later he drove into the car park of a pub that was situated on the outskirts of the town. A couple of plastic tables with large umbrellas shading them from the sun, stood outside, under the windows of the pub. The door to the tap room was open as he entered and walked up to the bar and ordered a pint and two cheese sandwiches. Paying the bartender he picked up his pint and sandwiches, before going outside and sitting at one of the tables. Leaning back in his chair, in the shade of the large umbrella that was fixed in the centre of the table, he contemplated the situation at hand, tucking into his light meal as the busy traffic went by. He was just about to finish off his second sandwich, when his mobile rang. Reaching into his pocket, his mouth full of the cheese sandwich, he took out his mobile.

'Laxton here,' he mumbled into the mouthpiece, as he attempted to clear his throat.

'Ahh Robert,' said a voice on the other end. 'Wilberton here.'

The inspector swallowed the remainder of his food, as he adjusted the phone to a more comfortable position, then replied, 'Yes Chief, what is it you want?'

There was a pause as the sound of papers being shuffled around could be heard.

'I want you to get in touch with forensics and see if they have come up with anything regarding the human remains that were found at Mansell Road.'

Laxton nodded his head at the phone. 'Okay Chief,' he replied. 'I'll get over there right away.'

Picking up what was left of his pint, he tipped up the glass and finished it. After a quick wipe of his mouth with the back of his hand, he walked over to his car, climbed in and drove out of the car park. Twenty minutes later he was entering the building that housed the forensics department. A smart, attractive young woman approached him.

'Can I help you sir?' she enquired, a friendly smile on her face, as she looked up at the tall, ruggedly handsome man in front of her.

Laxton nodded his head and returned her smile as he introduced himself and told her in a soft tone of voice. 'I'd like to see Mr Howsell.'

'Follow me,' she instructed him as she turned and walked in front of him down a corridor, her hips swaying provocatively from side to side. A few seconds later she stopped and knocked at a door.

'Come in,' a voice boomed.

She opened the door and stuck her head round it. 'Inspector Laxton to see you sir,' she announced.

Howsell was out of his chair and halfway round his desk as Laxton entered his office. There was a broad smile on his ruddy face as he reached out and shook hands. 'Hello Robert!' he exclaimed jovially.

'What can I do for you?' he enquired as he pointed to a chair.

Laxton, smiling, nodded his head in acknowledgement at the balding man in front of him, as he pulled out the chair and sat down. He and Bernard Howsell went back a long way. 'I've come to see if there are any developments regarding the skeletal remains that were found at the house on Mansell Road that was burned down, Bernard,' he informed the head of forensics.

Howsell pulled out a drawer and took out a couple of sheets of paper. After running his eye over them for a couple of seconds, he placed them on the desk in front of the inspector. 'There you are Robert,' he announced. 'Not much to go on I'm afraid, but that's everything we've got.'

Laxton picked them up and studied them for a few seconds. On one of them was the print out of the skeleton, with each bone numbered and named. The other one gave a date, to the nearest number of years that the experts could say, as to the age of the remains and how long they had been under the floor boards where they were discovered. Laxton plucked at his bottom lip, as he ran his eyes over the gruesome details. 'Between fifteen and twenty years,' he muttered, almost as if to himself. Then he added with an almost imperceptible shrug of his shoulders, 'Not very precise, I must say.'

Bernard Howsell leaned forward, his elbows on the desk. 'The fire didn't help,' he offered, somewhat apologetically.

'Mmm… you are probably right,' replied the inspector, a deep frown on his forehead as he leaned back in his chair. Turning his attention to Howsell, he told him, his voice dropping in volume, 'It looks as though we'll have to inquire into the past residents of the property.'

Howsell nodded in agreement. 'The best place to start would be the council offices. They will probably have the records of all the past occupiers,' he suggested.

'I'll get down there right away,' rejoined Laxton.

Thanking Bernard for his help, he put his hands on his knees and got to his feet, he was just about to open the door, when Howsell enquired, 'By the way Robert, have you discovered anything about the arsonist?'

Laxton, his hand on the door handle, stopped and turned round. 'No, I'm afraid not. The only information we've got at the moment is that he may own a red Ford Consul,' he replied, before opening the door and leaving.

A couple of minutes later he was climbing into his car. There was a thoughtful expression on his face as he turned on the ignition, pushed the gear into first and drove carefully out of the small car park and on to the road before making his way to the council offices in Arnsford.

'Ahh, we meet again,' gushed Muriel, as he walked into the outer office in Arnsford.

The inspector suppressed a smile. He had a serious expression on his face as he leaned on the long counter and addressed her. 'Muriel, can you get me the list of past occupiers of the house on Mansell Road?'

She wrinkled her forehead questioningly.

'The one where the recent fire was,' he explained.

'Oh!' she exclaimed. 'I know which one you mean.'

With this she disappeared into the rear office. A few minutes later she came out with a batch of dog-eared documents and placed them in front of him.

'There you are,' she declared, telling him to take them over to a small table that was placed in the corner of the sparsely furnished office.

Thanking her, he did as he was bid and sat down at the table to peruse the documents.

After almost a quarter of an hour carefully scanning through the lists of addresses, he found what he was looking for – number six Mansell Road. Checking through the names of previous tenants, he discovered that there had been four since the property was first built in 1945.

'Just after the Second World War,' he muttered to himself, as he slowly ran his forefinger down the list of names.

He paused for a moment as he thought over the fact that the remains were estimated to have been placed under the floorboards between fifteen and twenty years ago. It was now 1982. After a little mental arithmetic, he worked out that he was looking for tenants between 1962 and 1967, he surmised, as he took out a pen and wrote down the figures.

He saw that Alan Parkinson, who was the last tenant of the now defunct property, had lived there for eighteen months. That ruled him out. The previous occupants before the Parkinsons were a family named Barringdon. The head of the family was a Jonathan Barringdon. He had a wife and four children. He took up residence in 1972. According to the statistics he was also ruled out as that would mean that he didn't take up residence until five years after the estimated time. The next name on the list was a Walter Roxeen. He had lived with his wife in the property for eight years. That meant that they had been resident in the property from 1964 to 1972, which covered three of the years in question. The other tenants, who were the first tenants to move in after it was built in 1945 were a family named Mullinger. The head of the household was Albert. He had lived there with his wife and two children until 1964, covering the other two years. Laxton stroked his chin for a few seconds as he thought over the implication of what he had discovered. It seemed that Walter Roxeen and Albert Mullinger were the two tenants during the time that the body was placed under the floor boards, making them the prime suspects. Reaching into his top pocket, he took out his fountain pen and wrote down the relevant facts in a note book that he kept in his wallet. He had a serious expression on his face as he carefully put away the note book in his wallet and replaced his pen back in his top pocket.

Muriel was just approaching him as he straightened up and sat back in the chair. 'Did you find what you were looking for?' she asked him.

He lifted his eyebrows, looked up at her and nodded his head, as she reached out for the heap of documents. 'Is there any way to find out where they moved to after they left the properties?' he enquired as she tucked the documents under her arm.

She paused for a moment, as she pushed back a wayward frond of her hair that had fallen over her eyes, before telling him, 'I do believe that we have records of the addresses of tenants after they move.'

'Would it be possible for me to see them?' he enquired.

'Yes of course you can see them!' she exclaimed.

'I'll get them for you.'

Laxton got his feet and followed her to the counter, where she disappeared once again into the back office. A few minutes later she reappeared holding a large, well-worn black book with the words, 'Tenants' addresses' written on the front of it.

'There you are,' she announced, as she placed it down on the counter in front of him.

The inspector nodded his thanks, as he leaned his elbows on the counter and opened the book. Running his finger down the list of names (which were in alphabetical order), he turned over four pages before he came to the name 'Mullinger'. Taking out his pen and notebook he wrote down the last known address of Mullinger, which was a country cottage, situated just outside Arnsford. He suppressed a smile as he saw the name, 'Dunroamin'. After turning over another couple of pages and checking further down the list he eventually came to the name Walter Roxeen and the person's last known address. After writing this in his notebook, he closed the thick book, thanked Muriel for her help and left the building.

Climbing into his car, he drove out of the car park and made his way out of Arnsford. Ten minutes later, after meandering through the open countryside he arrived at the rather isolated 'Dunroamin'. Smoke was coming out of the chimney of the old, somewhat dilapidated, white washed cottage, as he walked up the crazy paved path that led to a side door, being careful not to tread in the two piles of dog mess that looked to have been placed strategically in the middle of the path.

Reaching out for the cast iron door knocker, he gave two sharp raps on the old, warped door. The sound of a dog barking broke the silence. A man's gruff voice could be heard cursing the dog, this was followed by a squeal; a spell of silence followed as Laxton waited patiently for someone to respond. After a couple of minutes had gone by, the door creaked open. A bewhiskered old man, around five-foot-seven, stood in the doorway, an annoyed expression on his face. A strong smell of stale sweat and animals wafted through the door, as he looked up at the tall man standing in front of him.

'Mr Mullinger?' enquired the inspector, taking in the sparse strands of grey hair on the almost bald head as he looked down at the elderly man in front of him.

'Yes,' he snapped nastily, sticking his chin out belligerently as he hitched up his creased baggy trousers and straightened up to his full height.

Laxton looked down at the bedraggled man, and introduced himself.

The man's face visibly softened when he knew that he was talking to the police. 'Come on in then,' he muttered as he stood back.

Laxton ducked his head as he passed under the low door frame. He had a distasteful expression on his face as he followed the man into the lounge. A Jack Russell terrier stretched out on a well-worn stained settee, looked up at him and growled as he came through the door.

The old man picked up a newspaper and took a swipe at the offending animal which in turn squealed as it hastily jumped off the settee and scuttled across the room, its eyes rolling as it took refuge under a coffee table that stood in the corner. An old black and white television that had seen better days was standing on the table. He indicated with his hand, an easy chair, telling him, 'Sit yourself down Inspector.'

His visitor declined, informing him that he would only be a few minutes.

Laxton folded his arms and stroked his chin, before explaining that he wanted to ask him a few questions regarding his tenancy of the property on Mansell Road.

'Okay,' Mullinger told him with a shrug of his narrow shoulders. 'Go ahead.'

'Can you describe to me the situation when you lived there?'

Mullinger massaged the back of his neck, his eyes half closed; he looked up at the cracked ceiling as he thought over the police officer's statement for a few seconds before replying. 'Well, you are going back a few years. But I'll do my best,' he explained with a shake of his head, before continuing. 'I went to live there just after the war.' He paused for a moment, plucking at his bottom lip, as his mind went back. 'I'd just been demobbed out of the army. I had a wife and two children at the time and we were allocated the property, which was a council house.' He smiled, showing tobacco-stained teeth, as his mind went back. 'They were good times,' he muttered. 'Hard times, I'll admit, but we were happy as pigs in muck for sixteen years.'

'Go on,' urged Laxton.

Mullinger's face turned serious as he stroked his

whiskery chin. 'Sadly it didn't last. I lost my job and couldn't find another one. Annie and me kept falling out. After a year of this we realised it couldn't go on. Eventually she took the kids and left me.'

He gave a shrug of his shoulders. Laxton almost felt sorry for him. 'What happened then?' he rejoined.

Mullinger gazed down at his muddied shoes for a few seconds, before raising his head and looking up at the inspector; there was a sombre expression on his face as he continued. 'Well…' he started, a little hesitatingly, then went on. 'A short time after she left, I was informed by the council that I would have to give up the property. A couple of years later we were divorced, I haven't seen her since,' he explained.

Laxton was deep in thought as he mulled over what the scruffy little man had said. 'What was the colour of your ex-wife's hair?' he queried.

Mullinger, a deep frown on his forehead, snapped, 'Why do you want to know that? She's all right isn't she?'

The inspector, noting the serious tone of Mullinger's voice, pressed on. 'Will you answer the question please?'

Well, if you must know. Her hair was black. Pitch black.'

'Thank you that's all I want to know,' countered Laxton, assuring him, 'I'm sure she's all right.'

After thanking Mullinger for his co-operation, he turned to leave. A few seconds later he stepped out of the front door and took a deep breath of fresh air, before carefully making his way along the path that cut through the unkempt, weed-covered garden, to his car, where he sat for a couple of minutes checking his note book. Then, putting the book in his pocket, he drove off to his next destination, 21 Grainville Street, Louth. He checked his watch as he turned off the roundabout at Ulceby Cross. Twenty uneventful minutes later he turned into Grainville Street and slowly drove along the front of a neat row of well-kept semi-detached houses, eventually stopping at number 21. Climbing out of the car, he opened a small wooden gate and made his way down the flower-lined path. He nodded in appreciation as he took in the neat lawns on either side of the path. Reaching up he gave a sharp rap on the brass door knocker that was situated underneath a white painted '21'. A young girl, around six years old, answered the door. She had a questioning expression on her young face as she looked up at the inspector.

'Can I speak to your parents please?' he asked smilingly.

She turned round and shouted at the top of her voice, 'Mum, there's someone wants to talk to you!'

'All right! All right! You don't have to shout so loud,' the woman said breathlessly, as she hurried to the door.

Laxton looked at the short, somewhat skinny woman, her hands covered in flour. 'Mrs Roxeen?' he enquired.

The dark-haired woman pushed back a frond of slightly greying hair that had fallen over her blue eyes with the back of her left wrist, as she nodded her head. 'Yes,' she replied, an inquiring look in her eyes.

After telling her who he was, he went on. 'I would like to ask you a few questions,' he began.

'That's all right Inspector!' she exclaimed. 'Would you like to come in?'

Laxton smiled his thanks and followed her along a passage way into the rear kitchen. A table stood in the middle; on it was placed a large glass bowl full of partly mixed dough.

'I'm busy making bread,' she explained with a nod at the bowl. 'You will have to excuse the state of the kitchen,' she told him apologetically, placing her hands under the running tap to wash the flour from them.

He nodded his head understandingly.

'Now then what's this all about?' she enquired, a questioning expression on her round face, as she dried her hands on a towel and turned to face the tall man.

'First of all Mrs Roxeen, how long have you and your husband lived at this address?'

'Well, I've lived here about eight years.' She paused for a moment before going on. 'My husband moved in here with me. Before that he lived at Mansell Street in Arnsford.'

Laxton's brow furrowed as he thought over her reply. 'Oh,' he rejoined, telling her to carry on.

'*Well!*' she exclaimed. Her brow furrowed as she cast her mind back, before going on to tell him, 'We met and married eight years ago.'

'Was he married before he met you?' he asked her, his voice dropping in volume.

'Yes he was,' she replied sharply. 'But what has that got to do with you?'

'I can assure you Mrs Roxeen, it is relevant,' he informed her.

'Can you describe his first wife?'

She gave a shrug of her shoulders. 'Her name was Margaret and as far as I can tell you, she wasn't very tall.' She paused for a moment as she again cast her mind back. 'From what I've seen of her in Walter's photographs, she was just a slip of a woman.'

'Do you know what happened to her?'

'My husband did say that she ran off with a fellow.'

'Did he tell you when she left him?'

She scratched the top of her head with her forefinger and half closed her eyes as she attempted to recall what her husband had said. 'I think he told me it was in 1966,' she confided.

Laxton stroked his chin as he thought over what she had told him.

'Is Mr Roxeen at home?' he enquired.

She had a solemn look on her face, biting on her bottom lip to suppress her feelings, before shaking her head and telling him in a hushed voice, 'I'm afraid not. He died four weeks ago.' She paused for a moment to dab her eyes with a handkerchief, before going on. 'He'd been suffering from cancer of the prostate for over three years,' she explained tearfully. 'He left it too long before doing something about it.'

Laxton was taken aback by the news of Roxeen's death. After commiserating with her, he thanked her for answering his questions, then, with a thoughtful look on his face, he turned to leave. He had his hand on the door handle when he stopped and turned to her. 'Can you tell me what colour hair his first wife had?'

'Yes of course I can. It was ginger,' she informed him.

Laxton thanked her as he walked out of the door and pulled it shut behind him. He chewed on his bottom lip as he made his way thoughtfully down the garden path, to his car. There were deep furrows in his brow as he started the engine and drove off.

The drive from Louth to Lincoln was to say the least, tedious, as he followed one farm tractor after another. Finally, half an hour later, he arrived at headquarters in Lincoln. Wilberton greeted him as he walked through the office door. 'What have you discovered Robert?' he asked, as Laxton took a seat opposite him and proceeded to tell him in detail, what he had uncovered.

'Mmm,' muttered the chief, after he had absorbed the fact that Roxeen was dead and that his first wife had ginger hair. 'It looks as though we may have discovered something that points to who may be responsible for the human remains that were found in the fire.'

Laxton shook his head, as the constable came into the office with the obligatory coffees. 'I'm not so sure Chief,' he rejoined, after giving the constable a nod of thanks. 'Until we know for certain whether she is alive or not, the case is still open,' he explained, as he reached out for his drink and took a tentative sip.

'You are right of course,' Wilberton conceded with a nod of his head. He paused for a few seconds as he took a couple of sips of his coffee, then went on. 'But you must admit it does fit in.'

Laxton nodded his head in agreement, as he finished his drink. 'It does look that way,' he rejoined, as he placed his hands on his knees, got to his feet and turned to leave.

Laxton stopped for a second, his hand on the door handle, as he turned to the chief, a questioning expression on his face. 'Have we any more information regarding the arsonist?' he enquired.

'No,' Wilberton told him with a shake of his head. 'All we know at the moment is that we are looking for a man in a red Ford Consul and that the arsonist may be responsible for two other house fires in the area.'

Laxton nodded as he absorbed the information. After checking his watch – it showed six-thirty p.m. – he turned to leave.

'I'll get off now,' he said as he went through the door, adding, 'I'll look into Roxeen's details tomorrow.'

It was a pleasant evening, the sun was just beginning to wane, as Laxton drove through the Lincolnshire countryside on his journey back to Old Bolingbroke, but he was in no mood to enjoy it as he thought over the day's events. Arriving at his cottage he climbed out of the car, to be met by Horatio, meowing and weaving in and out of his feet, almost tripping him up as he wearily trudged to the back door.

'All right Horatio, all right!' he exclaimed, as he bent down and gently ran his hand along the cat's furry back before entering the cottage.

He was surprised to see that Annie, his help, was still at the cottage. She was just taking a meat and potato pie out of the oven as he walked into the kitchen. He stopped for a second and sniffed the air, before taking a can of Guinness out of the fridge; pouring it into a glass, he pulled a chair up to the table and sat down. 'Something smells good,' he told her, rubbing his hands together in anticipation, as she carefully placed the steaming hot pie and vegetables on a plate, carried it to the table and placed the appetising dish in front of him.

'Annie,' he confided, a broad smile on his face as he picked up his knife and fork. 'I could kiss you.'

Annie's round face reddened slightly as she looked at him out of the corner of her eye. She had become used to his bantering over the years that she had been looking after him. 'Get away with you,' she said, chuckling as she put her coat on. 'I bet you say that to all the girls.'

With this, Annie, still chuckling to herself, bid him goodnight and walked out of the door, as he tucked in to the inviting meal that she had placed in front of him.

After placing the last piece of pie in his mouth, Laxton washed it down with a long swig of Guinness. Leaning back in his chair, his eyes half closed and a smile on his face, he gave a contented sigh and massaged his stomach. 'Mmm… that really was something special,' he muttered to himself.

Then, after emptying his glass he got to his feet, went into the kitchen and placed his glass and the pots in the sink, before climbing the stairs to the bathroom for his shower. The feel of the water cascading down on him made him feel good. After a good rub down he felt a new man; donning his dressing gown, he went back downstairs and stretched out on the settee. Switching on the well-worn record player, he closed his eyes as he listened to his favourite piece of music by Johann Strauss. An hour or so later, he woke up to the sound of the record player clicking incessantly as it went round and round (the automatic switch off wasn't working). Pushing himself into a sitting position, he reached out, lifted the arm and placed it on its rest. Suddenly there was a loud 'dong' from the old grandfather clock that stood in the corner as it struck ten-thirty. Stretching his arms out wide, he yawned loudly as he ran his fingers through his wiry hair, before getting to his feet and wearily making his way up the stairs to bed.

4

It was a clear, moonlit night as Martin Danister stopped his car one hundred yards past the end of the drive that led to a detached bungalow. It was just after midnight. He had already checked that all the lights in the property were out. Quietly opening the boot of his car, he took out a one gallon can of petrol; tip-toeing down the driveway, he carefully opened the gate and made his way to the back door. Turning the door handle, his heart leaped when he discovered it was open. This was the fourth property that he had tried. The other three had been securely locked. Being as quiet as he could he entered the bungalow and commenced to sprinkle the petrol around the kitchen. At that moment a cat jumped out in front of him, almost tripping him up. It squealed as he accidentally trod on its paw, making him spill the inflammatory liquid, soaking the lower part of his trousers. Cursing under his breath, he stopped for a few seconds and listened carefully. Everything was quiet. He gave grunt of satisfaction. Holding the can containing what was left of the petrol in his left hand, he reached into his pocket, took out a box of matches and struck one.

Seventy-year-old Walter Endleby climbed into bed beside his wife Mary. He gave a contented sigh as he snuggled up to her and closed his eyes. Twenty minutes went by and he was just beginning to fall asleep, when she poked him in the ribs with her elbow.

'What now?' he mumbled irritably.

'Have you locked the back door Walter?' she asked him in a low voice.

'I'm not sure,' he replied sleepily, as he scratched his balding head and made himself more comfortable.

'Well you'll just have to make sure won't you?' she told him, a sense of urgency in her voice, suddenly bringing him to his senses.

Walter shook his head from side to side, suppressing a sharp reply, as he pushed the blankets back and sat up. After pausing for a few seconds to gather himself, he swung his feet out of the bed; he knew when he was beaten. 'All right! All right!' he exclaimed irritably, before giving a deep sigh. 'I'll go and check the door.'

Climbing out of bed, he hitched up his baggy pyjama bottoms (which were in danger of falling below his knees) and put his bedroom slippers on. This was followed by tentatively feeling his way across the dark bedroom. He was just about to open the bedroom door when he heard the cat squeal. His hand froze on the door handle, as the hair on the back of his neck stood up. Turning away from the door, he carefully made his way towards the wardrobe where he kept a baseball bat.

'What's the matter?' whispered Mary fearfully, as he reached into the wardrobe and took out the formidable weapon.

'I think there's someone in the kitchen,' Walter told

her in a low voice, as he made his way stealthily back across the bedroom and carefully opened the door with the baseball bat over his shoulder ready for action.

'Be careful Walter,' his wife told him nervously.

Taking a deep breath, he tip-toed along the hallway; he made no sound as he eased open the door and stepped into the dark kitchen in his slippers. He sniffed the air. There was a strong smell of petrol, as he saw a shadowy figure strike a match.

'What the hell do you think you are doing?' he raged, as he stepped menacingly towards the intruder, swinging the baseball bat as he moved forward.

Martin Danister had just struck the match and was about to throw it on the petrol-covered floor. He jerked his head up in alarm as the well-built figure came at him, swinging the baseball bat. It caught him on the shoulder, knocking him off balance, causing him to spill what was left of the petrol in the can, over his clothing and making him drop the match; which landed on his foot. There was a '*whoosh*' as the match ignited the liquid and flames shot up from his petrol-soaked clothing. He screamed and ran out of the bungalow, as the flames enveloped him.

Walter picked up a carpet and smothered the flames that were coming up from the petrol that Danister had poured on the floor; after ensuring that the fire wouldn't break out again and still hanging on to the carpet, he ran out, into the garden, to where the man who was engulfed in flames, had run. He was rolling over and over on the lawn yelling and screaming, as he tried in vain to extinguish the flames that were consuming him. Walter ran across to the suffering Danister and wrapped him in the carpet. A few minutes later he unrolled the carpet, recoiling at the horrific sight of the badly burned man in front of him; his face was covered in blisters and the rest of his body was badly burned. He was obviously in pain as he moaned through badly swollen lips. 'Help me! Help me.'

Walter Endleby stood up and massaged the back of his neck, as he thought over what he should do next. It was obvious that he couldn't do anything to ease the badly burnt young man's suffering. 'I'll get on the phone and call an ambulance,' he muttered to himself, as he turned and ran into the bungalow.

'What's happened?' cried Mary agitatedly, her curlers bouncing up and down, as she ran out of the front door and saw the stricken man. Walter didn't answer as he brushed past her and went back into the bungalow and picked up the phone. 'Hello, is that the ambulance service?' There was an urgent tone to his voice.

After telling them what had occurred, he gave them the address.

Fifteen minutes later the ambulance was turning into the drive, its headlights lighting up the scene. After quickly placing the injured man on a stretcher, they lifted him into the ambulance, before driving off at speed, lights flashing and siren wailing, as they made their way to A & E at Lincoln County Hospital.

Robert Laxton woke to the sound of the bedside phone ringing; bleary-eyed he reached out and picked it up. 'Hello!' he exclaimed sleepily into the mouthpiece.

'Robert,' a sharp voice snapped, bringing him

abruptly to his senses. It was Wilberton. 'There's been another fire reported, just outside Louth. I want you to go there as soon as you can and get all the details.' He went on to tell him the address.

'Right Chief, I'll get off as soon as I've had something to eat.'

The hall clock was chiming five a.m. as he climbed reluctantly out of the comfortable bed, bent down and put on his slippers. Shuffling sleepily into the bathroom, he shaved and took a quick shower.

Fifteen minutes later, after towelling himself vigorously, he made his way back into the bedroom, humming away to himself, as he swiftly dressed. Walking over to the window as he fastened his tie, he looked out over the hills that surrounded the village. The moon, that had bathed the countryside with its pale light, was just beginning to disappear behind some heavy clouds that were gathering over the distant hills. *I feel good*, he told himself as he took a deep breath before turning to go downstairs. Horatio, repeatedly meowing, followed him as he entered the kitchen.

'All right I've got the message!' he exclaimed, a broad smile on his face as he reached into the cupboard and took out a tin of smelly cat food. Horatio unceremoniously pushed his hand out of the way to get at the food, as he forked it out on to an old plate.

With the cat purring away as it devoured its meal, he turned to his own breakfast. After a bowl of corn flakes and a couple of slices of toast, washed down with a mug of tea, he was ready to face the day in front of him.

Closing the door behind him, Laxton looked up at the sky. Pulling his face at the heavy clouds that had gathered overhead, he went out to his car. *Quite a contrast*, he told himself as he opened the garage doors, climbed behind the steering wheel and started the engine. Spots of rain were beginning to hit the windscreen, as he switched on the lights and drove off.

It was just coming daylight as, half an hour later he arrived at the address given him by the chief. The property, a bungalow, was surrounded by four-foot privet. A drive ran down the side of it. He frowned as he noticed a red Ford Consul parked along the lane, just past the bungalow.

Pulling into the driveway, he disembarked and knocked on the door. There was a strong smell of petrol as the door opened. A heavily built elderly man wearing a woolly grey pullover that matched the unruly grey thatch on his head stood in the doorway, an enquiring expression on his face. 'Yes,' he said, a little gruffly. 'Can I help you?'

'My name is Laxton, er, Inspector Laxton,' he offered, pausing for a moment before going on to explain to the old man that he was there to investigate the break in and the subsequent circumstances.

'Come on in Inspector,' said the man, a welcoming smile on his creased, ruddy face. 'My name is Walter Endleby,' he told him as he stood back from the doorway.

Laxton smiled in return and followed him into the hallway and along a passageway that led into a comfortable lounge containing a well-worn three-piece suite. He cast his eyes around the room as he sat down in one of the two easy chairs. He noticed a couple of amateurish water colours hanging on the walls. *Probably done by Endleby*, he thought as he shuffled his backside to make himself more comfortable.

'Mary,' called out the old man, in a loud voice. 'Bring in two mugs of tea.'

His wife who was in the kitchen, could be heard grousing about 'men living the life of Riley' amid the clatter of pots and the sound of the kettle being filled.

Endleby sat on the settee that was positioned opposite the chair that Laxton was in. 'Now then Inspector,' he began, leaning forward, his elbows on his knees. 'What do you want to know?'

Laxton relaxed into the soft back of the armchair, his hands in front of him, on his lap. There was a serious expression on his face as he interlocked his fingers. 'I would like you to start at the beginning and describe to me exactly what happened last night, Mr Endleby,' he asserted.

'Well,' began the old man, 'I had just gone to bed, when Mary, er, that's my wife, asked me if I had locked the door.' He paused for a moment, a faraway look in his small gimlet like, brown eyes as he gathered his thoughts. He went on. 'Realising that I might not have locked it, I decided to get up again and check it out. I was just about to open the bedroom door when I heard a noise coming from the kitchen.'

He stopped talking and looked up irritably, as his wife Mary came into the lounge carrying a tray with two mugs of tea on it.

'I hope I'm not intruding,' she announced, placing

her ample figure between the two men, as she bent over and put the tray on a coffee table that was in front of them.

'Mary!' he exclaimed, stretching his neck as he attempted to look round her broad rump.

'How can I explain to the inspector what happened last night, if you keep coming in and out?'

'Well you asked for the tea,' she snapped back at him as she flounced out of the room and banged the door shut behind her.

Laxton suppressed a smile as Endleby took a deep breath to calm himself, before going on with his narrative. 'As I was saying, I heard a noise in the kitchen. I went to my wardrobe, to where I keep a baseball bat.' He looked the inspector in the eyes before telling him, with a shrug of his shoulders, 'I keep it there in case of emergencies.'

Laxton picked up his mug of tea, took a sip, and nodded his head, letting him know that he understood, then listened attentively as the old man went on to tell him how he'd seen the figure of a young man in the act of setting fire to the bungalow.

Endleby paused for few seconds, his eyes wide with excitement, as he cast his mind back to that nerve racking moment. 'I challenged him!' he exclaimed, his unshaven chin jutting out aggressively. 'Then I went for him with my baseball bat, catching him a glancing blow on his shoulders.' He stopped and took a deep breath as he tried to compose himself.

'And then what happened?' urged Laxton.

Endleby slowly rubbed the palms of his hands together as he gathered his thoughts. Then after taking a long drink of his tea and wiping his mouth with the back of his hand, he told the inspector. 'He dropped the lit match on his foot and in a few seconds, he was engulfed in flames.' He raised his arms shoulder high to emphasise the point before going on to tell him, 'By the time I had put out the fire in the kitchen, he had run outside. A few minutes later I went out to him. He was engulfed in flames and rolling about on the front lawn screaming. I wrapped him in a carpet and set about putting out the flames then I got on the phone and called for an ambulance.'

He looked at Laxton, a helpless expression on his face as he gave a shrug of his shoulders. 'I know it was self-inflicted, but I felt sorry for the young man,' he explained with a shake of his head before adding a little apologetically, 'what else could I do?'

Laxton finished his tea, got to his feet and gave the old man a pat on the back. 'Under the circumstances, Mr Endleby, you did a good job,' he said, as he went to the door and prepared to leave. He had a serious expression on his face as he stopped for a moment and turned to face the old man, 'I wouldn't feel so sorry for him if I were you. He asked for everything he got.'

Endleby, who had followed him to the front door, shrugged his shoulders, telling the inspector that he still didn't like what had happened to the intruder as Laxton opened the door and went out.

He glanced up at the cloud-laden sky, as he closed the door behind him and walked down the flower-lined footpath. He stood for a moment and checked the spot in the middle of the lawn – there was an area of burnt grass where the stricken man had lain. Slowly shaking his head from side to side, he turned away, muttering, 'God doesn't pay his debts in money.'

The rain was just beginning to come down heavily as he climbed into his car and drove off. He had a lot to think about, during the journey through the countryside to the sound of the wipers rhythmically swishing from side to side, as he made his way to police headquarters in Lincoln. Wilberton was waiting for him in his office when he arrived. Laxton pulled the chair out from under the desk and sat down opposite him.

'What have we got then Robert?' Wilberton enquired, his arms folded.

The inspector went on to tell him of the arsonist's attempt to set fire to the bungalow that was situated just outside Louth. He went on to describe to him, how the fire raiser had been disturbed in the act of starting the fire and of how, in the process of committing the act he had accidentally set fire to himself.

Wilberton, who had been listening intently to the inspector, asked him, 'Which hospital have they taken him to?'

Laxton gave a shrug of his shoulders, as he told him that he wasn't sure. 'Probably Lincoln,' he suggested.

Wilberton picked the phone up and made a few enquiries. He held the phone to his ear for a couple of minutes. 'Okay,' he said into the phone. 'I've got that.'

Placing the phone back on its cradle, he turned his attention to Laxton. 'You were right!' he exclaimed with a slight nod of his head. 'He's in Lincoln County Hospital, in the burns unit.' He looked Laxton in the eyes over the rim of his glasses and told him, 'I want you to go down there straight away and see if you can get any information regarding the recent fires out of him.'

Putting his hands on his knees, Laxton prepared to rise. He had just got to his feet and was turning to leave, when Wilberton told him, 'By the way, we've had a phone call from Walter Roxeen's solicitor. It seems that Roxeen has left a sealed letter with instructions that it is to be only opened after his death, by the police.'

Laxton, an enquiring expression on his face as he asked him, 'Do you want me to call in at the solicitors and pick it up?'

Wilberton shook his head. 'No!' he exclaimed. 'He tells me we should be receiving the letter this afternoon by special delivery.'

'That should be interesting,' rejoined Laxton, as he pushed his chair back under the desk before walking out of the office. He gave a quick nod to Bellows as he passed through the outer office and out on to the car park. A few spots of rain were beginning to fall as he quickly made his way to his car; climbing in, he sat for a few seconds to gather his thoughts before turning on the ignition. The rain was beginning to come down heavily as he guided the car out of the car park and drove off. He switched the wipers on as he joined the heavy traffic.

His mind was full of differing thoughts as he drove the short distance to the hospital. After finding a parking spot in the large car park, he climbed out of the car and walked swiftly through the heavy rain to the glass swing doors; pushing his way through them, he approached the long reception desk.

'Can I help you?' asked a pretty young woman, as he leaned on the long counter.

Reaching into his pocket, took out his credentials and showed them to her, then asked which ward the young man who had suffered serious burns was in. He explained to her that he didn't know the man's name.

The young woman flicked through some notes on her desk. 'Oh, yes, here we are,' she muttered, then told him with a shrug of her shoulders, 'We don't seem to have his name either.' She then explained to him, 'What I can tell you is that he is in the burns unit.'

He nodded his head as she directed him to the appropriate ward. Thanking her, he strode along the busy corridor that led to the unit. On arrival he approached a male nurse and introduced himself. 'I'm looking for the man who has recently been admitted to the burns unit,' he told the young man.

The nurse directed him to a bed that had been curtained off. A doctor was just pushing back the curtain and coming out as they approached the cubicle. 'This is Inspector Laxton, Doctor Shinda,' he told him.

The doctor, a rather short man of Indian origin, looked up at Laxton over thick-rimmed glasses and nodded his head in acknowledgement. 'How can I help you?' he asked, in perfect English.

The inspector explained to him that he would like to question the injured patient.

Doctor Shinda ran his fingers through his thick black hair and adjusted his glasses, before addressing Laxton, in a measured tone. 'You can go in and see him,' he told him, holding the curtain back. 'But I must emphasise… no questioning.' He paused for a moment before adding, 'Anyway, I don't think you would get much out of him in his present state.'

Laxton ducked his head as he stepped into the cubicle and walked up to the bed. He looked down at the pitiful figure in front of him. It was obvious that the badly disfigured man wasn't in any state to answer any questions. He turned to the doctor, a deep frown on his forehead. 'When do you think he will be in a fit condition to talk?'

Doctor Shinda half closed his eyes, as he plucked at his bottom lip for few seconds before telling the inspector, in a serious tone of voice, 'I'm afraid he won't be in any state to talk Inspector, he has suffered over eighty per cent burns.'

'Doesn't that mean he isn't likely to recover?' Laxton put to him.

'Yes, I'm afraid it does look that way,' he replied, a note of finality in his voice, before looking him in the eyes and assuring him, 'we'll do our best for him.'

Thanking the doctor for his co-operation, the inspector walked out of the ward and back down the corridor as he made his way to the exit. He was deep in thought as the double glass doors closed behind him; striding across the car park, he climbed into his car and carefully drove out of the car park, round the one way system and out on to the busy main road.

The rain was beginning to abate and there were blue gaps appearing in the clouds, as he drew up in the headquarters car park and climbed out of the car. Sergeant Bellows, a half smile on his ruddy face, greeted him with a nod of his head, as he entered the outer office. He gave a nod of his head in return as he made his way across the floor to the chief's office before opening the door and entering.

'I'll send you a drink in,' he called after him, as he went through the doorway.

'Ahh Robert!' exclaimed Wilberton, as Laxton entered the room and took a seat. A white envelope lay on the desk in front of the chief; picking it up, he handed it to the inspector. 'Read that,' he told him, a grim expression on his face.

There was a questioning frown on Laxton's forehead as he reached out and picked it up. Holding it out in front of him, he ran his eyes over the wording on the front of the envelope. 'To whom it may concern.'

Poking his fingers inside the envelope, he pulled out a folded sheet of paper and opened it. On it was written:

To the police department.

Being of sound mind, I wish to confess that I am solely responsible for the death of my first wife Jane. It was caused accidentally after an argument at the top of the stairs. She lunged at me. I dodged to one side to avoid her fists. She overbalanced and fell to the bottom of the stairs. When I checked her, I discovered that she was dead. She had probably broken her neck. After placing her body under the floor boards,

I told everyone that she had left me and gone off with another man.

Walter Roxeen.

At that moment the sergeant came through the door carrying two cups of tea and placed them on the desk. Wilberton nodded his thanks and picked up one of the cups.

Laxton, who was still holding the letter in his hand, had a deep frown on his forehead, as he absorbed the information before raising his eyebrows and looking across the desk at the chief. 'It looks as though we can close the book on this one,' he intoned as he reached out and picked up the other cup of tea.

Wilberton leaned back in his chair and looked at Laxton over the rim of his glasses. 'Yes I agree with you,' he rejoined in a quiet voice. Sitting up, he enquired, 'What have you come up with regarding the arsonist?'

The inspector paused for a moment as he raised the cup to his lips and took a long drink, then he leaned forward, placed his cup on the desk and went on to tell the chief in detail, of the condition that he had found the arsonist in. 'According to the doctor, he probably won't survive the horrendous burns that he has suffered,' he informed Wilberton. He went on to tell him, 'The nurse in charge told me that he hasn't been identified yet?'

The chief, deep in thought reached out, picked up the phone and made a few enquiries. After nodding at the phone for a few seconds, he put it down and turned to Laxton. 'I've been informed that our arsonist's name is one, Martin Danister. He has been incarcerated in an institution for five years, after being caught setting fire to his parents' home.'

He stopped for a second to adjust his glasses which had fallen on to the end of his nose, before continuing, his voice lowered in tone. 'It seems that he was released from the mental institution six months ago.'

'Well, that's a bit of a coincidence!' exclaimed Laxton, pausing for a moment as he finished drinking his tea before reaching out and placing his cup on the tray. 'First of all we have Walter Roxeen, who has admitted involvement in his wife's death, has years later, succumbed to cancer. Then we have Martin Danister, the arsonist, in hospital with injuries caused by his own depraved action, at deaths door.'

'Mmm' grunted Wilberton. 'What you might call… 'Justice deferred'.'

End

Red Triangle

Alfred Hawsford put the small case he was carrying down on the ground and stretched his thin arms out wide. Taking a deep breath, he looked up at the clear blue skies through half-closed eyes. The sun was just beginning to show, as he breathed out slowly and checked his watch. It was nine a.m. A half smile played on his lips for a second as he nodded his head. 'It feels really good to be on the outside again,' he muttered to himself, as behind him the gates of Lincoln prison banged shut.

'See you again, Alf,' had been the parting shot of the warder manning the gate, a knowing expression on his face.

'Not if I can help it,' the puny man growled in reply, shaking his head, as he reached down and picked up his case, before turning his back on the twin turrets that stood like sentinels each side of the heavy wooden gates and walking off.

Hawsford, known inside as 'the runt' because of his small stature, had a string of convictions against his name, from probation in his teens to short sentences for minor acts of breaking the law, he had eventually hit the big time by becoming involved with a gang of bank robbers. He had joined them against his better judgement, having been attracted by the promise of making a killing that would set him up for life. According to inside information, they were told that the rear door of one of the large local banks would be left unlocked. All they had to do was walk in and fill their bags. The police must have got wind of it and were in hiding waiting for them; they pounced on the gang as they were in the act of breaking into the safe. Shaking his head in disgust, he cast his mind back to that fateful day. He had often wondered if the whole episode had been a deliberate ploy, set up by the police to catch them in the act, a trap that they had been stupid enough to walk into.

He had just completed three and a half years for being involved in the first (and the last, he promised himself) bank robbery that he had attempted, having had one and a half years cut from the original five for good behaviour. He made a vow to himself that he would never fall foul of the law again; he had decided that from now on he was going to go straight.

His narrow shoulders were hunched as he made his way to the nearest bus stop, some fifty yards down the road from the prison.

'What's your hurry Alf?' a voice called out loudly as he neared the bus stop.

Hawsford stopped in his tracks when he heard the familiar voice call out. Looking over his shoulder, he saw that a car had pulled up just behind him; its driver had leaned over and pushed open the passenger door. 'Jump in, Alf,' the driver, a well-built, hard-looking man, called out to him. 'I want to have a word with you.'

The little man shook his head emphatically, from side to side, he knew what was coming. 'Leave me alone,' he called back, a hint of annoyance in his voice, as he ignored the big man's request.

Alfred Hawsford carried on walking, knowing full well what was expected of him, but he had made his mind up that he would not be dragged into another scam. The heavily built man climbed out from behind the steering wheel, grabbed Hawsford's arm and forcefully dragged him back to the car, then unceremoniously bundled him into the back seat. 'You'll do as I bloody well tell you,' snarled the big man as he put the engine into gear and drove off. The diminutive Hawsford cowered in the plush leather seat as the car gathered speed.

At Lincoln city police headquarters, Chief Inspector Wilberton called D.I. Robert Laxton into his office; he pointed to a chair opposite him in front of his desk as the six-foot-three detective came through the door. Laxton nodded his head in acknowledgment and sat down, his long legs jutting out in front of him. He had an inquisitive expression on his ruggedly handsome face as he folded his arms and looked at the chief inspector behind the desk.

'What is it Chief?' he enquired.

Wilberton, his dark, well-groomed hair giving him a distinguished look, adjusted his gold-rimmed spectacles on the bridge of his nose, then leaned forward, placed his elbows on the desk and clasped his hands in front of him, as he looked Laxton in the eyes. 'We've been informed by one of our sources that there is a scam going on. Our contact has told us that Alfred Hawsford, who, as you know, has recently been released from Lincoln Prison, may have become involved.'

He paused for a moment, sat back in his chair and gazed down at his well-manicured fingernails, deep in thought, before raising his eyebrows and looking up at the inspector over the rims of his glasses and telling him in a low voice, 'I want you to place him under surveillance and see if you can find out what is going on.'

Laxton chewed on his bottom lip for a few seconds as he thought over the instructions that the chief had given him, before nodding his head. He recalled sending the skinny little man down after they had caught him among a gang who were in the act of breaking and entering a local bank. He shook his head ruefully as he leaned back in his chair and ran his fingers through his iron-grey hair. Alfred Hawsford just couldn't stay clean.

'I'll get on to it straight away,' he replied with a nod of his head as he got up out of the chair and turned to leave the office.

'There's just one more thing to tell you,' Wilberton called after him, stopping him in his tracks. Laxton, his brow furrowed, had a questioning expression on his face as he turned and faced the chief. 'Jane has handed in her resignation. She told me that Spencer has asked her to marry him and she's accepted. When they get married they are going to live in Australia. Spencer has been offered a good position by his firm.' Wilberton gave a deep sigh. 'I'll miss him.'

He coughed and turned away, his eyes blinking. Spencer was his only son and together with his three daughters, he loved them deeply. 'He's old enough to know what he wants I suppose,' he said with a shrug of his shoulders, before going on to explain. 'He has asked her to leave the police force. He said he was worried about her safety.'

'What did she say about that?' asked Laxton as he reached out for the door handle.

'She asked me for my opinion. I advised her that it would be better if she left the force.'

Robert Laxton nodded his head in agreement. He paused for a moment as he cast his mind back. Jane Bullyn had been an asset to him in the past, as his partner. Her resemblance to her mother Nancy was always a reminder to him (see Blind Stab).

He gave a deep heart-felt sigh, as he opened the door and prepared to walk out of the office, when the chief called after him. 'You'll have to go it alone for a while Robert. We are a bit short of staff at the moment. I'll assign you a partner as soon as I've got someone available.'

Laxton raised his hand in acknowledgement as he left the office; pulling the door shut behind him he made his way across the station car park, to his car.

His mind turned to the job in hand as he climbed behind the steering wheel, put the key in the ignition and started the engine.

He paused for a second to pop a peppermint in his mouth, before guiding the car out of the car park and driving off, his destination was Louth. Reaching out he turned on the radio as he made his way along the main highway that ran through the open Lincolnshire countryside. Soft, pleasant music filled the air as he contemplated the job in hand. The head office had received information that Hawsford had been frequenting the auctions that were held twice weekly.

Turning the car into one of the car parks, he found a parking spot. Switching off the engine he bought a ticket out of the machine and stuck it on the windscreen. He smiled to himself; he didn't want to fall foul of the attendants who were pretty keen on ticket dodgers. A few minutes later he approached the sales room where the auctions were to be held. He paused for a few seconds as he saw Hawsford scurrying along, about thirty yards in front of him; quickening his step, he followed him into the auction room. He was surprised that the little man had become involved in whatever the scam was, Hawsford had told him that this was going to be his last time in jail when he had charged him with the attempted bank robbery. 'But then,' he muttered with a grim smile on his face, 'they all say that.'

Hawsford made his way to the front of the crowd that had gathered round the auctioneers table, Laxton stayed at the rear in an attempt to be inconspicuous.

Anthony Mackennon, an artist of some considerable skill, had a problem. He wasn't selling enough of his work, and consequently was finding it difficult to pay his bills. Stretching his six-foot frame on the well-worn settee, the only piece of furniture in the lounge of his flat which was situated on the outskirts of Louth, the twenty-three-year-old ran his fingers through his thick black hair, his eyes half closed, as he contemplated the different ways of marketing his paintings. He'd tried exhibiting them in one or two of the local shops. He'd even hung a couple of them in the local pubs. It seemed that people got a lot of pleasure out of viewing them, but not many of them were interested in buying them. Then he had an idea. 'Why not try them in the local auction?' he muttered to himself. It was the one thing that he hadn't tried. He got to his feet and picked up the local *Standard*.

Searching through the ads columns in the paper, he saw that there was one to be held in Louth tomorrow, Wednesday, starting at ten a.m. He decided that he would place one of his paintings in the auction. Suddenly the phone rang. He reached out and picked it up.

'Hello Anthony darling, have you missed me?' a young woman's voice enquired.

It was Jill Downing, his twenty-two-year-old girl friend, a petite five-foot-two ash blonde; she'd been away for two weeks visiting friends. She was calling him on her mobile phone, from Louth bus station, where she had just arrived.

'Of course I've missed you Jill. I can't wait to hold you in my arms again,' he told her, his husky voice betraying his emotions.

'I'll be there shortly,' she promised him.

Half an hour later she arrived at the flat; she threw herself into his arms. With her hands clasped around his neck, her blue eyes gazed lovingly up into his brown ones. Giving her a long, hard, passionate kiss, he picked her up and swung her round the room. A few minutes later he sat down on the settee with her and told her of his decision to place one of his paintings in the local auction.

'What a good idea darling!' she exclaimed. 'I'll go with you.'

The next morning they arrived at the entrance to the imposing building where the auction was to be held, at nine a.m. Anthony had one of his painting with him. 'Just to test the water,' he explained to Jill.

After giving his painting to the auctioneer's assistant, they had a look round the large room that was packed with bric-a-brac and old furniture. Along one wall there stood a row of paintings, a mixture of watercolour and oil paintings, which were to be put to the bidders. *Around two dozen at the most*, thought Anthony as he saw the assistant place his painting among them.

Casting his eye over them he came to the conclusion that one or two of them were poor specimens. He couldn't see them drawing a bid. A few feet away from him a small man was looking studiously at the paintings with a magnifying glass, he seemed to be spending an unusually long time on one of the poor specimens – it was a medium-sized acrylic painting with what looked to be an expensive, ornate, thick frame. A few minutes later the auctioneer climbed up onto a rostrum that was situated at one end of the room and announced, over the heads of the congregated crowd that were sat in the rows of seats in front of him, that the auction was about to start. Anthony and Jill stood at the rear of the large gathering of potential buyers to watch the proceedings. After all the bits and pieces that were laid out on the long tables were sold, the auctioneer, a large, red-faced man, his tie almost sinking out of sight in the folds of fat around his neck, finally came to the paintings.

His voice boomed out, echoing around the large hall. 'Lot twenty-six is a watercolour painting by a local artist.' He paused for a few seconds as his assistant held the painting up for the punters to see. He cast his eyes around the packed crowd, before continuing in a loud clear voice, 'Now what am I bid for this?'

It was Anthony's watercolour. For a few seconds the auctioneer's announcement was greeted with total silence.

'Come on, there must be someone here who is interested in the arts,' he wheezed. 'Who is going to start me?'

Still no one spoke up, it seemed the gathering were still reticent. Anthony's head dropped. Maybe his painting wasn't as good as he thought it was, he wondered.

'Who will start me at forty pounds, it's got to be worth that?' the fat man pleaded.

A hand in the middle of the crowd shot up.

'Thank you sir,' he said, nodding his head at the bidder. 'Now then,' he went on, 'how about forty-two pounds.'

Another hand went up. Eventually, to Anthony's relief, the painting was knocked down for eighty pounds. The auctioneer went on to the other paintings, some of which he had great difficulty in getting bidders for. In the end he had to almost give them away.

He turned to Jill. 'It's obvious that the paintings are not in favour this week,' he told her in a low voice. She nodded her head in agreement.

Finally the auctioneer came to the acrylic painting that the little man had been studying so closely with his magnifying glass. Anthony leaned down, close to Jill's ear. 'I can't see this one going, it's about the worst one in there,' he whispered to her.

'Now what am I bid for this er, hem, work of art?' the big man called out, a little derisively.

A ripple of laughter went round the crowd.

'Who will give me twenty pounds?'

The little man who had shown so much interest in the painting put his hand up. The auctioneer nodded to him, telling him, 'Thank you sir,' before turning his attention to the rest of the congregation. He asked them, 'Now who will make it, twenty-two pounds?

There was a pause before a tall man, standing at the rear put his hand up. The auctioneer turned his attention back to the little man at the front.

'Twenty-five pounds?' he put to him questioningly.

The man nodded his head.

'Thirty pounds,' the auctioneer called out, deliberately raising the ante.

The tall man put his hand up again. And so it went on between the two bidders. It was finally knocked down to the small character; the one that had shown so much interest in it earlier, for the unlikely sum of one hundred and fifty pounds.

Anthony was gobsmacked.

'That was unbelievable,' he whispered to Jill as they went to collect the money for his painting. Beside him, paying out from a handful of crumpled ten and five pound notes, was the man who had bid one hundred and fifty pounds for his purchase of what Anthony had thought was a mediocre work of art. On impulse he addressed the small man who was putting the remainder of his money in his pocket. 'I don't wish to pry, but can you tell me what it was that attracted you to that painting?'

The man paused for a moment as he waited for a receipt. Then he turned and looked up at Anthony through narrowed eyes. 'It's none of your business,' he retorted nastily, as the painting was being handed over to him, then, after giving him another black look, he turned and walked sharply away, holding the fairly large painting firmly in his hands.

'Who was that?' Anthony asked the cashier as she counted out his payment of eighty pounds, less the percentage charged by the auctioneers.

'I'm sorry sir,' the cashier smiled with a shake of her head. 'I'm not in a position to tell you.'

Anthony gave a quick glance at the book and saw that the little man had signed himself as A. Hawsford.

The cashier reached out and quickly withdrew the book, giving him a look of disapproval as she did so. The young man turned and walked away slowly, a thoughtful expression on his face.

'What are you thinking?' asked Jill, in a low voice.

Anthony gave a slight shake of his head and shrugged his shoulders. 'I'm just puzzled that's all.'

At that moment the tall man who had been bidding against the man called Hawsford, brushed past them on his way out of the building. Anthony grabbed his arm and stopped him in his tracks. The man turned towards him, a look of annoyance on his face. There was a questioning look in his eyes.

'I… I'm sorry,' said Anthony falteringly. 'I just wanted to ask you, why did you bid so high for that painting?' He paused for a moment before adding. 'It was worthless.'

Laxton looked at him for a few seconds, a half smile on his face. 'I know it was worthless,' he replied, agreeing with the young man.

'Then why did you bid for it?' Anthony countered, with a slight shrug of his shoulders.

Laxton paused for a moment, his brow furrowed, before telling him sharply, 'I'm a police officer, now who are you and why are you so interested?'

Anthony hesitated for a couple of seconds, a little taken aback, before giving his name and explaining to him that he was an artist.

Laxton went on to explain that he had Hawsford under surveillance and wanted to see how high he was prepared to go. 'I'm as much in the dark as you are,' he confided to the younger man. 'But undoubtedly, there's something fishy going on.'

Suddenly he stiffened. 'Our friend is leaving.'

Anthony scribbled on a piece of paper and handed it to the police officer. 'This is my phone number. I would like to help.'

Laxton nodded, pushed it in his pocket and in two strides was out of the door.

Back at the flat Anthony was deep in thought, his brow deeply furrowed. 'Jill, what I would like to know is, what was that man, Hawsford looking for with the magnifying glass?'

'To see if it was authentic?' ventured Jill.

The young man shook his head slowly from side to side. 'No!' he exclaimed. 'Anyone could see that the painting wasn't worth much.'

He plucked at his bottom lip for a few seconds, deep in thought, his brow furrowed as he summed up the situation; eventually he turned his attention to Jill. 'I've got an idea,' he told her. 'We'll go to the next auction preview and check the paintings carefully before they go on sale.'

Three days later, equipped with a magnifying glass, they arrived at the sale rooms just as the doors were opening. They went over to where a dozen or so paintings that would be going on sale were situated. After checking them thoroughly with the magnifying glass, he stood back, a disappointed expression on his face. 'I can't see anything out of the ordinary, Jill,' he told her in a low voice as he shook his head slowly from side to side.

'Check the full stop after the signature on the third one,' a voice confided from behind him.

Anthony swung round. It was inspector Laxton, he had a grim smile on his face. The young man leaned over and held the magnifying glass closer. The full stop was a *red triangle.*

Anthony, a questioning look on his face, turned and addressed the inspector. 'What does it mean?' he asked.

'I'm not sure,' Laxton replied with a slight shake of his head. 'It could be some sort of a sign.'

At that moment the inspector saw Hawsford through a side window as he approached the salesroom. The little man glanced across at them as he entered the room. He gave the inspector a hard look.

'I think he's recognised me,' Laxton told them in a low voice.

After a few seconds thought, he looked at Anthony. 'Would you do something for me?' he asked. The young man nodded his head as Laxton went on to tell him, 'When he leaves, I want you to follow him and let me know where he's staying?' adding a serious tone to his voice. 'Whatever you do don't let him see you.'

Laxton pulled a leather wallet out of his inside pocket and opened it. He took out a card, and gave it to Anthony. 'You'll find me at this number,' he told him secretively.

With this he turned away from the young couple and quickly strode off, just as Hawsford entered the sales room.

Anthony and Jill carried on looking at the articles that were for sale. At the same time they kept an eye on Hawsford, who was taken up by the paintings that were on display. Ten minutes later they left the saleroom and went to their car, where they sat waiting for Hawsford to come out. After another fifteen minutes had gone by he came out of the building. They ducked down as he slouched past them and went to an old Ford Escort. He had a look of deep concentration on his face as he climbed in, then with a cloud of smoke issuing from the exhaust, he drove off.

They followed him at a discreet distance. Twenty minutes later he stopped the car outside an old, run-down, dilapidated, detached cottage, situated on a country lane, on the outskirts of Louth. There was one other vehicle parked up outside it.

Their quarry climbed out of his car and entered the cottage. He had a worried expression on his face as he went to the window, pushed the grubby curtains aside and peered through the small square panes. He nodded his head. 'I thought so,' he muttered to himself when he recognised the young couple who he had seen at the auctions, parked a little further along the lane. 'They've followed me. How much did they know?' he asked himself, a look of apprehension on his face. He broke into a cold sweat as he ran his fingers nervously through his thinning hair. 'If I was caught again I would get ten years,' he told himself. He suddenly made his mind up. Tomorrow was going to be his last. He was going to get out. At that moment the door behind him creaked open. He turned round. A large figure was framed in the doorway.

'Well Hawsford,' the big man growled. 'Did you check which one it was?'

'Yes,' he answered, his tongue flicking nervously across his lips as he nodded his head.

The big man's eyes narrowed, as he stood looking down at him for a few seconds, sensing there was something not quite right. 'What's the matter with you man?' he snapped nastily. 'You look scared to death.'

Hawsford drew himself up to his full five-foot-six and looked the big man in the eyes. 'I've decided that tomorrow will be my last job,' he pronounced defiantly, telling him in no uncertain terms, 'I've had enough and I'm getting out.'

'You'll pack up when I tell you,' snarled the big man, reaching out and grabbing him by the throat.

Hawsford twisted out of his grip and stepped back.

'If you lay a finger on me I'll tip off the Old Bill and take you down with me,' he threatened.

His adversary took a step forward and lashed out, catching Hawsford with a glancing blow to the side of the head. He fell against a table. His hand grasped a heavy marble-based ink pad that was standing on the table and threw it at his opponent, who fended it off. He, in turn, knocked the little man to the floor. Dazed and bewildered Hawsford reached for a large poker that lay in the hearth. Then, screaming his defiance, he clambered to his feet and attacked his tormentor with it. The big man caught the blows on his brawny forearms before wrenching the poker out of his hand and smashing it against Hawsford's head.

Repeatedly he swung the poker until all that was left was an unrecognisable bloody pulp.

Meanwhile the young couple outside were sat in the car keeping their vigil, oblivious to what was going on inside the cottage.

'I think he's seen us,' whispered Jill, seeing the curtains move.

'You may be right Jill,' Anthony replied. 'I think we should get to the nearest phone and contact inspector Laxton.'

At that moment they heard screams coming from the cottage. Anthony looked at Jill. There was a serious expression on his face. 'I'm going to check what's going on,' he declared.

'I'm coming with you,' Jill told him firmly as he climbed out of the car and ran across the lane, Jill following close behind him. Cautiously they made their way round the back of the property. There was a gate and a path that led to a back door that was open. They went through the gate and crossed the small back yard. Jill held Anthony's hand tightly as they entered the house; it had an unlived in damp smell as they stepped inside the gloomy front room. A stream of sunlight from the window fell on the macabre scene that greeted them. The battered body of the man that they had followed lay crumpled on the floor, in a pool of blood. Jill swayed and almost fainted when she saw the bloody carnage. Anthony put his arm around her shoulders and steadied her.

'I'll nip to the car and inform Laxton,' he whispered in her ear. 'Will you be okay?'

She nodded her head as he turned and went out of

the door, leaving her alone with the body.

Jill felt the silence close in on her when Anthony left. She shuddered as she saw the bloodied poker on the floor near her feet. Suddenly a shadowy figure came towards her. She screamed and reached for the poker. The large man pushed past her and ran out of the door. She heard a distant engine starting, then all fell quiet again. A few minutes later Anthony returned and saw Jill with the poker in her hand.

'Jill, whatever are you doing with that poker in your hand?' he declared in a shocked voice. 'It's evidence. You've probably wiped any fingerprints off it with yours.'

She told him of the man who was still in the house after he'd left. He nodded his head and told her that he had seen a man climb into one of the cars that were parked on the lane. 'You still shouldn't have picked up the poker,' he insisted.

'I picked it up to defend myself,' she explained, her voice dropping in volume.

As she spoke the police, forensics and an ambulance arrived, headed by inspector Laxton. He listened intently as Jill explained to him that she had picked the poker up to defend herself as she thought the killer was going to attack her.

'Right you two,' he told them. You've done very well and I'd like to thank you for your help, although the handling of the poker may cause us some difficulties.' He paused for a few seconds before telling them, 'I want you to go home now and leave everything to us. I'll get in touch with you later.'

Anthony and Jill left the scene of the crime and

arrived home some twenty minutes later.

They both flopped down on the settee, utterly exhausted. They felt much better after taking a shower, followed by a meal, after which, they sat and discussed the day's events over a cup of tea. Jill picked up her cup of tea. Anthony suddenly reached out and grabbed her wrist, a look of deep concentration in his eyes. 'What's that mark on the palm of your hand?' he mumbled through a mouthful of biscuit.

Jill, a questioning expression on her face, turned her right hand palm up. There was a black mark across it. She went to the bathroom and attempted to wash it off. She could make no impression. 'I must have picked it up from the handle of the poker,' she told him as she dried her hands on an old towel.

'Never mind, it will soon wear off,' he assured her.

Laxton was deep in thought. He folded his arms and tugged at his ear lobe as he carefully studied the murder scene in front of him. Blood was spattered everywhere. During a comprehensive examination of the crumpled body of Hawsford, he noticed the black ink stain on the dead man's right hand. After a thorough search he found the reason. A marble-based indelible ink pad lay in the corner of the room. A black mark showed where it had hit the wall. Laxton wondered if the little man had managed to hit his assailant. 'It would be a fact to keep in mind,' he muttered, telling himself, 'more to the point, how would the paintings be collected now that Hawsford was dead, and who would bid for them?'

After another half an hour had gone by studiously

examining the area around the body, he turned to leave the murder scene. 'It's all yours now,' he called out to forensics as he threaded his way through the paramedics and camera men and went to his car. The journey over the Wolds was an uneventful one as he made his way, deep in thought, back to headquarters in Lincoln.

Arriving back at the main office, he was informed that the chief wanted to see him. 'Now then,' declared chief inspector Wilberton sharply, his arms folded as he leaned back in his seat and addressed Laxton, who had taken a seat opposite him. 'You don't seem to be having much success in this case so far,' he intoned, nodding his head at the paperwork that he had just put down on the desk. 'You were supposed to keep an eye on Hawsford. Now we've lost him, our only contact and we now have a murder on our hands.'

Laxton, unabashed by the tirade directed at him, proceeded to give the details of his investigation so far. Wilberton listened intently. 'Mmm, so you think they will carry on in the same manner?' he grunted.

Laxton nodded his head. 'Yes,' he replied, adding emphatically, 'I don't see why not.'

Wilberton drummed his fingers on the desk top for a couple of seconds. 'Right then,' he declared, as if suddenly making his mind up. 'I'll go with you to the next sale,' adding as an afterthought. 'I'd like a word with the young couple who are involved.' He paused for a moment before turning to Laxton, and asking him, 'Have you got their address?'

Laxton nodded his head and took out a slip of paper from his pocket; it had the young man's address written on it.

Making their way through the outer office, they made an odd pair, with Laxton towering over his companion. Arriving at Anthony's flat, Jill answered the door bell and invited the two men in. Laxton introduced the chief to the couple, who led them into the rather sparse but homely lounge. After they had taken a seat on the somewhat worn settee and made themselves comfortable, the chief leaned back, folded his arms and turned his attention to Jill.

'Now then young lady,' he began, a serious expression on his face. 'It seems that you have been in contact with the probable killer. Do you think you would recognise him again?' he asked her.

Jill shook her head slowly from side to side. 'I didn't see his face,' she told him, adding, 'the only thing that I noticed was that he was a big well-built man.'

Wilberton stroked the bridge of his thin nose reflectively for a couple of seconds as he mulled over what she had said. Suddenly she butted in on his thoughts.

'There is one thing I would like to show you,' she informed him.

'And what would that be?' he enquired, his brow furrowing.

She held out her right hand to reveal the black marks on the palm of her hand.

'I got that when I picked the poker up to defend myself,' she intoned. 'The killer must have picked up similar marks on his hand when he handled the poker.'

'That could be a good point,' conceded Wilberton, nodding his head as he rubbed his chin thoughtfully with back of his hand. He turned to Laxton, who had been listening intently to the conversation and asked him, 'What's your opinion Robert?'

The inspector, who had been sat back, relaxing on the settee, paused for a moment as he studied the situation, then leaning forward, his elbows resting on his knees, he told the chief, 'The auction is being held again tomorrow. I think it would be a good idea for Mr Mackennon and Miss Downing to be there in case something jogs their memory.'

The young couple nodded their heads and agreed to be at the auctions the following morning. With this the two policemen got to their feet and bid the young couple goodbye, before leaving the flat and making their way to their car.

Wilberton and Laxton arrived at the auction preview early. The inspector took out a magnifying glass and checked through the paintings that were on display.

'This one has got a red triangle on it,' he declared, a hint of satisfaction in his voice as he pointed at the painting in question.

Wilberton, who fancied himself as an art expert, picked the painting up and studied it carefully. 'It's an Italian scene, very amateurish,' he stated as he held it up and looked at it closely. 'It's signed by what looks like an Italian artist and has a moulded frame.'

He checked three other paintings by the same artist. 'The one with the triangle on it seems to be a lot heavier than the others,' he concluded.

The auction room was beginning to fill up. Anthony and Jill had just arrived and the proceeding were about to begin. Laxton and Wilberton positioned themselves inconspicuously at the rear of the congregated potential bidders. Anthony and Jill were near the front. The auctioneer, a small man, took his position on the rostrum.

Jill gave Anthony a gentle poke in the ribs with her elbow and told him in a low voice, 'That's a different auctioneer, Anthony.'

Her companion glanced across at her and nodded his head in agreement, as the proceedings commenced.

Half an hour of bric-a-brac sales went by. Then it was the turn of the paintings. The auctioneer held up the painting that they had been waiting for. The chief strained his neck to see over the crowd. Laxton had no such problems.

'Lot one-six-eight,' he called out. He paused for a couple of seconds before going on. 'A watercolour of an Italian scene by an Italian artist. Do I see forty pounds?'

There was no response from the gathering. Laxton was beginning to look anxious.

'Go on then, thirty pounds,' called out the auctioneer.

An arm went up in the middle of the crowd. The bidder had a cap pulled down over his face. Suddenly Jill tugged at Anthony's arm. 'Look,' she gasped. 'There's a black mark on his hand.'

The auctioneer ran his eyes over the rest of the

potential bidders, before carrying on.

'Any advance on thirty pounds? I'm selling at thirty pounds.' There was no response. The gavel came down with a bang on the desk in front of him.

Wilberton and Laxton pushed their way swiftly across the room. Anthony was weaving through the crowd from the front. The man had seen him. He turned to go out. Anthony went to cut him off, in an attempt to block his escape route. He reached to grab the man, who was over six feet tall. They grappled. Anthony was thrown to the floor. The big man made for the door; Robert Laxton stepped in front of him. He was knocked to the ground with a savage blow to the head. Chief Inspector Wilberton was the only obstacle in his way. He stopped and looked down at the smaller man who was confronting him. His lip curled in contempt as he threw himself at Wilberton, who ducked under the outstretched arm, pivoted on his left foot and executed a perfect hip throw. His adversary sailed through the air and hit the wall with a resounding thump. Laxton looked on in amazement as the big man slid to the floor.

'Cuff him,' ordered Wilberton calmly, as he adjusted a lock of hair that had fallen over his face during the fracas.

At that moment Jill arrived on the scene. 'That's the auctioneer from the last auction,' she told them breathlessly. 'Look at the palm of his right hand, it's got a black mark on it.'

'Whoever he is, it looks as though we've got our man,' remarked Wilberton, looking down at the prostrate figure on the floor as Laxton bent down and checked the suspect's hand; a black mark could be clearly seen on his palm.

'That's John Penniford. He's one of the local auctioneers,' a voice called out.

A man pushed his way through the watching crowd. It was the present auctioneer.

Laxton turned to him. 'Do you know anything about the paintings?' he enquired.

'All I can tell you is that they were placed in the sale by an Italian source,' he told them with a shrug of his shoulders. He went on to tell them, 'We've been getting quite a few lately.'

Wilberton looked down at Penniford, who had just come round. He was sitting up shaking his head and looking around groggily. 'We'll take him down to the station for questioning,' announced the chief. Turning to the auctioneer he informed him, 'I'll make an order for these four paintings to be sent to forensics for examination.'

At that moment two burly, uniformed policemen approached Penniford, clicked the handcuffs on him and took him into custody. An hour or so later he was being interrogated in a back room at the police station. He denied any knowledge of the killing. 'I don't recollect being at the cottage that you are talking about.'

'Hold out your hands,' Laxton ordered him.

He held out both his hands palm-down. The inspector reached out and turned them over. The right one had a black ink mark across the palm.

'How did that ink mark get on your hand?' he

demanded.

Penniford shrugged his shoulders, there was an innocent expression on his face. 'I haven't a clue. It could have come from anywhere,' he retorted, shaking his head.

'I suggest it came from the poker that you killed Hawsford with,' countered Laxton.

'I want my lawyer,' snapped Penniford, realising that things weren't going too well for him.

Although the police officers were certain that he was the man who had killed Hawsford, they still didn't have enough evidence to convict him, then Laxton remembered the blood-spattered room in the cottage.

'We'll search his flat,' he announced. Accompanied by a constable, he left the police station and went to his car. Ten minutes later they arrived at the flat where Penniford was staying.

After a thorough search of the premises, they found a case containing trousers and a pair of shoes; these were sent to forensics and minutely examined. Two hours later the phone rang – Wilberton picked up the receiver. It was forensics. The chief nodded his head at the phone as he took the message, the grim smile on his face told it all as he replaced the receiver.

'We've got him,' he enthused as he smashed his right fist into the palm of his hand. 'They've found spots of Hawsford's blood on his shoes.'

Penniford was confronted with the evidence. His shoulders slumped. 'I'm saying nothing,' he told them, shaking his head vigorously from side to side.

Then he repeated, 'I want my lawyer.'

At that moment the phone rang again. The chief reached out, picked it up and put it to his ear. It was forensics again. After a few minutes he put the phone down; there was a grim expression on his face as he explained to them, 'The paintings have been carefully examined and have discovered that the frame of the suspect painting was solid. The other three were found to be hollow. The frame had been filled with a mixture of heroin and a binding substance, making it like putty. It was found that there was over a kilo of the substance in the frame with a street value of around one hundred thousand pounds. The Italian police have informed us that the paintings and frames have been traced back to their source and arrests have been made.'

This was followed by him thanking everyone for a job well done. Penniford was duly charged with murder and dealing in drugs. He was found guilty and sentenced to life imprisonment. Anthony and Jill received a reward for their part in apprehending Penniford.

Robert Laxton congratulated them. 'What will you do with the money?' he asked the young couple.

They looked at each other and spoke in unison. *'Have a fabulous honeymoon.'*

End

Just Desserts

Tom Roeder, his flat cap dripping with the rain that was coming down heavily, pulled his coat collar tighter round his neck. It was just going dark as he approached the invitingly lit up doorway. A strong gust of wind and rain followed him as he pushed open the heavy oak door of the Red Lion and went in. The sound of lively music emanating from a well-worn juke box standing in the corner of the smoke filled room was almost drowned out by the voices of the clientele as he shouldered his way to the crowded bar of the old pub, which was situated in the centre of Lincoln. He had just been released from Lincoln prison, where he had served three years at her majesty's pleasure for G.B.H. He had originally been put away for five years, but it had been reduced for good behaviour. He had spent the last twenty years in and out of jail, mostly *in*. His life as a law breaker and general low life began when he was twenty; he was now forty-two. The years of imprisonment that had been meted out to him did not seem to have made a lot of impression, even though the judge had given him a stark warning, telling him that if he was caught breaking the law again, he would go away for a very long time.

'Pint of bitter,' he rasped, raising his voice over the hubbub of the chattering customers, slapping the bar top with the palm of his hand as he did so, to attract the attention of the barman, who had just finished serving a customer at the other end of the long bar. The barman, his bald head glistening with sweat, acknowledged him with a nod of his head and proceeded to carefully pour the beer until there was a thick white top on it.

Sliding the pint glass across the bar, he addressed the rough-looking individual. 'That'll be one pound fifty.'

Roeder reached into his pocket and counted out the money before handing it to the barman.

Picking up the inviting drink, he held it out in front of him for a few seconds, some six inches from his nose, his eyes gazing at the amber liquid, anticipating the long-awaited pleasure before placing his lips against the glass; tipping his head back, he took a long swig. He gave a satisfied nod of his head as he reached out and placed the just over half a pint that remained in the glass on the bar top, leaving a line of froth along his top lip, almost covering the jagged scar that ran from the corner of his mouth to just under his left nostril, a relic of his time in prison, when a fellow prisoner had struck him with a broken bottle after a heated exchange.

'Ahh that's better,' he muttered to himself. Taking a deep breath, he reached up and wiped the froth away by rubbing the back of his hand over his bristly mouth which was puckered into a half smile by the scar. Lifting his cap, he ran his hand over his close-cropped black hair, his half-closed eyes sweeping the smoke-filled room. Suddenly the door swung open, letting in a blast of cold air and lashing rain. A slightly built, elderly, white-haired man, holding on to his black trilby that was dripping with rain with one hand and a leather briefcase in the other, pushed his way through the door and limped to the bar. Roeder moved to one side, making room for the old man as he pressed his chest against the bar.

Roeder looked down at him out of the corner of his eye as he took another drink of his beer; the old man, placing his trilby on his head, nodded and smiled back at the rough looking man, as the well-built barman, wiping his hands on a well-worn towel, approached him. 'Yes Mr Twigg,' he said, a broad welcoming smile on his round face, as he half turned and tossed the towel on to a shelf at the rear of the bar. 'What can I do for you?'

It was obvious that the little old man was well known locally.

'A double whisky Ron,' he croaked, as he placed his brief case on the bar before taking off his leather gloves and vigorously rubbing his hands together.

Roeder's eyes narrowed as he saw 'Mr Twigg,' reach into his inside pocket, pull out a fat wallet, and peel off a twenty pound note from a thick wad. Tilting his glass, he quickly downed the rest of his pint. Placing his glass on the bar before nodding his thanks to the barman, he wrapped his coat collar tight around his neck and went out of the pub, leaning into the cold wind and rain as he closed the door behind him, the darkness swallowing him up as he made his way along the footpath; after he had walked about forty yards he came to an alleyway. Stepping inside the alleyway he waited in the dark shadows, a callous expression on his face.

After what seemed an eternity the door opened and the slight figure of the elderly Mr Twigg, came out of the pub, the wind almost blowing him back inside as he fought to close the door behind him. Gathering himself, he leaned into the wind and lashing rain before setting off to where he had parked his car, holding grimly on to his hat.

Tom Roeder, the turned up collar of his jacket covering half his face, pulled his cap down over his eyes as he waited in the dark alleyway for his quarry to draw near. As the old man, struggling against the strong wind and rain, drew level, Roeder stepped out in front of him, knife in hand, stopping the little man in his tracks.

'Your wallet, quick,' he demanded hoarsely, holding the knife six inches from the elderly man's throat.

Twigg, holding his trilby on his head with his hand, looked up into the cruel, unshaven face of the man standing menacingly in front of him. He thrust his chin out aggressively. 'Get out of my way,' he shouted, waving his free hand that was holding the briefcase. Pushing past the nasty piece of work who was threatening him, he staggered on.

Roeder stepped behind him as he went past and wrapped his arm around his victim's neck, gripping him tightly, his knife held threateningly at his throat.

'Your wallet or you're dead,' he snarled into Twigg's ear.

The old man struggled in vain to free himself. Suddenly his body stiffened. His eyes opened wide as he reached up and grabbed his throat. Giving a choking sound he collapsed to the ground, his trilby, which had fallen off, rolling and bouncing along the pavement, carried by the strong wind.

Roeder bent down, reached into the helpless, grey-haired man's pocket and took out the wallet. Extracting the thick wad of notes, he callously threw the empty wallet on to the inert body. At that moment a group of people came out of the pub, their laughing and joking suddenly, coming to an abrupt halt, as they took in the scene in front of them.

'What are you up to?' one of them shouted angrily as they saw Roeder bending over the elderly man's crumpled body the floor.

The old man's attacker, a startled expression on his face, turned and looked at them for a few seconds, then set off at a run, splashing through the puddles as he disappeared into the dark night.

The group rushed to help the stricken man. Two of the younger ones went after Roeder, who had run down the nearby alley which led to the main thoroughfare. He was breathing heavily as he burst out on to the well-lit, busy town centre. Pausing for a few seconds to get his bearings, he decided to make for the far side of the square.

Threading his way through the traffic, ignoring the sound of car horns from angry motorists as they braked to avoid him, he eventually made it to the far side. His heart was in his mouth as he glanced over his shoulder and saw that one of his chasers was talking to a policeman and pointing his way.

Still breathing heavily from his exertions he stopped for a couple of seconds and looked up and down the rain swept thoroughfare frantically for a way out; suddenly he spotted a car at the traffic lights which were on red. Noting that the passenger seat was empty, he ran up to the car. Reaching out, he tried the door handle; he was in luck, it was unlocked. Swinging the door open, he scrambled in and pulled the door shut behind him, just as the driver was accelerating away.

The constable who had given chase stopped as he saw Roeder get into the car. Taking out a mobile phone he contacted the police station, informing them of the car's colour and the first four digits of its registration, which he could just make out in the diffused light from the overhead street lights as it pulled away.

Detective inspector Robert Laxton and his partner D.C. John Rowland were returning to headquarters in Lincoln when they received the call over the intercom.

'Robbery suspect, armed with a knife, may be dangerous, last seen entering a blue car, possible hijack, first four digits of car registration, X122. The car is travelling on the A46 between Lincoln and Skegness.'

Laxton, who had just negotiated the centre of Lincoln, reached through the side window and placed a blue flashing lamp on the roof of his car, then pressing his foot down on the accelerator, he set off in pursuit of the vehicle indicated.

'I reckon he can't be too far ahead,' he told Rowland, a grim expression on his face.

The car surged forward as he gunned the engine, swerving in and out of the traffic as they made their way out of Lincoln and on to the A46. The windscreen wipers were working overtime as the heavy rain bounced off the front windows as they gave chase.

'There it is!' exclaimed Rowland, pointing excitedly at the blue car that was being held up by a lorry, a hundred metres or so ahead.

'Phew.' David Helm rolled on to his back and pushed his muscular young body up into a sitting position, his thick black hair plastered to his forehead as Gloria Anston reached out with her hand. Her well-manicured fingers gripped his forearm, as she attempted to prevent him from getting to his feet, her long blonde hair falling provocatively over her face, almost covering her blue eyes as she did so.

'Come back to bed David,' she implored him huskily, her voice full of sexual undertones. 'Victor won't be home for at least another two hours.'

He turned and looked down into her half closed eyes, shaking his head from side to side. 'You are insatiable,' he grinned, resisting her offer as he gently lifted her hand from his arm and swung his long hairy legs off the bed. Gloria's eyes followed his virile, naked young body as he climbed off the bed, got to his feet, walked across the bedroom and went into the bathroom, where he turned on the shower.

He was playing a dangerous game and he knew it, he told himself as the water cascaded over him. He had a good position as assistant manager in Victor Anston's computer business. He knew that if he were to be caught out playing with the boss's wife he would be finished. Victor had been good to him in the past, taking him on at the end of his term at university when he had been finding it difficult to get a job. And this was how he was repaying him. He gave a deep sigh as he raised his face and let the refreshing water cascade down on him. A strong feeling of guilt went through him as he stepped out of the shower, reached out and pulled the cord to switch it off. He resolved to put an end to the affair before it was too late, warning himself as he vigorously towelled himself down before walking back into the bedroom with the towel wrapped around him. He cast a glance at Gloria, who was still reclining on the bed in her dressing gown, one side of which was open, displaying a shapely leg, almost up to her thigh.

Dragging his eyes away from her, he quickly got dressed, stopping for a moment to look down at her voluptuous, inviting body; there was a look of incredulity on his face, as Gloria, her arms outstretched, beckoned him to come back to bed. He gave a deep sigh, before bidding her goodbye as he turned to go out of the bedroom door.

Vincent Anston stopped the car and sat for a couple of minutes staring at his knuckles as they gripped the steering wheel. He was deep in thought as he cast his mind back to when he had left home earlier that morning, recalling the moment when had been a little sharp with his wife Gloria. He had been going through a difficult time with his business and had lost patience with her when she kept going on about them not going out and enjoying themselves. He shook his head imperceptibly. He had to allow for the fact that she was much younger than him. 'Fifteen years to be exact,' he muttered to himself. He gave a deep sigh as he opened the car door and climbed out. Pulling a face at the rain that was lashing down, he slammed the car door shut behind him and quickly made his way into the shopping centre. He had made his mind up, telling himself that he would call at the florist in Lincoln on his way home to buy his wife Gloria a nice bunch of flowers and promise her that in future he would take her out more.

'That should make her feel better,' he muttered to himself as he reached out and opened the florist's door.

The pleasant aroma from the display of flowers met him as he entered the shop. After picking his way through the large baskets of different species of colourful flowers, he approached the attractive young woman who was standing behind the counter.

'Can I help you sir?' she enquired of the older man.

'I would like a large bunch of roses please,' he told her.

'Someone's birthday?' enquired the florist, a broad smile on her face.

He shook his head slowly from side to side and smiled back. 'No,' he replied, with a shake of his head. 'Just a treat for my wife,' he told her.

'How nice,' she gushed as she carefully wrapped the large bunch of red roses and placed them on the counter. 'That will be four pounds fifty.'

Nodding his head he reached into his inside pocket and took out his wallet, peeled off a five pound note and handed it to her, telling her to keep the change. After thanking the young woman behind the counter, he picked up the beautifully arranged flowers, turned and left the shop. The rain, driven by the strong wind, seemed to be coming down heavier, as he made his way swiftly back to the car, being careful to protect the flowers.

Instead of working late (which he usually did) he had decided to finish early and surprise his wife Gloria. For weeks they had done nothing but argue and fall out. He couldn't understand her attitude. Okay, she was fifteen years his junior, but he'd worked hard for their lifestyle and lovely home. 'It seems that she's never satisfied,' he muttered to himself as he climbed into the car. 'Still,' he grunted out loud as he started the engine, 'some of it is my fault. I do seem to have neglected her lately.'

Taking a deep breath, he accelerated and pulled out into the traffic, the wipers swishing from side to side, as they fought to clear the heavy rain that beat down on the windscreen.

'That is all going to change now,' he muttered to himself with some conviction.

'From now on I am going to show her how much I really love her.'

Arriving at their home, he turned the car into the wide drive that fronted the mansion-like detached house. Leaning over, he carefully picked up the bunch of flowers from the passenger seat, where he had laid them, before climbing out of the car and going to the front door. Taking out a bunch of keys, he tut-tutted impatiently as he fumbled for a few seconds to find the right key. At that moment the door swung open. Confronting him was his young business associate David Helm, his mouth wide open in surprise. The young man took a step back, a shocked expression on his face at seeing his boss home early.

'What the hell are *you* doing here?' Victor demanded, a questioning frown creasing his forehead.

'Er… I… I was just visiting,' the young man spluttered, somewhat inadequately, his face reddening guiltily as words failed him. With this he slipped by Anston and quickly disappeared into the mist and rain.

Victor Anston, a puzzled expression on his face as he slowly closed the door behind him, walked into the hallway. His wife, Gloria, was just about to descend the long winding stairway.

'Oh, David, I'm so glad you've decided to stay…' Gloria, in a flimsy see-through negligee, called from near the top of the stairway.

She stopped short, her face blanching when she saw that it was her husband, Victor. He was standing at the bottom of the stairs, a large bunch of red roses clutched in his hands. He stood for a moment, nonplussed, a look of disbelief etched on his face.

'You two-timing bitch,' he growled, shaking his head from side to side, his face purple with anger as he approached her, climbing the stairs two at a time.

He threw the bunch of roses at her as she turned to go back up the stairs. She was on the top stair when he reached out and grabbed her by her shoulders and wrapped his arm around her neck. She struggled to break his choking grip. Her face was turning blue. Realising he was being too rough, he loosened his hold on her. She pulled away from him as she felt him release her.

Suddenly she became unbalanced as she teetered for a few seconds on the top stair before making a desperate grab at the banister rail to steady herself. Unfortunately the rail was just out of reach, this was followed by a terrifying scream as she fell back. He reached out and tried to grab hold of her, to no avail. She pitched head first to the bottom of the stairs.

Vincent Hanson looked down in horror at the broken body of his wife as she lay on the floor of the hallway, her unseeing blue eyes wide open. His face was white with shock as he quickly descended the stairs and bent over her. Reaching out he checked her pulse. There was no beat. His face froze as he realised that she was dead.

'The fall must have broken her neck,' he told himself, a look of disbelief on his face as he stood back and looked down at the broken body of his wife. 'What have I done?' he called out dejectedly, his arms out wide as he looked up at the ceiling, his heart full of pain. In one uncontrollable moment he had destroyed everything he loved. If there was one thing he knew for certain, it was that he couldn't live without her. 'Why did she have to taunt me with her sordid affairs?' he declared out loud. 'Well she's gone too far this time,' he concluded, almost sobbing as tears of pain welled up in his eyes. Shaking his head slowly from side to side, he took a deep breath as he attempted to control himself.

Suddenly the enormity of what he had done struck him. His life was finished. He tugged at his bottom lip nervously, as he studied the situation confronting him for a couple of minutes.

Then he came to a decision.

'There is only one solution,' he muttered to himself.

Going back upstairs to the bedroom, he brought out a blanket and rolled her body in it. After carefully checking the roadway for traffic, he slung the blanket-wrapped body over his shoulder and swiftly carried it out to the car. It was dark and the rain was still bucketing down as he struggled to place the body in the back seat.

Breathing heavily from his efforts, he flopped down in the driver's seat and sat for few moments to regain his senses. Taking a deep breath to steady himself, he started the engine and slowly manoeuvred the car out of the driveway and on to the road. His mind was in turmoil as he drove through the heavy rain, the windscreen wipers monotonously swishing from side to side as they fought against the deluge. His eyes were open wide, seemingly unseeing, as he made his way through the centre of Lincoln. He was approaching the traffic lights, putting his foot down on the brake when he saw they were changing to red. Suddenly there was a blast of cold wind and rain as the car door swung open. He looked across the car, a questioning expression on his face. A scruffy-looking individual, rain dripping from his cap, had scrambled into the car brandishing a knife.

'What the hell do you think you are doing?' Anston growled.

'Carry on driving as normal,' snapped the intruder, holding the knife to Victor Anston's throat, as he closed the car door behind him. The lights turned to green and the car picked up speed as Anston, a confused expression on his face, pushed his foot down on the pedal and accelerated.

Roeder took out the thick wad of twenty and fifty pound notes from his pocket. He smiled inwardly as he looked down at it. *At last*, he told himself. *I've found a way out of the life that I was leading.*

Suddenly he looked up in alarm. They were on a forty mile an hour stretch of road on the outskirts of Lincoln. Victor Anston, his eyes two slits as he pressed his foot down on the accelerator – fifty miles an hour – sixty miles an hour.

'Steady on you'll attract attention,' he snapped, a note of alarm in his voice.

Anston, displaying a crazed look on his face, leaned forward over the steering wheel, completely ignoring him.

'Slow down you fool,' snarled Roeder, fetching blood as he pressed the sharp point of the knife into the driver's jugular vein.

Victor Anston turned his attention away from the road ahead and looked his uninvited passenger straight in the eyes. There was a suicidal expression on his face and a look of madness in his eyes, as a rivulet of blood ran down his neck. 'What are you going to do, kill me?' he declared mockingly, sticking his chin out as a grim smile transformed his face.

Roeder looked out of the rear window to see if they were being followed. A car with blue lights flashing could be seen in the distance. It was rapidly gaining on them. His mind was racing. *The police must be on to me*, he told himself. At that moment Roeder noticed, out of the corner of his eye, something on the rear seat of the car; he turned round and looked down at the woman wrapped in a blanket, laid out on the back seat, her head lolling to one side, exposing the purple bruises on her face, her sightless eyes gazing straight at him. His brow furrowed as he attempted to take in the spectacle in front of him. Pausing for a moment, he turned and looked at Victor Anston and saw his wild staring eyes. Then the truth suddenly dawned on him. 'She's dead,' he gasped, a look of horror in his eyes. His voice croaking, he added, 'You've killed her.'

Victor Anston, wide-eyed, was leaning over the steering wheel, staring straight ahead, a maniacal expression on his face.

The car slowed down. A farm vehicle was holding

up the traffic. Vehicles were approaching at speed down the other side of the road, headed by an eight wheeled articulated lorry. Suddenly Anston spun the steering wheel, the car swung violently across the highway into the path of the oncoming traffic. He pressed his foot down on the accelerator, laughing hysterically, as the large vehicle bore down on them.

Roeder screamed as he threw himself in front of Anston. Twenty and fifty pound notes scattered around him as he fought for control of the steering, to no avail. The car hit the heavy lorry head on.

'What's he doing?' gasped Rowland as they saw the car they were following, deliberately pull out in front of the articulated lorry. 'Oh my god!' he exclaimed, his eyes widening in horror, as he saw it smash head-on into the massive vehicle, fly into the air over a hedge, and land on its roof in a field, rolling over to finally come to rest on its four wheels.

'Call an ambulance,' Laxton called out to Rowland as he pushed his foot down hard on the brakes causing the car to screech to a stop. Quickly opening the car door, he jumped out, scrambled through the hedge and made his way to the stricken car which was emitting thick smoke. Wrenching the wrecked car's rear door open, he bent down and looked inside. He could just make out the body of a woman draped over the back seat and the mangled bodies of two men in the front. He reached inside and checked the woman's pulse. She was dead. After quickly leaning into the wrecked car and making a summary check on the other two bodies it was obvious to the inspector that they were all dead. Bank notes were scattered all around and there was a strong smell of petrol. Flames were licking round the smashed engine as Laxton, his face blackened by the fumes, withdrew his head out of the car.

'Look out, it's going to go up!' shouted Rowland frantically to his partner.

The inspector reluctantly drew back from the badly damaged vehicle and the three dead occupants. A few seconds later the car exploded in a sheet of flames. The ambulance and fire engine arrived five minutes later.

Laxton, who had climbed back on to the road, looked at the inferno in front of him. Shaking his head slowly from side to side in disbelief, he turned to Rowland.

'What a way to go.'

End

A Meeting of Hearts

1

Forty-seven-year-old Caroline pushed back a frond of her slightly greying light brown hair from over her brown eyes, as she slowly placed the phone back on its cradle. There was a tear in the corner of her eye, her heart was full of joy. She had just heard that her twenty-five-year-old daughter Jane and Gary, her husband, were expecting their first child; she was over the moon. Jane was the eldest of two daughters. At that moment the front door banged open as her younger daughter Lisa, who was staying with her boyfriend Ronald in a flat in Nottingham, bustled in.

'Hi Mum,' she carolled as she made her way into the kitchen, where her mother was just putting the kettle on. Caroline, a somewhat secretive expression on her face, turned to her and gave her a peck on the cheek.

'Lisa I've just heard some good news,' she confided, as she took two cups and saucers out of the wall cupboard and placed them on the table that stood in the centre of the modern kitchen.

'What would that be Mum?' enquired her twenty-two-year-old slim, blonde, good-looking daughter, as she nibbled at a cream biscuit that she had taken out of the dish that had been placed on the table.

Caroline poured out two cups of tea. She paused for a moment as she turned and placed the teapot on the worktop that ran down one side of the kitchen, before going on to tell her daughter, 'Our Jane is having a baby!'

'Having a baby?' gasped Lisa, a look of disbelief on her face.

The biscuit stopped just short of her mouth as the news struck home. The serious expression on her face slowly changed to a broad smile. Popping what was left of the biscuit in her mouth, she flung her arms around her mum and hugged her. 'That's wonderful news Mum,' she mumbled through a mouthful of biscuit. 'I'll bet Dad will be thrilled when he gets home from work.'

William, Caroline's forty-eight-year-old husband had always said that he hoped his first grandchild would be a boy. Having had two girls (who he loved dearly), he had always expressed his regret that they hadn't had a son. After the two girls were born she had trouble with her womb and had to have a hysterectomy, thereby stopping her from having any more children. After enjoying the cup of tea together and spending ten minutes or so discussing the happy moment, Lisa got to her feet and prepared to leave, giving her mother, who had walked her to the door, an affectionate peck on the cheek before bidding her goodbye.

'I'll drop in on our Jane on the way home Mum,' she informed her mum as she went through the door and walked down the flower lined path to where her car, a Mini, or a 'small box on wheels' as her dad jokingly called it, was parked. A few seconds later, to the sound of Lisa's car revving up as she drove off, breaking the silence, Caroline turned to go back in the kitchen. She looked up at the clock on the wall – it showed five o'clock. William was due home from his job at the local superstore, where he had recently been promoted to manager. She was worried about him.

After having a few funny turns which had left him feeling weak, he had been to the doctors and following a thorough examination, he was told that he was being referred to the local hospital for a blood test. A letter had arrived this morning, although it was addressed to him, she was on tenterhooks and couldn't wait until William got home. Her hands shook slightly, as she put on her glasses and opened the letter. It told him that he had to attend next Thursday morning at ten o'clock.

'Now let me see,' she muttered to herself. 'That will be four days from now.' A worrying frown wrinkled her forehead, as she absorbed the information. 'Four days,' she mused, as she prepared her husband's meal. 'That's short notice.'

Something told her that his condition was serious. Her mind went back to when William's father had gone through the same procedure and it was discovered that his blood was thick. The doctor had informed him that he would have to take precautions to ensure that he would be able to carry on a normal life. He was given warfarin tablets to keep his blood in order.

'Although he is now seventy-five, he hasn't had a very good time of it,' she told herself.

Shaking her head, she cast off the feeling of foreboding, placed the letter in the top drawer of the kitchen unit and turned her mind to the present. When William heard the news that Jane was having a baby, she was sure that it would make him feel better. She was just putting the finishing touches to the pan of curried rice (William's favourite meal), when the door burst open and he walked in, a broad smile on his face as he approached her from behind, reached out and put his arms around her waist. He squeezed her gently and gave her an affectionate kiss on the back of her neck.

'Stop it William,' she giggled, telling him as she attempted to wriggle out of his embrace, 'you'll make me spill your meal.'

'Something smells good,' he enthused as he released her, walked across the kitchen and hung his jacket in what they called the 'cubby hole', that was under the stairs.

Rubbing his hands together in anticipation he went into the fridge and took out a can of Brown Ale; pouring it into a glass, he sat down at the table.

'There you are my dear,' announced Caroline as she placed a large plate of curried rice in front of him, before taking a seat opposite him with a much smaller portion. Without further delay he tucked into his meal. Ten minutes later he leaned back in his chair and rubbed his stomach, a satisfied smile on his still ruggedly handsome face.

'I really enjoyed that,' he told her as he pushed the empty plate away from him and reached out for what was left of his drink. Glancing over the rim of his glass as he tilted it back to finish it off, he couldn't help but notice the worried look on Caroline's face and the way she was tentatively picking at her meal. Placing the empty glass on the table, he got to his feet and went over to her. 'What's troubling you luv?' he enquired, a questioning expression on his face, as he leaned over and placed a comforting arm around her shoulder.

She looked up at him out of the corner of her eye for a few seconds, then she got to her feet and went over to the kitchen cabinet. Opening the top drawer, she picked up the envelope that contained the letter that had come from the surgery, then, without a word, she handed it to him. A deep frown creased his forehead; he had a puzzled look in his eyes as he took the letter out of the envelope and carefully read it, plucking slowly at his bottom lip as he did so.

'Mmm,' he muttered as he ran his eyes down the letter. 'I wonder why they are sending for me so quickly.'

He well remembered other times when he'd had dealings with the local hospital. It had usually taken them weeks to see him. *In fact*, he told himself. *At times I'd thought that they had forgotten me.*

Caroline placed her arms around his neck and looked up into his warm brown eyes. 'What do you reckon Will?' she asked him in a low tone of voice. 'Do you think it's serious?'

'I'm not sure,' he rejoined, shrugging his shoulders, as he ran his fingers through his thinning hair, adding, 'we'll know more when we get to the hospital.'

Taking her arms from around his neck she stood on tiptoe and gave him a gentle kiss on the bridge of his nose. 'I love you William Daneman,' she told him huskily.

He looked deep into her eyes for a few seconds. A broad smile enveloped his face as he gave her a kiss on the forehead, telling her in return, his voice low, 'And I love you Caroline.'

Going out of the kitchen he went into the hallway and picked up the evening newspaper from the floor near the front door, a few seconds later he went into the lounge for his evening read, which was followed as usual, by a nap. The following morning he informed the management that he had an appointment at the hospital to take a blood test.

The next three days went by slowly, as they contemplated the possible consequences. Early on Thursday morning, William and Caroline climbed into the car and set off for Nottingham Hospital. On arrival they were shown to the cardiac department, where they were given a seat and told that they would eventually be called in. The next twenty minutes were taken up by scanning through the large collection of old magazines that were scattered about on the table that stood between the rows of seats.

Suddenly a female voice shrilled, 'Mister William Daneman!'

They both looked up at the stern-looking nurse dressed in a white uniform standing in front of them. William jumped to his feet. 'That's me,' he informed her.

'Follow me,' she ordered him, a little brusquely.

'Can I go with him?' Caroline asked the nurse falteringly.

'Of course you can,' the big woman assured her, softening her voice a little. 'Follow me,' she again instructed the couple, as she turned to leave.

Led by the nurse, the couple set off at a brisk pace down the corridor, which resembled a rabbit warren with its many doors.

'Here we are,' she announced, opening one of the doors in the long corridor, with the name Doctor Stevens on it. Waving them in, she told them to take a seat. William and Caroline entered the room and sat down.

'Now let me see,' intoned the young doctor who was sat at a desk, dipping his head as he looked at them over thick-rimmed glasses. 'Mr Danman isn't it?'

'Er, Daneman,' William corrected him. 'William Daneman.'

'Sorry,' said the dark-haired young man, waving his hand in acknowledgement of his mistake. He paused for a few seconds as he ran his eyes down a sheet of paper in front of him. A troubled expression clouded his face as he turned to William and informed him that he had been called to attend hospital because of a serious complication regarding his blood pressure, which had been taken at the local surgery.

'Your doctor has indicated that there may be something awry and that we should take a sample of your blood and examine it,' he told them as he ran his eyes over the sheet of paper that he held in front of him. At that moment a well-endowed nurse dressed in blue, indicating that she was senior, came through the door. She was carrying two large, somewhat menacing syringes, wrapped in a cloth in her hand.

'Nurse Singleton will be taking a blood sample from you!' exclaimed the doctor, getting to his feet, as she approached William, taking out the syringes as she did so.

'I'll leave you in the capable hands of the nurse and see you when we get the results through,' he told the couple as he made for the door.

Nurse Singleton approached William and asked him to roll his sleeve up, then told him in a comforting tone of voice, 'You will just feel a slight prick.'

William concentrated his eyes on the top of the nurse's hat as she bent over and inserted the large-looking needle. He flinched slightly. Caroline screwed her eyes up as she watched it go in. A few seconds later the nurse withdrew the needle, placed the blood sample on a glass shelf and told him in a quiet voice, as she reached out and picked up the other one, 'Just one more sample and that should do it.'

After completing the task, she took the two glass phials (which were full of blood), to be analysed, then she instructed the couple to go back to the waiting room, from where they would eventually be called to see the doctor again.

William and Caroline dutifully took two seats in

the waiting area. After an hour or so of chatting and again reading the numerous outdated magazines and gazing at the watercolour pictures of local scenes that were hanging on the blandly painted walls, they were called in by a young nurse, who led them to the appropriate office. They were met by a solemn-looking Doctor Stevens. He was studying a sheet of paper on the desk in front of him, patting his bottom lip with his pen as he did so. A few seconds later, he raised his eyes and indicated for them to take the two seats in front of him. After giving the couple time to settle down, he turned his attention to William and informed him, 'Mr Daneman, I'm afraid I've got some rather unpleasant news for you.'

William gave a slight nod of his head in acknowledgement, before enquiring, 'And what would that be doctor?' Before he could reply, he told him, 'And I want you to give it to me straight.'

Doctor Stevens leaned forward, placed his elbows on the desk and looked him in the eyes; he could see the strength there. He nodded his head approvingly. 'All right I will!' he exclaimed, then went on. 'It seems that your blood is thick and that you could suffer from a heart attack at any time.'

Caroline's hand went to her mouth in shock when she heard the diagnosis. 'Is there anything you can do about it?' she enquired tremulously, her heart pounding in her breast.

The doctor paused for a moment before explaining to the couple that he could give him special tablets to thin his blood.

'What are they?' asked William.

'Warfarin,' intoned the doctor.

'Warfarin,' repeated Caroline, a look of incredulity on her face. 'Isn't that rat poison?'

'Sort of,' was the reply. 'And it is very effective.'

He instructed William that he must take one tablet a day, emphasising that he must not take more. With this the couple got to their feet and thanked the doctor, before shaking hands with him and walking out of the office, after being told that they could pick up a prescription at the hospital pharmacy which was situated just outside the hospital.

Picking up the prescription they made their way to the car. After paying the obligatory parking fee, William, deep in thought, proceeded to guide the car carefully out of the car park, then drove the rest of the way home in silence.

On arrival home Caroline broke down in tears.

'Don't cry my love,' comforted William, putting his arm around her shoulder telling her, 'I'll be all right. Look at Dad, he's been taking warfarin for the same complaint and he's still going strong at seventy-five.'

What he didn't say was that his dad had been just a shadow of his former self since he had suffered from heart trouble.

Caroline dabbed her eyes and looked up at him. 'I know you are right darling, it's just that I…' her voice trailed off as she reached up and kissed him.

'Right,' said William, giving her a pat on the backside. 'Let's have something to eat and a cup of tea, I'm hungry.'

The following weeks and months went by and Caroline noticed that William was looking frailer by the day. The firm where he worked was very helpful towards him by appointing an assistant manager to take some of the strain. Occasionally he had to go home because he was too ill to carry on. Eventually the time came when he had to be off work and on the sick almost permanently.

'I don't know Carol,' he confided. 'I'm not much good to you, am I?'

She turned round on him, a shocked expression on her face. 'Don't you ever say that William Daneman,' she told him with feeling. 'Most of the men out there aren't fit to wear your boots.'

He smiled wanly and shook his head slowly from side to side, placed his arms around her waist, drew her to him and told her huskily, 'No wonder I love you so much.'

'And I love you,' she breathed as he pressed his lips on hers.

At that moment the back door swung open and Jane walked in holding her hands on her tummy, as if she were supporting it.

'Hi Mum. Hi Dad,' she announced as she walked across the kitchen and gave them both a kiss on the cheek. She had a concerned expression on her face as she took in the weak state of her father. 'Are you okay Dad?' she put to him as she looked up into his eyes.

William gave weak smile as he reached out and patted her on the back of her head, telling her in a soft voice, 'I'll be all right darling, when I've regained my strength again.'

A couple of days later Caroline was preparing herself to do some shopping. William was sat in the lounge reading the morning paper. 'I think I'll go with you,' William told her, putting his paper down, jumping out of his armchair and getting to his feet.

'Are you sure darling?' she enquired, looking at him a little apprehensively.

'Yes,' he assured her, telling her, 'I feel a little better at the moment, the fresh air and the walk will do me good.'

'Well, so long as you are going to be okay,' she told him.

'Yes. I'll be all right,' he told her confidently, as he walked to the large mirror in the hallway to put his tie on. He was humming away to himself.

Caroline sat in the comfortably furnished lounge, waiting patiently for him to get himself ready to go. Suddenly the humming stopped. This was succeeded by the sound of choking, followed by a loud bump.

'Are you all right William?' she called out. There was no reply. She got to her feet and went into the hallway, a worried frown on her forehead.

'Oh my god!' she exclaimed, her eyes open wide with shock. William was lying in a crumpled heap on the floor in front of the mirror; one of his hands was still holding the tie that was hanging round his neck, the other hand was clutching his throat. She went down on her knees, reached out and rolled him on to his back.

Her hand went to her mouth, she quickly drew back, a horrified expression on her face at the sight of William's face screwed up in pain, in front her.

His lifeless eyes gazed back at her. It was obvious that he'd suffered a heart attack. Quickly getting to her feet she went to the polished table, picked up the phone and dialled 999. A calm, feminine voice on the other end asked her which service she wanted.

'Ambulance please,' she replied falteringly. Taking a deep breath, she added, 'It's urgent. My husband's collapsed, I'm almost certain he's had a heart attack.'

After giving the woman at the other end of the phone her address, she contacted both of her daughters and gave them the news.

A few minutes later the ambulance arrived amid a wail of sirens.

The medics, carrying a stretcher, made their way swiftly to the stricken man. One of them went down on his knees and placed his ear against William's chest. After what seemed an eternity he straightened up and turned his attention to a weeping Caroline. He shook his head slowly from side to side.

'I'm afraid he's gone my dear,' he informed her solemnly.

At that moment Jane and Lisa came through the door and saw their dad stretched out on the floor. 'Is he all right Mum?' they both asked falteringly, a shocked expression on their faces.

Caroline, dabbing her eyes with her handkerchief, shook her head negatively. 'We've lost him,' she told them, sobbing uncontrollably as the medics placed him on the stretcher and carried him to the ambulance.

The neighbours were all out on the street, watching as the popular William, was taken away; they crowded round Caroline, offering her their condolences.

The next few days were taken up organising the funeral which they had placed in the hands of the local Co-op. Their professionalism was greatly appreciated, as the ceremony went without a hitch. After the funeral Caroline went to stay with her daughter Jane until such times as she could manage on her own. Three weeks had gone by and Caroline was beginning to show signs of getting back to normal. The hurt still dwelt in her eyes, but they also showed an inner strength. She turned to her daughter, reached out and placed her hands on her shoulders, looked into her eyes and told her huskily, 'Jane, I've made my mind up, I'm going home.'

'Are you sure you know what you are doing Mum?' Jane enquired worriedly, her brow deeply furrowed at the thought of her mum living alone in her bungalow.

'Yes my love, I know it will be hard on my own, but I've got to pull myself together. I can't spend the rest of my life moping around like a lost soul.'

Jane took her both of her mother's hands in hers, looked in her eyes and gave them a squeeze. 'I know you are right Mum,' she told her with feeling. 'Just give me a minute, then I'll get the car out and run you home.'

Twenty minutes later Jane was stopping the car outside her mother's bungalow. 'Here we are Mum,' she announced, a broad smile on her face.

Caroline sat for a few seconds gazing through the car window, as she took in the neat front garden that she and William had spent so many hours planting out. She smiled to herself, then, giving a deep heartfelt sigh, she shook the thoughts from her head as she climbed out of the car and made her way up the flower-lined path to the front door. There was some resistance as she unlocked the door and pushed it open. A pile of letters lay on the floor, most of them junk mail, bending down, she gathered them up and carried them into the kitchen; after dropping them on the table, she put the kettle on.

'Are you going to have a cup of tea with me before you leave Jane?' she asked her daughter who had followed her into the bungalow.

'Mmm,' Jane paused for a couple of seconds as if making her mind up, then told her with a nod of her head. 'Just a quickie Mum.'

Twenty minutes later she finished her tea and got to her feet. 'I'll be off now Mum,' she announced. There was a questioning look in her eyes as she enquired, 'Are you sure you will be okay?'

Caroline waved her hand, assuring her daughter that she would be able to manage now.

After a month living on her own had gone by, although she was sad, she decided to pull herself together and get on with her life. Encouragement from her neighbours and her daughters went a long way to help her through. There was nothing too much trouble for them to do for her.

The next day her phone rang, it was her friend Betty.

'Hello Caroline, how are you getting on?' she enquired, after having heard of her loss.

'Not too bad considering,' Caroline told her.

'I was just thinking,' Betty continued. 'Do you fancy a night out?'

'Just depends what you mean by 'a night out'.'

'Well, I was wondering if you would like to go to Coleman's dance hall with me,' Betty suggested.

'Oh I don't know Betty,' replied Caroline, a little reluctantly. 'I haven't been dancing for years.'

'Neither have I,' her friend replied. 'I just thought it might do both of us good to get out for an evening.

Caroline went quiet, as she thought over what Betty had said, then after taking a deep breath she made her mind up. 'Okay Betty I'll give it a go. By the way when is it?'

'On Wednesday, I'll pick you up at eight p.m. That should get us there for eight-thirty or thereabouts.'

Caroline placed the phone back on its rest and turned to go into the kitchen, her heart was pounding with excitement as her mind went back to the odd times when she and William used to go dancing at Coleman's. William hated it, he always said that he had two left feet. After she became pregnant with her first daughter Jane she gave up dancing, much to William's delight.

Today was Monday, that gave her two days to prepare herself for the big night out. After having her hair set the following day she was ready. Wednesday duly arrived. It was almost eight o'clock and she was waiting for Betty to pick her up. A few minutes went by before her friend arrived in her Mini. Caroline got into the passenger seat and they were on their way. It was just going dark as they arrived at Coleman's. After parking up they went the lit up doorway of the dancehall. A man was stood at the door as they approached. 'Are you on your own ladies?' he asked them.

They looked at each other. 'We are,' they replied somewhat mystified. 'Why?' they enquired in unison.

'All ladies must be accompanied by a gentleman,' he explained apologetically.

'What's the problem?' a voice behind them interrupted, as they turned to walk away.

'We are not allowed in without an escort,' Betty told the two elderly men who were about to enter the hall.

'Don't worry about that girls, we'll book you in,' one of them offered.

'Thank you, you are real gentlemen,' Betty told them, a relieved expression on her face as they followed the two men through the door. After settling down at a vacant table, the two men asked them what they would like to drink, then left to go to the bar. Although the two women weren't exactly smitten by their two new friends, they decided to stay with them for the time being. They returned a few minutes later with the drinks. After a quarter of an hour of meaningless chit-chat had gone by the two men asked them if they would like to dance. Caroline smiled at the grey-haired man and nodded her head in acceptance, a few seconds later she was clumsily swept on to the floor. Caroline told her partner

Bernard, that she would sit the next one out. Finishing his drink, he told her that he was going to the bar for another one. Betty was still on the floor at the start of the next dance, she looked as though she was enjoying herself. Caroline was sat on her own at the table, when a smart, tall man about her age came to her and asked her if she would like to dance. She smiled at the rather handsome dark-haired man and accepted, a thrill went through her as he took her in his arms and swept her out on to the dance floor.

2

Edward and Josey Barnes were pulling together qu

ite well, despite the difficulty of bringing up six children, but they were managing it quite well. Since Edward had been de-mobbed out of the R.A.F. with three children, it had been hard going. After a spell at Maltby, where he had lived next door to his brother David, he had eventually, after buying and selling various properties, arrived at his present address on Rawmarsh Hill, Rawmarsh. Although it was a substantial property, it needed a lot of renovation, a job which Edward had taken on.

He was just about to change jobs, having originally taken up employment as a steel worker at the large steelworks at Templeborough. After spending over nine years at the firm in which he had learned how to use an oxy-acetylene torch, he was made redundant. His boss told him that there was a vacancy going at a nearby firm, as an oxy-acetylene burner; the name of the firm was 'Slag Reduction'. He was one of a gang of fifteen men. Their main task was to cut up discarded railway wagons and other large items into sizes that could be fed into the furnaces at, what was known as the Templeborough Melting Shop, which was situated about a mile away. The pieces of metal were loaded onto railway wagons and shunted the short distance to the furnaces. His relationship with his wife Josey was beginning to get very strained and wasn't going very well, in fact they had come close to splitting up on a couple of occasions.

Arriving onsite, he prepared himself for his usual hard stint. Three large cast iron water valves stood on edge. They were about two feet thick and stood five feet square. They were joined to sheets of mild steel and held together with mild steel bolts.

'I want you to split them up Eddie,' said the foreman with the warning. 'Be careful, they don't look too safe to me.'

Eddie nodded his head in agreement as he walked round the valves, carefully assessing the safest way to tackle them. After making his mind up he got stuck into them. After safely dismantling two of them, the third one presented a more difficult proposition. Its close proximity to the other two made it awkward to get at, as it had sheets of soft steel bolted to it. As it stood it resembled a large metal box. He found that he could cut the plate along the outside, but it was dangerous where it stood close to one of the other valves. He looked round the yard, the crane was on the other side of the site. He scratched the back of his head as he thought the situation over. Then, making his mind up, he decided to cut round the mild metal strip that was fastened to the valve. He reckoned that if he left a strip of about six inches, it would hold it up until he could finish it inside, from a safer position. Having accomplished what he intended, he stood back and surveyed the scene to check if it was, indeed, safe. After assuring himself that it was, he squatted down and reached under it to cut through the six inches of metal that was holding it at the bottom. Suddenly there was a loud crack. His heart was in his mouth, as he struggled to step back out from under it – to no avail. He felt the pressure of the heavy piece of metal across his back, pinning him to the ground. The last thing he remembered was the one ton valve bearing down, crushing the life out of him, his last thought was, *What will Josey think?* as everything suddenly went black.

Opening his eyes, he took in the sea of faces looking down on him as he attempted to piece together what had happened. The faces faded away then came back again, as he went in and out of consciousness. The funny thing was that he didn't feel any pain.

'Keep your eyes open Eddie!' voices urged him.

'Don't go to sleep,' others advised him.

Another held a cigarette to his lips, he gave a slight shake of his head. 'No thank you,' he croaked. 'I don't smoke.'

He smiled inwardly at his comments. *What did it matter if I indulged in the habit or not in such a serious situation?* he asked himself, as his workmates stood back and let the ambulance men through. A few minutes later they were lifting him into the ambulance. He felt, slightly, the prick of a needle in his upper arm, as one of the medics injected him. A few seconds later he passed out.

When he opened his eyes, he was lying in bed; a cage had been placed over him to keep the weight of the sheets from his injuries to stop them causing him discomfort. A nurse, who looked to be in her forties, was bending over him, a beaming smile on her freckled face. 'Welcome to the land of the living young man,' she gushed as she pumped the pillow up under the back of his head.

Eddie's brow furrowed, as he looked up at her questioningly.

'We almost lost you!' she told him, explaining that he had been unconscious for almost two days, during which time the surgeon and his hospital staff had a battle on their hands, as they fought to keep him alive. When they told him the extent of his injuries, he wasn't surprised. They consisted of: six broken ribs, a fractured spine, internal injuries, both feet and ankles smashed, and a badly burned hand. It seemed that his body had been folded up into a space of six inches by the one ton water valve. He was told that it took fourteen men to lift it high enough to enable them to drag him out.

'Someone to see you Mr Barnes,' the nurse's voice told him.

Turning his eyes sideways (he could barely move his head), he saw Josey, dabbing her eyes with a handkerchief, approaching the bed, accompanied by Rita and Marylin, their two youngest daughters. She leaned over and kissed him affectionately on the forehead. 'What have you done?' she whispered in his ear, shaking her head from side to side. Eddie smiled wanly. He had no answer to her query, but it was nice to hear her caring comments. It made a change from her attitude towards him over the last twelve months.

'How are you managing for income?' he asked her worriedly.

'Your firm's manager has been in touch with me. They have agreed to carry on paying your wages, while you are incapacitated.'

'That's good of them,' Eddie told her.

'Well, you did nearly get killed working for them,' Josey put to him.

Eddie nodded his head slightly in agreement. At that moment the nurse approached the bed and addressed Josey. 'I'm afraid you will have to leave now Mrs Barnes.'

Josey got to her feet, thanked the nurse for looking after Eddie, before leaning over and kissing him again on the forehead and squeezing his good hand reassuringly, then after Rita and Marylin gave him an affectionate kiss on his cheek, they all turned and left the ward.

The following days and weeks, Eddie was made as comfortable as possible by the hospital staff, although at times it was quite painful, as he slowly recovered from his unfortunate mishap. After four weeks, even though he couldn't stand on his badly injured feet, he was able (with some difficulty) to wriggle his body out of the bed and onto a wheelchair, in which he travelled round the wards chatting to other patients. Then two week later, after an operation on his left foot and ankle and a resetting of his right ankle, he was sent to Rosehill Hospital at Rawmarsh to further his recovery. He was to stay there for eight weeks until he was capable of standing with the aid of crutches, after which time he was allowed home.

It was now late August and Eddie spent most of his time stretched out on the lawn in the front garden of his home which overlooked Rawmarsh Hill, talking and joking with the passers by. This was when the trouble started with Josey. 'I saw you chatting to those women while you were out front,' she snapped at him accusingly, when he came in the house.

'So what? I was only being friendly,' Eddie replied, his eyes wide with surprise at the sudden outburst from his wife.

'I'm not wasting my life looking after a man who spends his time ogling and fancying other women,' she told him angrily.

Eddie shook his head slowly from side to side, an expression of disbelief on his face. He knew that Josey was inclined to be a little jealous, but he never expected anything like this. This went on day after day. He was becoming fed up with the continuous tirade. After a month had gone by, he received a letter from the Industrial Injury department, telling him that they had found a place for him at Firbeck Hall rehabilitation centre, near Maltby. It was used for the recuperation of injured miners. It meant that he would have to be away from home from Monday to Friday. He wasn't very keen on leaving home, although he had to admit that it would make a welcome change from the incessant bickering that he was having to put up with from Josey.

3

It was Monday. Eddie, struggling along on two walking sticks, was waved off by the family, as he climbed into the ambulance that had arrived to pick him up. A few minutes later the vehicle set off on its journey to the former stately home, which was set in pleasant surroundings in the countryside. On arrival he was allocated one of the forty beds that were situated in a long room. He shook his head and smiled to himself, as he put his sticks down and sat on the edge of the bed that had been allocated to him; it reminded him so much of his spell in the R.A.F. After placing his belongings in the steel locker provided, he was taken to the man who was in charge, where he was given instructions of what he could and could not do. This was followed by signing in. then he was introduced to all the other inmates, who were all injured miners. It wasn't long before he made quite a few friends. He was informed that the day was split up into different exercises which depended on how badly injured you were. Eddie was one of the worst injured and would need extensive treatment, which consisted of numerous exercises to strengthen his back, legs, and ankles.

The weeks that followed consisted of hours spent on an exercise bike, presumably for his feet and ankles, and regular spells of light weight lifting for his back. After a few weeks had gone by, he found that he could stand on his feet longer and that he only needed one stick. Once a month the inmates at Firbeck were invited to local working men's clubs, where they received two free pints of beer and a couple of sandwiches each. They were great times for the injured men, making them forget their aches and pains, as they broke out in song and thoroughly enjoyed themselves. After eighteen weeks Eddie was told by his doctor, who came to visit him at regular intervals, that although he had improved immensely, it would be necessary for him to have another operation on one of his ankles, as it wasn't reacting favourably to treatment.

Two weeks later he left the rehabilitation centre to go in hospital for the operation. Bidding the other inmates farewell he left in the ambulance and was taken to the general hospital in Sheffield, where the operation on his ankle was performed. After ten days of attention by the hospital staff, he was sent home. On completion of his latest operation, he found that he could get about a lot better, albeit with one stick. Meanwhile, his wife Josey, who had only been seeing him at the weekends, continued harassing him, making him extremely unhappy.

Two years went by and Eddie, who was by now getting about a lot better, was sent on a government joinery course in Hull, where he made many friends. During his stay he was given lodgings at a large house in Hull, which also provided accommodation for seven other men. He and one or two of the others spent many an evening at the local working men's club. Halfway through the course, he was accused by

Josey of having an affair. Her jealous attitude towards him was beginning to have an effect on their relationship. After the end of the course he returned home and got himself a job at a local caravan manufacturer. He was managing to cope with the job quite well until, after becoming more experienced, he was asked to take up a position on the production line, which meant that he would be stood on his feet all day. After a week had gone by, he found that it was too much for him and that the pain from his injuries was becoming unbearable.

'It's no good,' he told the foreman with a shake of his head. 'I can't carry on like this George, standing on my feet all day is crippling me; the pain is almost unbearable.'

After much discussion he was told by the management that there wasn't another job on the site that he would be able to do and accordingly the firm would not be able to employ him any longer. A disappointed Eddie accepted the inevitable and left. Twelve months later he was offered another training course for book keeping at Portland Training College; it was situated near Mansfield in Nottinghamshire. Nine months into the ten month course, after a lot of falling out, Josey called him up on the phone and informed him that she didn't love him and that she had met someone else. Eddie was devastated. His studying, that had been going quite well, suffered over the ensuing days as he began to lose interest. The weekend came and he went home. Josey wasn't in, it seemed that she was having one of her driving lessons.

I wonder if the driving instructor is the man she is involved with? he asked himself. After giving the idea some thought he decided he would check on him when his wife arrived back home. Sitting at the front window he waited patiently for her return. Twenty minutes had gone by, when a sleek car pulled up outside the house. Eddie, who had been waiting for this moment, jumped to his feet in readiness to go out and tackle the driving instructor. Suddenly he stopped in his tracks as the instructor got out and opened the driver's side door for Josey. Eddie's brow furrowed as he ran his eyes over him; he was about five feet tall, he had a fat paunch and long greasy hair. He gave Josey a friendly smile as she turned away from the car and made her way to the front door. Eddie stroked his chin as he pondered the situation. 'There is one thing certain,' he muttered to himself. 'That can't be the bloke she's interested in. She would have to be really hard up to take to him.'

The door opened and Josey came in. She paused for a moment and looked Eddie in the eyes; judging by her expression, he wasn't about to get the usual peck on the cheek that she always greeted him with.

'Well,' he began with a shrug of his shoulders. 'What's this all about?'

'I've met someone else,' she told him a little unfeelingly. 'I am sorry Eddie but I have to tell you that I don't love you.'

'Who is it?' he demanded, a little aggressively.

She shook her head. 'I'm not telling you,' she replied.

After ten minutes cajoling, she gave way. 'All right if you must know, it's someone who I knew before I met you.'

Eddie's brow furrowed. There was only one person he could think of. 'Arthur Clinton?' he put to her.

She nodded her head. 'I met him two weeks ago in the supermarket. I told him how unhappy we were.' She gave a shrug of her shoulders and went on to explain that she had been seeing him and had fallen in love with him again.

'What do you intend to do now?' Eddie asked her.

'I haven't put it to him yet, but I hope he will agree to him and me setting up home together.'

'And if he agrees?' Eddie put to her, a little icily.

Her answer said it all. 'I would be over the moon,' she breathed, her eyes half closed.

All the feeling that he had for Josey went out of Eddie at her blunt answer. He could see that they had no future together after this. There was only one way for him now, he decided.

'I'll pack my things and move out,' he rejoined, telling her, 'I'll leave everything for you to arrange.'

4

Eddie went back to the training college with a heavy heart. He went through the routine of training for his pass certificate, which he had to sit for during the following week. Derek, one of his fellow trainees, saw the unhappy expression on his face. 'What's up Eddie?' he enquired.

Eddie took a deep breath and sighed, then told him about his marital troubles.

Derek plucked at his bottom lip for a few seconds before giving his opinion. 'If I were you Eddie, I would shake the whole episode out of my mind and try to make a new way in my life.'

'It's easier said than done,' Eddie replied with a shake of his head.

'All you've got to do is get out and enjoy yourself,' Derek advised him.

After the day's training was over Eddie went to the room where they were staying, took his jacket off and flopped down on the bed. He was on his back gazing at the ceiling, his mind in turmoil, when Jimmy, another of his friends came up to him. 'Eddie can you do me a favour?' he asked.

Eddie took his eyes from the ceiling and turned his head towards him. 'Just depends what it is,' he rejoined.

'Well,' began Jimmy, sitting on the edge of the bed, 'I'm in a predicament.' He paused for a moment before going on. 'I met a woman at a dance last Wednesday and I made a date to meet her tomorrow night at nine p.m.' He stopped for a few seconds and gazed down at his clasped hands.

'Go on,' urged Eddie as he listened attentively. 'What's the favour that you want me to do?'

'I know it may sound a bit silly of me,' Jimmy confided, his face reddening slightly, before going on to tell him, 'since then I have met another woman and made a date with her for the same evening.'

'Well!' Eddie explained with a shrug of his shoulders. 'Why don't you keep the date with one of them and drop the other?'

'Oh, I can't do that Eddie, it wouldn't be right.'

'What are you going to do about it then?' enquired Eddie.

'Well that's where you come in,' replied Jimmy, going on to tell him, 'I was going to ask you to meet the first one and make an excuse for me.'

'Whoah, hold on,' exclaimed Eddie, holding his hands out. 'I don't want to get involved in the problems of your love life.'

'You won't get involved. All you will have to do is tell her that I can't see her as I have had to go to Grimsby,' explained Jimmy. 'There will be a couple of pints in it for you,' he added.

Eddie stroked his chin for a few seconds as he thought over what his friend had told him. *I haven't been out for a couple of weeks*, he told himself. It was about time he started to enjoy life. 'First of all, what is the name of the dance hall?'

'Coleman's, it's in Nottingham.'

'Coleman's,' Eddie murmured to himself. He cast his mind back to the one time that he had been there, as he recalled, it had been an enjoyable experience. 'Okay,' he rejoined, a little reluctantly. 'I'll do it, now tell me what is the woman's name and what does she look like?'

'Her name is Jean. She is what you might call a big girl, she's about five-foot-nine and has long blonde hair, you can't miss her,' explained Jimmy. Reaching into his pocket and taking out a fiver, he gave it to Eddie, telling him, 'That will do for the drinks. Oh and thanks for helping me out.'

The following evening Eddie got himself ready for his night out. He intended to get there for around nine p.m.

It was eight forty-five when he arrived at Coleman's. The double doors were open and music could be heard emanating from the large dance hall as he turned into the almost full car park. Finding himself a spare space, he parked up. It was spotting with rain as he climbed out of the car and made his way to the welcoming, lit up doorway. There were half a dozen couples gliding round the highly polished floor to the haunting sound of 'My Way', as he threaded his way through the tables to the bar, where he ordered a pint of bitter.

'That will be one pound twenty sir,' the portly barman told him, a broad smile on his ruddy face, as he slid the pint across the bar.

Eddie thanked him and raised the glass to his lips. Taking a good swig, he placed the glass on the bar and ran his eyes around the large hall. There was only one woman with long blonde hair and she was slightly built and about five-foot-four. *Hardly what you would call big*, he told himself. After taking another drink he noticed a woman sitting at a table on her own.

Why not? he asked himself as he approached her and asked her for a dance, she smiled as he took her in his arms, stepped out on to the dance floor and swirled her round to the sounds of 'The Last Waltz'.

She looked up into his eyes; he had a sadness about him, she thought, as his arm held her gently.

At the end of the dance he walked her back to the table where she had been seated. After thanking her, he went back to his original position at the bar. Caroline's friend Betty returned with her partner. Leaning across the table, she asked her friend in a low voice, 'Who was that you were dancing with?'

Caroline shrugged her shoulders, as she told her, 'I didn't ask him his name, but he seemed a nice man.'

A few minutes later the man came across to their table and asked Caroline if she would like to dance again. She smiled her acceptance and got to her feet; she was swept out onto the dance floor to a quick step. After ten minutes or so of energetically traversing the dancing area, they came to a stop at her table. The two men, who had signed Caroline and Betty in, had gone to the bar to get a couple of drinks. Eddie asked the two women if they minded him joining them; they both told him he was welcome to take a seat beside them.

'What about the two fellows who are with you. Will they mind?' he put to them as he pulled another chair up to the table and sat down.

'They are not with us,' the two women told him, explaining that the two elderly men had just signed them in.

'What are your names?' he enquired.

When they had told him, he gave them a gentle shake of their hand and told them that his name was Edward. 'Eddie will do,' he informed them, smiling as he did so.

Caroline, detecting a northern accent, asked him where he came from.

'I was born and brought up in Sheffield,' he confided, 'but I haven't been back there for some years now.'

At that moment a man came up to them and asked Betty if she would care to dance. She accepted and was led on to the dance floor.

'Would you like to dance Caroline?' asked Eddie. She nodded her head and a couple of seconds later they were stepping out to a rendition of 'Strangers in the Night'.

Caroline's face was flushed and her heart was beating fast as they glided round the floor. *I haven't felt like this for a long time*, she told herself.

The evening was magical, as the two of them danced the night away. They only had eyes for each other, as they had the last dance together.

'Will I see you next week Caroline?' enquired Eddie, as the music stopped and they walked off the dance floor to their table.

'If you want to see me again, I'll be here,' she enthused, a serious expression on her face.

'And I'll be here too,' he assured her, as he helped her put on her coat. 'How are you getting home?' he asked the two women as they left the dance hall.

'We came by car,' they informed him as they walked out to the car park.

Bidding them goodnight, Eddie shook both their hands and gave Caroline a peck on the cheek, before going over to his car and climbing in. With a wave of his hand he drove off.

Caroline was in a world of her own as she fastened her seat belt.

'You were really taken up with him, weren't you?' Betty put to her.

Caroline's face reddened a little as she looked across at her friend. 'Does it show that much?' she rejoined.

Betty smiled, as she started the car and drove carefully out of the car park. 'I'm pleased that you enjoyed yourself Caroline, but take my advice and be careful, I don't want to see you hurt again.'

Caroline nodded her head as she told her friend, 'I know what you are telling me, but he was a nice man wasn't he?'

'Are you seeing him again?' asked Betty, glancing at her out of the corner of her eye.

'He says he wants to see me at the dance next week,' she confided.

'You don't know much about him,' rejoined her friend, a note of caution in her voice as she reached out and switched on the main beam, lighting up the darkness in front of them as they made their way along an unlit country lane.

'Well I've only just met him,' replied Caroline a little sharply.

'I know, I know!' exclaimed Betty, in a soothing tone of voice. 'All I'm saying is that you don't even know if he's married or not.'

Caroline went quiet as she absorbed what her friend had just said. Betty was right of course, she told herself before deciding that she would ask Eddie when she saw him next week.

Ten minutes later Betty stopped the car outside Caroline's bungalow. 'Here we are,' she remarked.

Caroline unfastened her seat belt, opened the car door and stepped out on to the pavement, telling her, 'I'll see you next Wednesday.'

5

Eddie was deep in thought as he drove back to the training college. The woman he had met at the dance hall had made a strong impression on him. He looked forward to seeing her again.

The next few days were taken up with studying for his book keeping test which was to be held the following week. That was also the week that the course ended. His biggest worry then would be where he was going to stay after he left the college. The manager of the college had told him he could stay on the premises over the weekend until the end of the course.

The days passed quickly and it was Wednesday again. Eddie had found it hard to concentrate on his studies as his thoughts were on Caroline. He was full of feeling as he drove out of the Portland training college car park and set off on the short journey to Nottingham. He checked his watch as he turned into the car park at Coleman's. His heart was beating fast as he climbed out of the car and walked through the entrance to the hall. Reflections from the large glass ball that hung over the dance floor, sent a myriad of flickering coloured lights around the large dance hall, where quite a few couples were gliding round the spacious floor to the sound of romantic music. He cast his eyes around the chattering people that were sat at the tables that were placed around the hall, his face breaking into a smile as he spotted Caroline sitting at a table with her friend Betty. Carefully making his way around the edge of the dance floor, he eventually reached the table, pulled out a chair and seated himself by the side of a smiling Caroline, her face showing her pleasure at seeing him.

'Would you like to drink?' he asked the two women politely. They both nodded and asked for a glass of orange juice. Getting to his feet again, he went over to the bar and ordered himself a pint of bitter and the ladies a glass of orange juice each.

'We'll bring them to you sir,' the smiling barman informed him, nodding his shiny bald head. Eddie thanked him and went back to his seat. The waitress duly turned up carrying the drinks on a tray. Placing them on the table she turned to Eddie. 'That will be three pound fifty sir,' she trilled, a pleasant smile on her pretty face.

Eddie held up his hand as Caroline reached for her handbag. 'I'll get them,' he intoned, reaching into his pocket and taking out four pounds and handing it to the young waitress, telling her to keep the change.

'What are you doing at Portland training college Eddie?' asked Betty, as he was taking a drink of his beer.

He paused for a moment to wipe the froth from his lips before answering her. 'I'm taking a course on book keeping,' he told her. 'Actually, I take my final exam tomorrow.'

'Does that mean that you will have to leave Portland College?' she persisted, much to the annoyance of Caroline.

'First of all I've got to pass the exam, then I'll have to find myself a job,' he explained, a rueful smile on his face.

'Aren't you going to ask me for a dance Eddie?' asked Caroline, butting in on Betty's questioning. There was a hint of annoyance in her voice as she got to her feet.

Eddie, a half smile on his face, placed his arm around her waist and swept her out onto the floor to a rendition of the romantic 'Please Release Me'.

'I hope you weren't offended when Betty was questioning you,' she whispered in his ear as he held her close.

He looked deep into her brown eyes as he executed a reverse turn. A shudder went down her spine as he told her in a low voice, 'I wasn't offended. It's only right that you should know more about me.'

'You don't know anything about me either,' she replied.

'We can soon put that right,' he told her, adding, 'first of all what do you want to know?'

She was silent for a few seconds as they glided round the floor. Suddenly she looked up into his blue eyes and asked him straight out, 'Are you married?'

Returning her look, he chewed on his bottom lip before telling her firmly, 'I am.'

Her heart missed a beat as she turned her head and looked away.

Seeing the hurt expression on her face, he whispered in her ear, 'I'm estranged from my wife.'

She looked up at him again, a questioning expression on her face as the music stopped.

'Come on,' he told her as he held her firmly by the arm and walked her to an empty table where they both sat down.

Leaning forward, his elbows resting on the table, he reached out, took her hand in his and looked deep into her eyes for a few seconds before going on to tell her what had happened between him and his wife Josey. After he finished talking he sat back, the expression on his face telling her that it had been a hurtful experience. She patted his hand, an understanding look in her eyes. 'Never mind Eddie, you are a strong man, you will get over it,' she confided with feeling.

His face broke into a smile as the band began to play a lively quick step. He got to his feet gave an exaggerated bow before asking her, 'May I have this dance my lady?'

Caroline smiled and moved into his arms, a strange feeling of relief going through her as they stepped onto the dance floor and joined the swirling couples.

'Now it's my turn,' he asserted as they strode out to the music.

She looked up at him questioningly.

'Are you married?' he put to her.

'I was,' she replied. There was a pregnant pause before she went on to explain to him that she had lost her husband to a heart attack and that subsequently she was a widow.

'I'm sorry to hear that,' he told her with feeling.

She gave a slight shrug of her shoulders, telling him, a sad expression on her face, 'It's all in the past now.'

The music stopped; he gave her a sympathetic smile as they walked off the floor hand in hand and joined Betty. 'Where have you two been?' she enquired as they sat down.

'Opening our hearts,' replied a smiling Caroline as she reached out and squeezed Eddie's hand.

'Good,' said Josey, a smile on her face as she noted the affectionate way that they were treating each other.

After a few more dances, the band leader informed them that this was the last waltz. Eddie checked his watch; it was almost eleven o'clock as they moved out onto the floor, held each other close as they danced, somewhat appropriately, 'The Last Waltz'.

She looked up at Eddie as they glided round the dance floor. She was getting feelings that she thought had gone forever. She felt as though she was floating on air as she laid her head on his chest. He looked down and smiled, giving her a gentle kiss on the top of her head. All too soon the music stopped, putting an end to the magical moment. Eddie gave a deep sigh as he followed her to the table where she picked up her handbag. Betty gave her a knowing smile as they made their way out of the dance hall and into the cool night air. Eddie stood for a moment and looked up at the star filled clear sky; he turned to Caroline, 'Would you like me to visit you at the weekend?'

She nodded her head. 'I'd love that Eddie,' she replied, with feeling.

'Saturday afternoon, say one o'clock?' he put to

her as they walked across the car park.

'Okay, I'll see you then,' she told him as she climbed into the passenger seat and joined Betty.

Eddie stood by his car as they drove out on to the road, giving a wave as the two women disappeared into the night. Getting into his car he made his way out of the car park, his mind was in a whirl as he drove through the night back to Portland College.

The following morning, after breakfast, he made his mind up to take his mind off the previous evening and concentrate on the job in hand, i.e. doing his best, as he and his fellow trainees went through the ordeal of the four hour exam, which he knew was going to be quite difficult.

The pages of work that he had to contend with seemed never-ending. Eventually the examiner's authoritative voice called out, 'Pens down.'

Eddie gave a sigh of relief as he put his pen down and sat back as the examiner's assistant gathered up the completed exam papers from the participants. A few minutes later they got to their feet and left.

'How do you think you went on?' asked Jimmy as the group made their way to the dining room for lunch.

'I'm not sure,' rejoined Eddie, shrugging his shoulders. 'We'll know on Monday.'

The next two days went by quickly and it was Saturday. Eddie's thoughts were all of Caroline as he drove to Long Eaton; he could hardly wait to see her again.

Caroline's face was flushed at the expectation of seeing Eddie again as she sat at the window, waiting for his car to pull up on the street in front of her bungalow. She looked at the clock on the stone fireplace; it was five minutes to one. Suddenly his red car drew up; she went to the door and opened it. Eddie was striding up the footpath, a broad smile on his face as he approached her; he reached out and took her small hands in his, leaned over and gave her a kiss on her cheek before following her into the comfortable, welcoming lounge. Caroline indicated with her hand for him to take a seat before leaving him to go into the kitchen. Smiling, he sat down on the plush settee, leaned back and relaxed as he ran his eyes round the spacious room, taking in the numerous paintings and photographs that were either hanging on the walls or standing on just about every shelf including the stone fireplace. Most of them were pictures of her two daughters and her smiling husband. It was obvious to him that before the loss of William they had been a very close, happy family.

'Are you hungry?' Caroline called out from the kitchen.

'I am,' he replied, raising his voice as she walked into the lounge and placed a plate full of sandwiches on the table. This was followed a few minutes later by her carrying in a tea pot.

'I hope I've got it right, making you tea?' she put to him, a questioning frown on her forehead, as she poured out two cups of tea.

'Spot on,' Eddie assured her, with a smile and a nod of his head as he reached out, took one of the cups and placed a spoonful of sugar in it.

Caroline went over to a CD player that was standing on the highly polished sideboard and switched it on before joining him on the settee. A strange feeling of contentment went through him as the rendition of the well-known classic 'Tales from the Vienna Woods', drifted round the room. He gave a heart-felt sigh as he took a sip of his tea. 'Caroline,' he confided in a husky voice, 'you really are something special.'

She smiled at his comment, leaned towards him, looked deep into his eyes and told him, 'You are not so bad yourself, you know.'

Smiling, he reached out and tenderly pushed back a lock of hair that had fallen over her eyes. She clutched his hand before he could withdraw it and held it against her face for a few seconds before kissing it and moving into his arms. Eddie ran his fingers through her silken hair, looked down into her eyes and gently pressed his lips against hers.

'You can do better than that,' she whispered as she put her arm around his neck and gave him a long, lingering kiss.

Suddenly the phone rang, breaking the magical moment. Reluctantly Caroline pulled away from him and got to her feet, her face flushed as she left him and went into the hallway to answer the phone. It was her daughter enquiring if she was okay. Caroline assured her that she was, before returning to the lounge and joining Eddie, who was on his feet straightening his tie.

'My dear,' he intoned. 'I think I should leave you now.'

'So soon!' she exclaimed, a look of disappointment on her face.

Eddie put his arms round her waist, pulled her close to him and looked down at her.

'Caroline there's nothing I would like better than to stay here with you,' he told her huskily, 'but I must get my life sorted out first.'

Her heart missed a beat as the thought went through her mind that he was making an excuse to drop her. 'Is that it then Eddie?' she put to him a little tearfully, realising she was beginning to have strong feelings for him and didn't want to lose him.

He smiled and shook his head from side to side as he told her, 'No my dear, that isn't it. But I must go back home and get everything right as regards the maintenance of my youngest daughter.' He paused for a moment before going on to explain to her, 'When I've sorted that out I've arranged to stay with my sister in Skegness for a while.'

'And what about us?' she whispered.

'As soon as I've settled in I'll come to you.' He looked into her eyes and added in a husky voice, 'That is if you still want me.'

'Of course I will want you,' she assured him, reaching up and giving him an affectionate kiss on the cheek, as he turned to leave.

Eddie had a contented smile on his face as he drove back to Portland College.

The following Monday Mr Humphries, the instructor came into the classroom with a heap of papers in his hands. Placing them on the table in front of him, he proceeded to pick up the papers one at a time and reading off the result of each one. They had to score forty-eight or over to pass. Eventually he came to Eddie's.

'Edward Barnes,' he called out in a stentorian voice. Eddie closed his eyes as the result was announced. 'Seventy-two.'

His face broke into a broad smile. He heaved a sigh of relief at the score he had achieved. The next ten minutes was spent on the members of the class congratulating each other. Every one of them had passed. Caroline was over the moon when he phoned her and told her the news. He informed her that he would be going back to Rawmarsh to put things right.

The weekend came and all the trainees made their farewells. Eddie drove out of the car park and on to the road that would take him back to Rawmarsh. A strange feeling of sadness was with him as he left behind him the friends that he had made during his stay at the college.

On arrival at Rawmarsh, he parked the car in the driveway, then, taking a deep breath he opened the door and walked into the house. Josey was at the sink washing some dishes. She looked up at him as she reached out for a towel to dry them. 'And what do you want?' she enquired sharply.

'I've come to make arrangements for our Lisa,' he told her calmly.

'What do you mean?' she enquired, her brow furrowed.

He paused for a moment before going on to explain to her that he wanted to settle on a monthly sum of money towards her keep. She chewed on her bottom lip for a few seconds as she thought over his offer to help. 'Would you be able to pay sixty pounds a month?' she put to him, a little tentatively.

He looked into her eyes and nodded. 'Yes, I reckon I can manage that.'

With this he reached into his pocket and pulled out his wallet. Taking out three twenty pound notes, he placed them on the table in front of her. 'That's for one month in advance,' he told her, before turning away from her.

He was halfway through the door when she called out to him, 'Eddie, I wish you all the happiness in the world.'

He turned a warm smile on his face as he replied, 'And you Josey.'

He gave a deep sigh as he climbed in his car and set off on his journey to his sister Marie's home in Skegness. He had arranged with her that he would do some jobs for her around the house for his board and lodgings. He went to stay with Caroline every weekend. After six months had gone by she told him that she wanted to see more of him.

'What did you have in mind?' he asked her.

She went quiet for a moment, her eyes half closed. Suddenly she blurted out, 'I've been thinking of selling the bungalow and moving to Skegness to stay with you.'

'Are you sure?' he put to her, a deep frown on his forehead.

'I'm sure,' she replied firmly.

Eddie put his arms around her and gave her a long, loving kiss. 'Caroline, I promise I'll make you happy,' he assured her huskily.

Two months later, after selling her property, she moved to Skegness and stayed with Eddie and his sister. After settling in, they searched the area for a bungalow; six weeks had gone by when they found what they were looking for, a nice little property on the outskirts of Skegness.

A week later they moved in. The happy couple stood at the bay window and looked out over the open countryside. Eddie had his arm round Caroline, his thoughts going back over the events that had led to this moment. 'Caroline,' he whispered in her ear; she turned her head and looked up into his eyes. 'It seems as though this was all planned for us.'

'What do you mean?' she asked.

'Well, when you think about it, events in your life led you to Coleman's and events in my life also led me to Coleman's.' He took a deep breath before continuing. 'It is as if the meeting of two hearts was meant to be.'

Caroline smiled, looked up into his eyes and kissed him on the lips before telling him, 'Eddie, I believe you are right.'

End

Well Met

The heavy rain was beginning to ease as Barbara drove her car into the small car park at the side of the solicitor's office that was based in the seaside resort of Skegness. She had been informed that the results of her divorce had come through and that the solicitor wished to see her regarding the settlement; climbing out of the car she made a quick dash to the entrance. Pushing open the glass door, she entered the reception room. A long counter confronted her as she closed the door behind her. Behind the counter, sitting at a desk, busy typewriting, was a frosty-faced woman. She turned her head and looked at her over her half-rimmed glasses.

'Good morning,' said Barbara smilingly.

The woman nodded her head. 'Good morning,' she replied, without the smile. 'Can I help you?'

Barbara explained to her that she had an appointment; taking out the letter that she had received and showing it to her. The woman ran her eyes over it for a couple of seconds before picking up the phone and speaking into it.

'There's a Mrs Wetteringham to see you sir,' she announced, before turning to Barbara, informing her that the solicitor would see her now, indicating with a wave of her hand, a door situated at the far end of the office.

Barbara thanked her, knocked on the door and walked in. A Mr Pullman greeted her as she entered his office. He was seated at a large desk; a glass frame on the wall behind him displayed the obligatory diploma. After requesting her to take a seat opposite him, he picked up a sheaf of papers and placed them on the desk in front of him, then with his thick-rimmed spectacles balanced on the end of his nose, he leaned forward, his elbows resting on the desk. He paused for a moment as he reached into his pocket, took out a handkerchief and coughed into it to clear his throat before commencing to read out the court's decision. Barbara, sitting stony-faced, gazed straight ahead as he droned on, her blue eyes concentrating on the shiny bald patch on his head as he looked down at the documents in front of him. The outcome of it all was that her ex-husband Harold, had handed over almost everything to her. It included the bungalow that he had so lovingly built for them, and the car.

'It seems that you have come out of the divorce quite well, Mrs Wetteringham!' exclaimed the solicitor, as he sat back in his chair and adjusted his glasses.

Barbara looked down at her clasped hands and nodded her head in agreement, a lock of hair falling over her forehead as she did so. 'Yes,' she replied as she reached up and flicked the wayward strand of hair back into place with her fingers, adding, her voice softening. 'Harold always was generous.'

She quickly looked away as the emotion showed in her eyes. Opening her handbag, she took out a handkerchief and dabbed them. The solicitor smiled sympathetically. He had seen it all before; some took it hard, others welcomed it.

Recovering her composure, Barbara put the handkerchief back in her handbag, got to her feet and thanked him. Pushing his chair back with the back of his legs, the tall, rather thin solicitor walked from behind the desk and opened the office door for her, smiling politely as he reached out and shook her hand before bidding her goodbye.

A few seconds later she stepped out of the local solicitor's office and pulled the door shut behind her; there was a distant look in her eyes as she stood on the step, paused for a moment and looked up at the sky. It had stopped raining and the sun was beginning to peer through a gap in the grey clouds. She smiled to herself. It was as though it was telling her that there always was a silver lining. Then, with a determined expression on her face, she strode purposefully to where her smart red Fiesta was parked.

What I have been waiting for has finally come to fruition, she told herself, as she climbed into the car and pulled the door shut.

Taking a deep breath, she placed her handbag on

the passenger seat and sat for a few seconds as she gathered her thoughts. The finality of it all had made her feel light-headed. It was hard to take in that after all these years her life with Harold was finished. *There will be no more men in my life*, she told herself doggedly, with a shake of her head as she reached out, inserted the key into the ignition and started the engine. She paused for a moment to clear her mind, before putting the gear into first, exiting the car park and pulling out into the busy Skegness traffic.

The sun, shining from a now predominately blue sky, was quickly drying up the pools of rain and the wet sand as she drove along the sea front. After negotiating the heavy traffic in the centre of the seaside town, she was finally driving along the road to Burgh Le Marsh, where she eventually pulled into the drive of her well-tended bungalow. Switching off the engine, she sat in the car for a few moments, her blue eyes glazing over as she took in the enormity of what she had done. A great calm descended over her as she realised that the days of arguments and heartbreaking turmoil in her life were finally over; after a prolonged struggle, she was alone.

Giving a heartfelt sigh, she dragged her thoughts back to the present; opening the car door, she climbed out and stepped on to the cobble stone driveway. She stood for a few seconds and cast her eyes around the colourful, well-tended garden. Her grey cat, Smoky, who was in the process of stalking a sparrow that was perched in one of the bushes that ran along the boundary, turned his head and looked at her momentarily, before carrying on with the more important task in hand. Betty closed the car door firmly behind her, the sound of which scared the sparrow, causing it to fly off, much to the annoyance of Smoky. She paused for a moment and admired the low stone wall that her now former husband Harold had built. She gave a deep sigh as she made her way along the concrete path that ran along the front of the property, to the front door.

At least I didn't come out of it too badly, she told herself, a satisfied expression on her face as she opened the door and went inside; she gave an annoyed, 'Tut! Tut!' as she almost tripped over the cat as he squeezed through the door in front of her, giving out a squeal as she caught his foot under her heel. Going into the lounge she threw her coat over the back of the settee, before flopping down in an armchair. Leaning her head back she half closed her eyes, as she contemplated her present situation.

'The past eight years have been a complete waste of my life,' she muttered to herself as she looked up at the landscape picture that Harold had painted during the earlier, happy periods of their twenty years together; it was hanging on the wall over the tiled fireplace.

Actually this wasn't quite true. For the first fifteen years of their marriage they had been perfectly happy, it wasn't until Harold came home from work one day and broke the news that he had lost his job at the caravan firm that was situated just outside Skegness.

'Fifteen years I've worked for them,' he raged as he stepped into the house and slammed the door shut behind him. 'Fifteen years,' he repeated, a look of exasperation on his face, as he banged his right fist into the palm of his hand. 'And what's my reward?' He paused for a moment before declaring angrily,

'One week's bloody notice.'

'Never mind dear,' she told him, placing her hand on his arm in an attempt to calm him, as he strode by her on his way to the bathroom. 'Something will turn up.'

The weeks and months went by and try as he might, Harold couldn't get another job. He kept telling her that he was on the scrap heap at forty-two, rambling on about the useless government, blaming them for getting the country into this position. As their savings dwindled, he got more and more frustrated. It was a blessing that they had no children.

'Harold,' she'd told him. 'This is 1986. There are four million other men on the dole with you. That's the problem.'

Eventually, after three years of arguing and disenchantment, they had a big bust up and Harold walked out of the door, slamming it behind him. That was two years ago. At first she was lonely and hurt, but after a while, although she found it difficult to get him out of her system, she settled down to a life on her own. It wasn't hard to do. She and Harold had never been ones for going out much.

'Why don't you come and live with me?' her mum had asked her over and over again. She smiled to herself; Mum meant well, bless her, but she preferred to be independent.

Suddenly the phone rang, jerking her out of her reflective thoughts. She picked it up; it was her friend Marjory, enquiring how she was keeping. Barbara told her that she was okay now that the divorce had been finally settled.

'How about going with me for a night out to celebrate?' her friend suggested.

'It depends on what do you mean by a night out,' she countered sharply.

There was a pause for a few seconds; this was followed by Marjory telling her hesitantly,

'Well, I don't know if you're interested Barbara, but I see there's a dance being held at the Festival Hall in Skegness on Saturday night.'

Barbara shook her head at the phone, exasperation in her voice as she replied, 'You know that's not my scene Marjory. I haven't been dancing for years.'

After a lot of pleading and cajoling from her friend, she finally gave in. 'Oh all right,' she rejoined, telling her grudgingly, 'just this once.'

'Saturday night then!' exclaimed Marjory excitedly. She went on to tell her 'I'll meet you outside the Festival Hall at eight o'clock.'

Barbara, despite agreeing to go to the dance with her friend, still wasn't all that keen; she shrugged her shoulders as she put the phone down. 'Well… it *will* make a change from staying in and watching television,' she told herself.

There was a half smile on her face as she cast her mind back to when she and Harold were younger. They often had an evening out at the Festival Hall. Harold wasn't much of a dancer; he always claimed that he had two left feet.

'That was just an excuse to stop me from getting him on the dance floor,' she muttered to herself, her eyes half closed as her mind went back. 'Actually he wasn't all that bad,' she conceded.

The Festival Hall was situated on the sea front. It was well lit up and music from the dance band could be heard drifting out over the dunes. The sun was just dipping out of sight on the horizon as Barbara drove into the festival car park. She saw that Marjory was waiting for her as she climbed out of the car and walked towards the entrance. There were two men standing beside her; one of them was talking to her animatedly.

'Here she is,' her friend announced, a wide smile on her face as Barbara approached them. Marjory formally introduced her to the two men. 'This is Martin and this is Walter.'

The two men politely nodded, smiled and shook hands with her.

'I hope you don't mind me springing them on you like this,' she confided as they walked along. 'They asked if they could accompany us to the dance at the festival.'

Martin, the one Marjory had been talking to, ranged alongside her, his paunch preceding him by a good six inches. He looked to be in his late forties, she surmised. Her thoughts went back to Harold. The last time she saw him he looked ten years younger than this bloke. She wasn't impressed as he lit up a cigarette after offering her one, which she declined with a shake of her head. The band was playing a lively quick step as they sat down at a table near the dance floor.

After the two men had been to the bar and got the drinks in, Martin asked her if she would like to dance; she got to her feet and was swept clumsily out on to the dance floor. One thing was certain, she told herself, he was no Fred Astaire. A few dances later, during which her feet had been almost crushed, she checked her watch (it showed ten fifteen p.m.). She decided to call it a night. She leaned over the table towards her friend. 'Marjory, I've had enough. I'm off home,' she whispered to her, as the two men went to the bar for another couple of beers.

'Okay Barbara,' Marjory replied with a nod of her head; realising that her friend wasn't exactly smitten by the company. 'I'll go and let them know that we are leaving then we'll get going.'

Getting to her feet, she went over to the bar, to where Martin and Walter stood waiting to be served and told them of their intentions.

'So soon?' remarked Walter, questioningly, as he paid for the drinks.

'Well…' replied Marjory hesitantly. 'It's Barbara, she doesn't feel well,' she lied.

Her face reddened a little as she turned away and left the two men, joining her friend, who was already walking towards the exit.

On the walk back to the car park, Barbara explained to her that at the moment she wasn't really interested in finding a new man; her friend put her arm around her shoulder and gave her a squeeze, apologising for spoiling her evening.

'It's okay Marjory, you meant well,' she told her. 'Anyway,' she conceded, with a slight shrug of her shoulders. 'I needed a break. Maybe I'll be all right after a while.'

Although she knew deep down inside her that this wasn't her way.

'Have you tried one of those friendship magazines?' suggested Marjory, worried that her friend was beginning to get into a rut.

Barbara turned and looked at her, a concerned expression on her face. 'Isn't that a bit risky?' she replied. 'You don't know who you're dealing with,' she told her.

'Well you don't *have* to give them your real name and address,' said Marjory, throwing her friend a meaningful look as they walked across the car park to their respective vehicles.

Barbara smiled at Marjory and bid her goodnight as she opened the car door, climbed in and drove slowly out of the car park.

The next morning as she lay in her bed contemplating her future, she thought over what Marjory had told her. She reached out and picked up a magazine that lay on top of the cabinet that was at the side of the bed and carefully flipped through it, stopping at a page headed, 'Lonely Hearts'.

She ran her eyes down the list, shaking her head and smiling to herself at some of the comments.

'Make my day – Unhappy brown eyes.'

'Maybe you were meant for me, signed – A man needing love.'

And so it went on. Some were funny, others quite sad, she thought.

Suddenly she stopped at one.

'Are you as lonely as I am, and need a friend? If so, get in touch.' It was signed, 'Raymond'.

Her eyes dropped to the bottom of the page, to where there were instructions on how to contact any of the writers. Underneath there was a box number. She looked at it for a moment, a little undecided, before shrugging her shoulders.

'Why not?' she muttered to herself. *He'll probably turn out to be a crank*, she thought.

After mulling it over for a few more seconds, she made her mind up and reached out for pen and paper. Chewing on the end of the pen as she made her mind up on what she was going to say, she thought of what Marjory had told her about using a fictitious name, at least until such times as when she knew more about the person she was communicating with.

Now what name should I use? she asked herself, as she rested her head back on the pillow as she thought deeply, running a list of names through her thoughts, before making her mind up.

'*Charlene*,' she muttered out loud, a half smile on her face, as she reminded herself, that was the name she'd always dreamed of giving her daughter, if she had one. 'That's it, Charlene.'

She gave a deep sigh as she started writing.

It was a formal letter, just saying that she was a divorced woman living on her own, then she went on to say that although she wasn't really interested in a new relationship, she thought it would be nice to help someone to get over their loneliness. She gave a box number for any reply and signed it, 'Charlene'.

After she had finished her breakfast she went into Skegness to do some shopping, posting the letter at the post office while she was there.

One week went by. She dropped in at the post office in Skegness to check her box number; the woman behind the counter turned round and went to a row of pigeon holes along the wall behind her. After quickly checking she came back. 'Just one,' she informed her smilingly.

Barbara's heart missed a beat as the brown envelope was pushed across the counter towards her. On it was written. 'Charlene', a box number was written underneath it.

Slipping it in her pocket, she went to the car park and climbed into her car. Leaning back in the car seat, she took out the envelope and looked at it carefully to see if she could see the post mark. It was impossible to make out the area where it had come from. Giving a shrug of her shoulders, she opened it. The first thing she noticed was that it was typewritten.

'Mmm,' she mumbled to herself as she flattened out the folded page. 'Maybe he's not a very good writer.'

The wording was similar to the one she had written. It was formal and not giving too much away. It started, 'Dear Charlene,' then went on to tell her that he was a man living on his own and was very lonely. Then he told her that at the present time he was working as a plumber. Like her, he was divorced and needed to communicate with someone, as he wasn't very good at making friends, specially the female kind.

The letter was signed, 'Raymond'.

As she read it she felt she had a strange sense of affinity with the writer. Driving out of the car park she called in on her grey haired seventy-two-year-old mother, who was a widow living on her own in Archer Road in Skegness, her dad having died five years earlier after suffering a massive heart attack.

'Are you all right my love?' enquired her comfortably plump mum, as Barbara came through the door; placing her arms around her daughter's shoulders she gave her a kiss on the cheek. 'You look a bit pale.'

Barbara walked into the cosy, lived-in lounge; she had a broad smile on her face as she sat down on the comfortable settee.

'Mum you always say that. Of course I'm all right,' she chuckled as her mum went into the kitchen to put the kettle on. She leaned back and ran her eyes around the room, taking in the watercolour painting of the local church that her dad had painted, hanging on the wall. A photograph of him in his younger days, which had been placed on the top of the tiled fireplace, smiled at her; a tear formed in the corner of her eye. She shook her head slowly from side to side as her mind went back to the happy times she'd had when she was a young girl. She blinked away the tear and rubbed the back of her hand across her eye as her mother came into the room with a tray in her hands, which she placed on a small coffee table, before sitting down in an armchair opposite her.

She went on to tell her mother about the letter that she had written to the 'Lonely Hearts' club, and the reply she'd had.

'You be careful our Barbara,' warned her mother as she picked up one of the cups of tea and handed it to her daughter. 'There's a lot of cranks about you know!'

'Don't worry Mum, I will,' she replied, as she reached out, took the cup and saucer from her and, before taking a tentative sip of the tea.

'Have you heard how Harold is getting on?' her mum enquired, a questioning expression on her face.

Barbara, who was just about to take another sip of her tea, raised her eyebrows and shook her head negatively in reply to her mother's query, looking her straight in the eyes as she did so; she paused for a few seconds to take sip her tea before replying. 'You know full well our Mum, that I've had nothing to do with him for over two years,' she countered, adding in a low, penetrating voice, 'and after the way he treated me I don't want anything to do with him in the future.'

'Well, I just asked,' replied her mum apologetically, shrugging her shoulders.

Barbara finished her tea, placed her cup and saucer on the table, before getting to her feet and going over to her mum. Putting her arm around her shoulders, she gave her an affectionate hug.

'I know you mean well Mum,' she told her with feeling, giving her a kiss on her wrinkled forehead, as she was about to leave, 'but my life with Harold is finished now and I've got to find another way.'

Barbara was deep in thought as she drove back to

Burgh Le Marsh. She was suddenly brought back to the present, braking sharply as a small dog ran across the road in front of the car, the front offside wheel missing it by inches. She heaved a sigh of relief as the dog, a Jack Russell, emerged into sight and scuttled on to the pavement. Tut-tutting, she shook her head from side to side, as she pushed the gear into first, before continuing, a little shaken, on her way. Ten minutes later she was turning the car on to her driveway.

'Am I *really* being silly?' she asked herself, recalling her mother's comments as she reached out and switched off the ignition; getting out of the car, a thoughtful expression on her face, she approached her front door. Her brow was furrowed as she placed the key in the door and unlocked it, opening the door she made her way along the hallway and into the kitchen.

After putting the kettle on and making a pot of tea, she poured herself a cup, then sat at the kitchen table and took out the letter, putting on her glasses she commenced reading carefully through it again. There was a lump in her throat as she detected a note of sadness in the words.

Taking a sip of her tea, she placed the cup down before reaching out for pen and paper and starting to write her reply. She told him that all she wanted was to be friendly and that they should keep it at that stage for the time being. Four days later she received another letter, which she answered. This went on week after week. The letters between them were becoming more and more intimate as the weeks went by.

There were times when she had tried to envisage what he looked like. He came across as someone who wasn't very happy with his life. Barbara suddenly realised that she was having strange feelings about a man that she knew very little about.

Should I tell him my real name? she asked herself. Then with a shake of her head she decided that, at the moment it wouldn't be appropriate. She felt that she wasn't ready for a new relationship just yet, although she must admit, she was *very* interested. 'Anyway,' she muttered to herself. 'He's only given his first name.'

It seemed no time at all before three months had gone by, then after the sixteenth letter Raymond suggested that, now they knew quite a bit about each other, they should arrange a meeting. He put it to her that she was to pick the time and place. After giving the idea a good deal of thought, she cast aside her inhibitions and agreed to meet him. *What have I got to lose?* she asked herself, with a slight shrug of her shoulders. *If I arrive at the meeting place fifteen minutes late, I can have a good look at him and see if he is how I had envisaged him.*

Deep in thought, she half closed her eyes as she tried to conjure up a picture of him. 'What if he's fat and ugly?' she whispered almost inaudibly. She shook her head from side to side, as she cast the thought out of her mind. 'If I don't like the look of him I can walk away.'

'Now let me see,' she muttered to herself, the pen poised over the writing pad. 'Today is Monday, if I suggest Saturday, that will give me nearly five days to prepare.'

They both agreed to meet in the Embassy in Skegness on the following Saturday at twelve noon. They were to carry a red carnation.

It was Saturday morning, and the sun was shining as she drove out of her driveway, on her way to the rendezvous that had been arranged; her stomach was churning with a mixture of excitement and foreboding, as she prepared for her meeting with Raymond. She had decided to arrive at fifteen minutes past twelve. Driving into the Embassy car park, she climbed out of the car, holding her carnation in her hand as she made her way to the front of the building and mounted the steps outside the Embassy. If she didn't like what she saw, she could quickly hide it. She reached out to push the swing door, when it was opened from the inside. She stood back to let the person out.

To her surprise it was Harold. He looked at the carnation in her hand. There was a questioning look in his eyes.

'Charlene?' he choked a look of incredulity on his face as he pointed his finger at the carnation in her hand.

She stepped back, her eyes wide with shock, holding her hand to her mouth as her heart missed a beat.

"'Raymond?'" she gasped, a look of disbelief on her face.

They stood transfixed for a few seconds, looking at each other. Then in one movement they both stepped forward and embraced, tears of happiness running down Barbara's cheeks as Harold's arms almost crushed her.

End

Troubled Waters

'When are you going to get off your backside and give me a hand?' demanded a harassed Betty angrily. 'You've been stretched out on that settee watching the telly all afternoon, while I've been working my socks off getting ready for tomorrow.'

'All right! All right! Don't get your hair off, I'm coming,' replied her husband Jim, as he sat up and swung his legs off the settee; reaching out, he picked up the control and switched off the telly, then, stretching his arms out wide, he gave a loud yawn and reluctantly got to his feet.

Jim and Betty lived in a small village in Lincolnshire. They were originally from Nottingham, but after a works accident which cost Jim his job, they had decided to up stakes and move to the countryside. After purchasing a plot of land in the village of Wainfleet, near Skegness, they bought a small caravan to stay in whilst they were in the process of building a bungalow. Almost two years later they finally completed the property that was to be their home and which they lived in up to the present time. They were now retired. Jim liked to do a bit of fishing and messing about on the water, so he had decided to buy a second hand two-berth river cruiser that had been advertised for sale in the local *Skegness Standard*. The cruiser was moored in a boat yard that was situated at the side of the river Witham at Dogdyke, near Tattershall.

When he and his wife Betty went to view the cruiser, she told him in no nonsense terms that it was nothing but a 'pile of junk'. Jim agreed that it needed a good bit of work doing on it before it was what you might call 'seaworthy', but it wasn't a lost cause. After spending an hour or so talking Betty round, she reluctantly gave in and they decided to buy it. After he had worked on it throughout the winter and into the summer months, it was now June. He had decided it was finally ready to be taken out on to the river Witham to begin its journey to a boatyard near Nottingham. They named the boat *Carp*.

Jim had always dreamed of travelling the waterways between Nottingham and the South of England. With his hands on his hips and a satisfied expression on his face, he stood on the jetty and looked proudly at his newly painted craft. He turned to his wife who was standing beside him. 'What do you think Betty?' he asked her as he admired his handiwork.

'You'll be lucky to get it out of the marina,' Betty

had told him sarcastically. She wasn't as keen as he was. Nevertheless, much to Betty's consternation, he had decided that they would move it to a Sawley boat yard on the river Trent where it would give them access to the waterways in the south and west. Sawley was situated on the other side of Nottingham, some eighty miles away by road. Travelling on the waterways would make the journey a good bit longer and far more time consuming. Jim had estimated that it would take four days to reach their destination. Today was Saturday. The couple had planned to leave early the following morning.

'I'll put the blankets in the car,' Jim told her, as she prepared a large pack of sandwiches to take with them on the first leg of their long journey.

The next morning they were up at six a.m. as they had planned. After a quick breakfast they were ready to go. The sun was rising above the trees at the back of the bungalow, burning away the heavy morning mist as Jim and Betty got into the car. 'It looks as though we are going to have a nice day for the start of our journey Betty,' he announced. There was a smile of contentment on his face, as he fastened his seatbelt and started the engine, before carefully backing the car out of the driveway and on to the road.

He took a deep breath as he put his foot down on the accelerator and set off on their journey to the boat yard. He was excited at the thought that, at last he was going to take his boat out on to the open river. After a pleasant fifty minute drive through the open countryside they arrived at the marina. Jim checked his watch. It was eight a.m. He and Betty climbed out of the car, then, loaded with the necessary equipment and food for the journey, they made their way to where the boat was moored up. Jim jumped aboard. Betty handed him the basket full of sandwiches then joined him, the boat swaying as she climbed aboard and made her way unsteadily to the prow of the boat in readiness to cast off.

'Ready Betty?' called out Jim after he had checked the fuel gauge to make sure that there was enough to take them as far as, what was to be, their first stop, Lincoln.

Betty, standing precariously on the edge of the boat as it swayed under her weight, barge pole in hand, waved her arm in acknowledgement, calling to him as she did so, 'I'm ready.'

Jim gave a grunt of satisfaction as he told himself, 'Up to now everything seems to be okay.' Reaching out, he pressed the starter, then, with a belch of black smoke from the exhaust at the stern, the old boat spluttered to life, before settling down to a steady 'putt-putt'. They were finally ready to start their long journey.

'Cast off!' he shouted to her, over the sound of the engine.

She leaned over, lifted the rope from its mooring peg before giving a push with the pole to guide the boat out of the mooring. Jim felt a thrill as he carefully steered the old craft out of the marina and on to the river Witham. He looked up at the blue sky. The sun was getting up by now.

'It's going to be a warm day,' he muttered to himself as the boat, cutting through the calm water, sent ripples outwards as they made their way up the river. Betty carefully made her way along the narrow footway that ran along the side of the boat before climbing down into the covered cockpit, making herself comfortable beside him in the passenger seat.

Waves fanned out behind them as they chugged their way towards Tattershall Bridge.

Along the river bank, as far as the eye could see, anglers were busy setting up their tackle. Jim, who was standing up peering through the cockpit window, leaned over, raising his voice over the sound of the engine as he addressed his wife. 'Judging by the number of anglers lined up on the bank Betty, it looks as though there is going to be quite a large fishing match on,' he told her as he steered well clear of the rods that were poking out on to the river. The anglers acknowledged him with a wave of their hands, as the boat chugged past them at a steady five miles an hour. Their first stop was to be the moorings in Brayford Pool in Lincoln, where they had decided to stay overnight.

'I reckon it will take us about seven hours to reach Brayford Pool, Betty,' Jim told her loudly, as the boat chugging away, passed under Tattershall Bridge.

'As long as that?' replied a disappointed Betty, shaking her head from side to side. She had hoped to be in Lincoln by lunchtime, thereby giving her chance to do some shopping before settling down for the night.

'Don't forget that we have to negotiate Bardney Lock,' he told her in a loud voice. 'That will be at least a half an hour job.'

Jim noted that the anglers, who were lining the

river bank, were waiting for the starting whistle as, some twenty minutes later the boat approached Tilney Lane End. Jim steered well clear of the fishing rods. At that moment the engine spluttered to a stop. Jim pressed the starter; nothing happened. Panic gripped him as the boat slowly drifted towards the anglers' rods. Betty, who had been relaxing with a book in her hand, jumped to her feet, frightened. She held her hands to her face as she saw the craft being pushed by the current towards the rods.

'What are we going to do?' she screamed hysterically at him.

'Cast the anchor in!' he shouted back at her.

Betty climbed out of the cockpit as quick as she could, looked round and saw the anchor on the deck. Quickly picking it up, she threw it out into the river. After a few seconds, to Jim's relief, it held. This didn't stop the boat from swinging across the river with the current and clattered into the rods of those anglers who hadn't been quick enough to withdraw them.

'What the hell are tha' playing at?' angrily yelled a voice with a broad Yorkshire accent.

'Get that damned wreck off the river,' was one of the more reasonable comments, with some more choice language being thrown at them by others.

Jim, his face red with embarrassment, ignored the caustic comments as he took the cover off the engine and checked the starter motor. After ten minutes or so investigating, he found what was wrong. There was water in the carburetter. After cleaning it thoroughly he turned to Betty. 'That should do it!' he declared confidently as he wiped his oily hands on a cloth.

He pressed the starter. After a couple of coughs, the engine burst into life. A sarcastic cheer went up from the anglers on the river bank.

'Tha' wants to gerrit in't scrap yard kid,' bawled one of them, as Jim and Betty thankfully upped anchor and continued upstream. The old boat, belching out a cloud of black smoke in defiance, chugged away.

An hour went by and the river had become devoid of anglers and other boats. The only life they came across was the water hens, a few ducks, and the odd heron standing sentry like in the shallow water on the edge of the river.

'It's turned quiet all at once Betty,' said Jim, a confused look on his face as he scratched the back of his head.

'Well it *is* Sunday Jim,' she called out to him over the sound of the engine.

Southery came into view, they could see the jetty and the pub on their right. A number of boats were moored up. A sign had been erected on the jetty. Betty, shielding her eyes from the bright sun, looked across the river towards it. She couldn't quite make it out.

'Did you see that sign Jim?' she asked him.

'No!' exclaimed Jim with a shake of his head. Having to concentrate on the river in front of him, he hadn't noticed it.

On the other side of the river a man was waving his arms frantically. Jim waved back.

'Friendly lot here,' he muttered to Betty.

As they approached the next bend in the river, a

rowing boat with four young men rowing energetically came into view on the same side of the river as they were on. They were heading straight at them.

'What the hell?' Jim snapped as he frantically manoeuvred the craft in an attempt to avoid a collision with them.

'Don't you know the river code?' he shouted at them angrily, as they went past.

'You bloody idiot,' they countered as they raised their oars to avoid smashing them on the larger boat.

A few seconds later they rounded the bend. To their horror, there were rowing boats of all sizes and shapes, coming towards them. There were hundreds of them, stretching into the distance. Jim's face was a picture of concentration as he turned the steering wheel to swing the boat from side to side in an attempt to avoid them. Oars clattered against the side of the cruiser, as it veered crazily among the oncoming boats. The oarsmen raised their oars to a vertical position as their boats drifted towards the much bigger river cruiser, others wandered helplessly into the reeds along the river's edge.

'You damn fool,' called out one of the stricken oarsmen. 'What are you doing on the river?'

Jim, a puzzled expression on his face, as he was assailed from all sides, raised his voice and shouted back at the angry oarsmen, 'What's going on then?'

'Don't you know that the river is closed to all motor boats until sixteen hundred hours?' the oarsman shouted angrily.

Jim, a vacant expression on his face, shook his

head and shrugged his shoulders. The man went on to explain. It seemed that they had ploughed into the annual Lincoln to Boston rowing regatta. Then Jim remembered that sign at Southery and the man waving his arms. His face reddened as he guided the boat over towards the bank side. 'There's only one thing to do now Betty,' he shouted over the sound of the engine. 'We'll have to find somewhere to moor up until all the rowers have gone through.'

A few minutes went by as they searched for a suitable mooring spot. On finding one he drew the boat close to the bank side. Betty was standing on the prow.

'Now don't forget Betty, jump when the boat touches the bank!' he exclaimed. He didn't want her to land in the river.

'Do you think I'm stupid?' she retorted sharply, over her shoulder, as she prepared herself, waiting for the right moment to jump.

A few seconds later the boat touched the bank. At that moment, grasping the mooring rope firmly in her hand, she took a mighty leap into the long, lush grass that was growing along the river bank. She let out a scream as she disappeared from sight. What they hadn't seen was the ditch that ran alongside the river.

All that Jim could see was a pair of legs waving about and Betty's knickers. She scrambled to her feet, grass sticking out from her hair, she was furious. Jim was fighting to hold back a wry smile. He jumped off and secured the boat to a steel rod which he knocked into the bank.

'That should do us until all the rowing boats have

gone by!' he exclaimed to her, as he gave the rod one final wallop with the hammer.

Betty, having got over her mishap, dusted herself down before pouring two mugs of coffee out of a flask. She handed one to Jim, who was sprawled out on a blanket on the ground, looking up at the clear blue sky overhead.

'This is the life,' he muttered as he took a bite out of the cheese sandwich that Betty had given him. He looked out onto the river to where the rowers were sweating it out as they vigorously swept by. He had a smile of satisfaction on his face as he took in the warm sun. Finishing his sandwich, he closed his eyes. All that could be heard was the sound of the water lapping against the river bank and the occasional squawk of the water hens in the reeds along the bank side. Betty sprawled out beside him, a contented expression on her face as she also closed her eyes. For once she was in agreement with Jim as she drifted off into a deep sleep. A couple of hours later she woke up. Jim was snoring, she sat up and shook him. He opened his eyes and looked up sleepily at her; suddenly he was awake. Swiftly pushing himself to a sitting position he looked out over the river; except for one boat, it was clear. He checked his watch. It was twelve o'clock.

'Good grief Betty,' he gasped. 'We've been asleep for two hours.'

He turned to the two oarsmen in the boat, who were rowing energetically, as they went by.

'Are there any more boats to come?' he shouted at the top of his voice.

'No,' one of them replied in a loud voice, adding, 'we are the last ones.'

Jim waved his thanks, before turning to Betty. 'We'd better get on our way,' he told her. She nodded her head in agreement before she carefully folded the blanket that she had been laying on and tossed it into the boat. Betty packed what was left of the food and flask away as Jim started the engine.

'It should be plain sailing now,' he told her confidently, as he turned the steering wheel to pull away from the bank and out on to the river. He had spoken too soon. There was a grinding sound. The boat wouldn't budge. 'What the hell's gone wrong now?' he growled angrily, shaking his head in disbelief, as he stopped the engine and jumped off the boat.

Betty, who had gone into the cabin, came out, a questioning look on her face. What's the matter Jim?' she asked worriedly. She had visions of being stranded miles away from nowhere.

Her husband shrugged his shoulders and scratched the back of his balding head. 'I'm not sure,' he replied, somewhat perplexed. 'It looks as though I'll have to get in the water and see what's stopping the boat from moving.'

With this he pulled off his shoes and socks and then, after a quick look around to make sure nobody was watching, he took off his trousers, leaving him in his underpants. Betty suppressed a smile at the sight of his bony legs, as he jumped into the water (which was about two-foot deep) taking with him, the boat hook. Then, using the boat hook he reached as far as he could under the stern. He discovered that the Z-drive and the propeller were stuck firmly in the mud.

'What's the problem?' asked a concerned Betty.

Jim chewed on his bottom lip for a moment, a look of deep concentration on his face as he studied the situation, before telling her, 'I reckon the boat's stuck on the bottom. I'll have to try and free it with the spade.'

He was deep in thought, shaking his head slowly from side to side, as he tried to work out how it had happened. Then it suddenly dawned on him. He turned to Betty. 'When we moored up we had plenty of depth!' he exclaimed, a look of disbelief on his face. 'The river must have gone down with the tide, during the time we have been waiting for the end of the Boston boat race,' he explained.

'What are you going to do about it?' queried Betty nervously.

She could see them waiting for hours for the tide to turn and the river to rise again.

'The only thing I can do is free it,' replied Jim as he used the spade to dig some of the mud from around the Z-drive, which was well and truly sunk in the mud.

After half an hour of struggling in the, by now muddied water, he straightened up. 'Right,' he declared firmly. 'I'll see if I can move the boat now.'

Using the boat hook as a lever and after a lot of grunting, sweating and swearing, the craft floated free. Heaving a sigh of relief, Jim climbed back on to the river cruiser.

'Look at the state you're in,' gasped Betty, pointing

at his muddied underpants and bony legs. 'I hope you are going to change before we get to Bardney Lock,' she laughed, visualising the reception they might get.

Jim shrugged his shoulders. 'We can't hang about, Bardney Lock is still nearly two hours away,' he countered, a smile on his face at her comment, as he started the engine and guided the craft out on to the river, still in his muddied underpants.

Betty went down into the cabin and came up holding out a pair of clean ones.

'You'd better put these on,' she intoned, telling him, 'I'll pilot the boat while you go inside and get yourself properly dressed.'

Jim nodded his head and stood aside as she took over, instructing her to keep to the middle of the river before he went into the cabin to change. A few minutes later he returned fully dressed. Betty looked him up and down. 'That's better,' she told him approvingly as she stood aside and let him take over the steering, before she made her way carefully to the front of the boat, where she stretched out and took in the quiet beauty of the Lincolnshire countryside, broken only by the putt-putt of the craft's engine and the occasional squawking of the water hens as they called out to each other.

'Probably complaining about the intrusion,' Betty smilingly told herself.

Two hours later they arrived at Bardney. They needn't have worried about onlookers there was no one about. Jim looked around for the lock keeper to no avail; the lock was deserted. He wondered how he was going to work the equipment. He needn't have worried; after a brief explanation of how the controls were manipulated, Betty proved quite adept at opening and closing the lock gates. Twenty minutes later they were once again on their way.

The sun was dropping over the horizon when Lincoln Cathedral came into view, the 'Three Sisters' rising majestically out of the mist.

'I hope we get there before dark Jim,' confided Betty, a little anxiously.

Half an hour later they reached Lincoln. Jim steered the cruiser carefully off the river and through the numerous swans that were gathered on the narrow waterway. Another quarter of an hour went by as onlookers, standing on the narrow bridge, watched their slow progress with interest as they passed under them and entered Brayford Pool. With a sigh of relief Jim switched off the engine as Betty disembarked and tied the boat to the mooring. Jim checked his watch; it was six o'clock. The journey had taken them ten hours. At that moment a man dressed in an orange and blue donkey jacket and wearing a peak cap approached them and told them he was the officer in charge of the moorings. He asked them how long would they be staying.

'One night,' Jim told him.

The man reached into his pocket and took out a note book; after checking the name of the boat, he wrote a few details in it, before handing Jim a slip of paper. 'That'll be ten pounds sir,' he announced in an official tone of voice.

Jim nodded in reply, pulled out his wallet and paid the man, before turning to his wife. 'Betty, I think we'll have a walk into town and have meal,' he told her as he put his wallet away, adding, 'I'm starving.'

'Good idea,' she enthused, putting her arm through his, as they set off walking briskly along the quay side to the nearest café.

An hour later he was rubbing his stomach in satisfaction as he pushed his empty plate away from him. The haddock and chips had gone down well. He turned and looked at Betty. 'I really enjoyed that,' he told her.

Betty nodded her agreement as he ordered two coffees. A few minutes later he paid for the meal and they made their way back to the boat.

The sun had just dipped below the rooftops of the buildings that surrounded Brayford Pool.

It was just beginning to get dark, as they strolled arm in arm along the waterside footpath; all that could be heard was the lapping of the water against the half a dozen boats that were moored up as they approached their boat, *Carp*.

Jim's eyes narrowed as they neared it. The cruiser was swaying from side to side. He suddenly stopped and gripped Betty's arm. She looked up at him, a questioning look in her eyes as she saw the grim expression on his face. 'What is it?' she enquired in a low voice.

He put his finger to his lips, indicating for her to keep quiet. Leaning towards her he whispered in her ear. 'I think there is someone in the boat. You go and get the officer in charge.'

'Will you be all right?' she asked anxiously.

He nodded his head, as she turned and ran as fast as she could to the office that was situated by the side of the pool. Betty banged on the door. There was nobody in. She looked around frantically. In the meantime Jim had stealthily climbed on the boat and picked up the boat hook.

Standing by the open cabin door, brandishing the boat hook, he called out, 'Right, whoever is in there, come out now.'

There was a scuffling sound from inside the cabin. A voice called out. 'Okay, I'm coming out. I wasn't doing any harm. I just wanted somewhere to sleep for the night.'

A few seconds later the head of a scruffy-looking individual poked out of the doorway. He looked to be in his twenties. As the young man emerged, Betty, who had just returned, shouted, 'Look out Jim he's got a knife!'

The young man, who had tried to conceal the knife, suddenly sprang out of the doorway and confronted Jim. 'Get out of my way or I'll slice you,' he growled menacingly.

At that moment the officer arrived on the scene. 'What's going on here?' he snapped.

'We've just caught him breaking into the boat,' explained Betty.

The officer took out his mobile and dialled a number. After a few words to explain the situation he nodded his head at the mobile, then put it in his pocket. 'The police will be here in a few minutes,' he announced.

After hearing this, the young man turned to Jim, a desperate look on his face. He lunged with the knife. Jim swayed to one side to avoid it. Then he brought the thick shaft of the boat hook down on the wrist of his assailant, knocking the knife out of his hand and on to the floor of the boat. The young man reached down and attempted to retrieve it. As he did so Jim brought the shaft down on the back of his head. He slumped unconscious to the floor. With the help of the officer they lifted him off the boat and laid him out on the quayside. At that moment the police arrived. The young man was shaking his head and rubbing the back of his neck as he pushed himself to a sitting position. The two policemen approached the group. One of them, a sergeant, looked to be in his forties, the other was a constable, he looked much younger.

'Now then!' exclaimed the heavier built sergeant. 'What's the problem?'

The rough looking young man was just getting to his feet. 'I've been assaulted by this bloke,' he grumbled as he massaged the back of his neck.

The sergeant looked closely at the unshaven individual. Suddenly his eyes lit up. 'Why!' he exclaimed, as he suddenly recognised the scruffy character in front of him. 'It's light-fingered William. So you've been at it again, have you?'

The would-be robber gave a sullen look at the police officer, who turned to the Brayford Lock official. 'What's he been up to this time?' he enquired, a knowing expression on his face.

Jim butted in before the official could speak. 'I caught him inside the boat cabin,' he paused for a moment before going on. 'He told me he was looking for somewhere to sleep. When he came out of the cabin, he went for me with a knife.'

'Are you okay?' enquired the constable, who had been taking notes.

Jim turned to him and nodded his head.

'What happened after he came at you?' enquired the sergeant.

'Well!' exclaimed Jim hesitantly. 'I, er, jumped to one side to dodge the knife then I clobbered him over the back of the head with the boat hook shaft.'

The sergeant listened carefully to what Jim had to say, then after a few moments contemplation, he nodded approvingly. 'Did he take anything?' he enquired.

Jim plucked at his bottom lip for a few seconds before answering. 'I haven't checked yet,' he told the police officer, with a shake of his head and a slight shrug of his shoulders.

'I left my purse in one of the lockers inside the cabin,' declared Betty, adding agitatedly, 'there was a ten pound note in it.'

'Can you do a quick search of the cabin sir?' requested the sergeant, turning to Jim.

Jumping down into the lower level, Jim went into the cabin. He came out a few minutes later; he had a thoughtful expression on his face. 'The tenner's gone out of the purse and my watch which I placed in a drawer is missing,' he stated meaningfully.

The sergeant a stern expression on his face as he turned his attention to the young man, who up till now had just looked guiltily down at his feet. 'Turn your pockets out,' he told him sharply.

The young man was unwilling to comply with the officer's request, he just shook his shoulders from side to side.

'I said *turn your pockets out.*' There was an ominous tone to the sergeant's voice. Reluctantly the young man reached into his anorak pocket and came up with a ten pound note, some loose change and a man's wrist watch in the palm of his hand.

'Okay you've got me,' he admitted in a low voice, his shoulders slumping as he handed over the stolen items.

The police officer heaved a deep sigh as he ordered the constable to charge the offender. Then he turned to Jim and Betty. 'Leave it with us,' he informed the couple, his ruddy face beaming. 'We'll do what's necessary.'

'Will you need us as witnesses?' asked Betty, as the two officers were about to leave with the charged man.

The constable stopped for a moment and turned to her. 'I doubt it,' he replied with a shake of his head. 'He's as good as confessed already.'

Jim nodded and gave a sigh of relief, as the two policemen walked to their car with the miscreant, taking a deep breath, he turned to Betty.

'We'd better turn in now after all that excitement my love. We'll have to make an early start in the morning,' he told her as they climbed on to the boat and went into the cabin. After a quick wash they got between the sheets. Within minutes they were fast asleep.

'Come on let's have you up,' urged Betty as she shook Jim. Bleary-eyed he sat up and took the mug of tea that she offered him. After drinking it he quickly washed and sat down to a breakfast of bacon, egg and tomatoes that Betty had cooked for them on the small electric cooker. After eating it he patted his stomach in satisfaction. He was ready to set off for their next stop on the journey, which was the locks at Torksey, where the river Witham joined the Trent. It was imperative that they reached their destination by twelve noon. They needed to catch the incoming tide that would carry them up the Trent. Jim checked the engine, which he noticed had been getting a bit hot, then after topping the oil up, he turned on the ignition. After the customary cough and a puff of black smoke from the exhaust, the engine started up. Betty untied the rope from the metal mooring ring, gave the boat a gentle push and scrambled aboard. A few minutes later the *Carp* was chugging its way out of Brayford Lock and back on to the river Witham. Betty sat beside him in the cockpit as he manoeuvred the boat through the narrow channel and out on to the wider river. The sun was just beginning to rise in the clear blue sky; Jim checked his watch, it showed eight-thirty. All being well, he told himself, they should reach Torksey comfortably before twelve o'clock, which was about the time the tide turned.

'We should make it comfortably,' he informed Betty, giving a contented sigh as the boat, hardly making a ripple, cut through the calm water of the wide placid Witham. They had the river to themselves; there wasn't another boat in sight. He turned to Betty. 'Would you like to take over for a while?' he asked her.

Betty's eyes lit up. I'd love to,' she answered, as she swapped places with him.

She pushed her chest out in a feeling of pride as she manoeuvred the *Carp* down the centre of the river. Jim clambered out of the cockpit and made his way along the narrow walkway that ran along the side of the boat, then, climbing on to the flat deck, he stretched out and closed his eyes. He felt calm and at peace with himself as the gentle breeze wafted across his face. All that could be heard was the clacking of water hens and the 'putt-putt' of the engine. They had been travelling smoothly for over an hour when the engine suddenly spluttered to a stop.

What the hell's gone wrong now?' growled Jim, as he jumped to his feet, threw the anchor into the river and joined Betty in the cockpit.

'How should I know?' replied Betty with a shrug of her shoulders. She brushed a tendril of hair from over her eyes as she told him, 'It just stopped.'

'I can't understand it,' protested Jim, throwing his arms out wide. 'Every time I let you take over something happens.'

Betty, still at the wheel, panicked as the pull of the water sent the boat swinging across the river, causing it to crash into the bank. Jim jumped off the boat, hammered the steel peg into the bank and tied up. Getting back on board he checked the carburetter. He shook his head in disbelief. 'We've run out of petrol,' he declared.

'You idiot Jim,' Betty snapped. 'Why didn't you fill up when we were in Lincoln?'

He let the remark go. Getting annoyed wouldn't help.

At that moment he heard the sound of a lorry in the distance. He stood up and looked across the field. It seemed that the river ran parallel with the road at that point. Picking up a large oil drum he set off across the field towards the road which was some two hundred yards away. Luckily there was a petrol station about half a mile along the road.

Half an hour later he returned, the five gallon drum on his shoulders. He was red in the face as he struggled to get the drum on board. 'I've brought five gallon,' he said breathlessly, as he poured the petrol into the tank and started the engine. A few minutes later the old boat was chugging away with Jim at the helm. 'That should get us the rest of the way to Torksey,' he told Betty confidently.

An hour later they drew in at the moorings at Torksey. A petrol tanker was parked up beside the river. Jim approached the driver and ordered ten gallons. Twenty minutes later the boat's tank was topped up in readiness for the rest of the journey. There were about a dozen boats of all sizes moored up in front of them. They were all waiting to go through the locks. Jim approached one of the boat owners, who was relaxing on the grassy bank side, smoking a pipe.

'What's the hold up?' he asked the stocky built man.

'There isn't enough clearance for the boats to get

over the bar,' the man informed him after taking a deep drag on his pipe and blowing out a stream of blue smoke.

At that moment the lock keeper bawled out, 'Only craft with a shallow draught are to be allowed through.'

It was explained to them, that the water level of the river was low and that a metal girder ran across the opening. This was situated some fifty yards from where the Witham led out on to the wider waterway of the river Trent. The girder was situated two feet below the surface and until the tide turned and the river had risen high enough, the larger boats couldn't get through. At the moment there was barely a two-foot clearance. A few minutes later a flat-bottomed narrow boat came in; when told the circumstances he stated that he was willing to take a chance as he thought his boat would just about clear it.

The other boat owners watched with bated breath as the narrow boat attempted a run at it. There was a loud scraping sound as the boat went over the metal girder. Then to a loud cheer from the onlookers, it floated clear; with a toot of defiance from its horn, the narrow boat set off on its journey upstream.

Jim, arms folded, stroked his chin thoughtfully, as he carefully studied the situation. Betty, I reckon *we* could make it,' he asserted in a low voice.

She laid her hand on his arm and looked up into his narrowed brown eyes. 'Are you sure Jim?' she asked nervously.

'Yes, I'm sure,' he told her with a nod of his head. 'If he can get over it, I'm certain we can.' He raised his arm to attract the lock keeper's attention. 'I'll give it a go,' he called out.

The lock keeper nodded his head. 'Okay,' he replied with a shrug of his shoulders. 'If you think you can make it, go ahead.'

'I'm certain we can,' Jim told him confidently.

He followed this up by steering the boat out into the main stream and approaching the gate. Betty closed her eyes, held her breath and silently prayed as the boat approached the girder; there was a grinding, scraping sound as the *Carp* went over the girder, a few seconds later, to the cheers of the other boat men they were cruising smoothly out on to the river Trent.

'There you are,' he declared triumphantly. 'I knew the old girl could do it.'

He patted the steering wheel as if the craft was an animal. Manoeuvring out of the calm of the Lock, they entered the Trent. Half an hour into the journey Jim felt the pull of the incoming tide. He went up a gear and accelerated. A cloud of black smoke erupted from the rear of the boat as she forged upstream, the strong current from the rising tide helping to push her forward. It took all Jim's strength to keep the craft on a straight course, as he carefully guided it through the notorious sandbanks, which were well known hazards.

'I reckon it will take about two and a half hours to reach Cromwell Lock!' he exclaimed, as he guided the boat up the centre of the river. With the existing low tide, he had to be careful they didn't hit any of the sandbanks.

Two hours later, earlier than Jim had anticipated, owing to the strength of the incoming tide. Cromwell

Lock came into view. The lock keeper waved them into the high-sided lock. A shudder went through Betty, as the gates closed behind them. It seemed as if they were trapped in a large metal box.

'Stay clear of the walls,' the keeper's voice echoed as he shouted down to them.

As if in a lift the boat rose slowly with the level of the water. A few minutes later after rising some twelve feet, they were at the same level of the river in front of them.

'You'll find the current strong. We've had a lot of rain,' the lock keeper told them as he opened the gates and signalled for them to go through.

Jim nodded his thanks, accelerating as the boat battled its way up river against the strong flow. He also took note that there was no incoming tide to help them now. He checked his watch as the *Carp* forged through the water as they made their way to the next stop, which was Newark. It was two-thirty p.m. 'We'll go for something to eat when we reach Newark, Betty,' he called to her over sound of the engine.

'Good,' she replied in a loud voice. 'I'm starving.'

An hour and a half later they chugged into Newark. After tying up at one of the moorings, they went to the waterside office and checked the boat in. The official, a big thickset man gave them a ticket, which they placed on the side of the boat before setting off to the nearest café, where they ordered haddock, chips and a mug of tea each. Jim rubbed his hands together in anticipation, as the young blonde waitress placed the heaped plate in front of him. Fifteen minutes later he leaned back in his chair, a satisfied expression on his face as he patted his stomach. 'Betty!' he exclaimed. 'I *really* enjoyed that.'

She smiled at his comments. 'You always say that,' she told him before going on to finish her meal.

'Don't you think time is getting on a bit Jim?' queried Betty, a worried expression on her face, as she placed her knife and fork on the empty plate in front of her.

'What do you mean?' Jim rejoined, his brow furrowed, as he reached into his pocket and handed a fiver to the waitress to pay for the meal, before getting to his feet in readiness to leave.

'Well…' she explained to him, hesitantly as she followed him out of the restaurant. 'It is going to be quite late when we get to Sawley.'

'Stop whittling Betty, we've got plenty of time,' he told her a little sharply, adding with a shrug of his shoulders, 'we should be there by eight o'clock. It will still be daylight.'

Arriving back at the boat, he paid the mooring fee to the official.

'I wouldn't wait about too long if I were you,' the official advised him with a shake of his head. 'You'll find the current will get stronger. We've had a lot of rain in the last few days.'

Thanking him for the advice, Jim explained to him that they wanted to be at Sawley Marina by, at the latest nine o'clock.

'Well!' the big man explained to him. 'As I've already told you, don't hang about too long.'

'We'll get off straight away,' said Jim, with a nod of

his head as he climbed on the boat.

After checking to make sure that they had sufficient fuel in the tank, he turned to Betty who had followed him onto the boat, telling her, 'That should get us to Sawley comfortably luv,' as he pressed the starter and carefully guided the craft out of the placid water of the Newark marina and back on to the strong current of the wide river Trent.

The pull of the downstream current was strong. It seemed at times, as though they were hardly moving. Jim gave the boat engine some extra revs to counter it. An hour or so later he was beginning to get extremely worried.

'We don't seem to be making much progress,' commented a worried Betty, as she noted the craft juddering, as it battled against the strong current.

'No, and the engine is beginning to overheat,' replied Jim, his brow deeply furrowed, as he looked apprehensively at the smoke from the engine that was beginning to fill the cabin.

Betty started coughing as the smoke got thicker. 'I can't breathe,' she gasped as she held a handkerchief to her mouth.

'Climb out of the cabin Betty and sit on the front of the boat,' Jim told her.

Betty clambered out of the cabin, still holding the handkerchief to her mouth as she made her way to the front of the boat, desperately hanging on the rail that ran along the side of the cabin, the boat dipping and swaying as it fought against the strong current of the swollen river.

Jim gave it a few more revs, to no avail. He was getting worried. The craft was still hardly moving and more smoke was pouring out of the engine as they slowly continued on their way.

Suddenly as they rounded a bend in the river, the jetty at Burton Joyce came into view. Jim heaved a sigh of relief. 'We'll have to give the old girl a breather!' Jim shouted over the noise of the smoking engine as he guided the boat towards the Burton Joyce Jetty.

Betty disembarked as the side bumped against the moorings and tied up.

'We'll give it half an hour to cool down,' Jim decided after checking the engine.

'I can't see us reaching Sawley tonight Jim, it'll be dark in a couple of hours,' announced Betty, her eyes looking out over the distant trees to where the sun was beginning to dip below the horizon.

Jim ran his hands over his grimy face. He hadn't anticipated the problems that they had encountered on the journey. He nodded his head in agreement. 'Well never mind luv, we'll stop for the night when we reach Stoke Bardolph,' he told her with a weary air of resignation.

After half an hour or so had gone by Jim checked the engine. He decided that it had cooled down sufficiently for them to continue on their journey. Jim looked up at the heavy clouds that had gathered in the sky above them, as he lowered himself down into the control cabin. It was beginning to rain as he made himself comfortable and turned on the ignition. 'Ready Betty?' he called out to his wife who was waiting to cast off.

'Ready,' she replied. The boat swayed as she cast off, jumped aboard and entered the cabin.

Jim pressed the starter, engaged the gear and they were on their way again. He decided that he would take it easy as they travelled the five miles to Stoke Bardolph. After another two miles of fighting against the strong current, conditions were beginning to get unbearable. The rain was beating down incessantly and the boat was still making little progress, as it battled against the force of the powerful downward flow of the river. Once again the cabin filled with blue smoke. Jim, his face black with the thick fumes, was coughing and spluttering as they laboriously approached the private jetty. It was owned by the Ferry Boat Inn which was situated about one hundred yards back from the river. Betty, her head covered by a plastic hood to protect her from the rain, was perched precariously at the front of the boat as they drew up to the moorings. She jumped off as it bumped into the wooden structure, and tied up.

'I hope they let us stay here,' spluttered Jim, as he thankfully switched off the engine.

He checked to see if he could find out what was causing the smoke. He almost swore when he discovered that the previous owner had replaced a couple of pipes that were fitted to the exhaust with ones that were made of plastic. It seemed that the heat had caused them to melt, resulting in the smoke being released in the boat instead of through the exhaust. He explained it to Betty, bending their heads as they walked through the driving rain to the Inn.

She shook her head. 'Jim, when you bought the boat you knew it was in a bad way,' she snapped angrily. 'You should have checked the engine thoroughly and put it right before taking it out,' she told him.

He shrugged his shoulders sheepishly as they arrived at the entrance to the Ferry Boat Inn. He wasn't going to argue, he knew that she was right.

The landlord of the Inn, a jolly-looking man, his double chin and long handlebar moustache giving the impression of a walrus, was in the act of pulling a pint for a customer. He looked up with some disdain at the somewhat dejected, blackened faces of the rain-soaked pair, as they entered the inn and approached the long bar. A jukebox in the background was playing a jazzy melody as he listened carefully to their problems. He paused for a moment as he slid the pint of draught bitter across the bar to a short fat man, before turning his attention to the unfortunate couple and telling them in a friendly tone of voice, 'You can leave it fastened to the jetty for the night,' adding with a shake of his head, 'but I'm afraid I won't be responsible for its safety.'

Jim nodded in response to the landlord's generosity before thanking him and asking him how much he owed him. The landlord raised his hand. 'Just put a donation in the tin, that'll do,' he advised him, indicating the tin with a slight nod of his balding head.

Jim smiled his thanks and pushed a fiver into the tin that was placed on the end of the bar. It had written on it, 'Cruelty to animals'.

'Can we use your phone?' asked Betty, somewhat

tentatively.

The landlord leaned over the bar and pointed to a phone in a cubicle in the far corner of the spacious room. Betty thanked him and wended her way through the tables to the phone booth.

Closing the door behind her to keep out the hubbub of voices, she picked up the receiver and phoned their daughter Chris, explaining to her what had happened. An hour or so later their son in law Clive and Chris arrived outside the inn to pick them up. A few minutes later, after again thanking the landlord of the pub for his help, they were on their way to a hot bath and a meal.

The following morning, after a hearty breakfast, they set off on the journey to Stoke Bardolph. It was ten a.m. and the sun was shining out of a cloudless sky when they arrived back at the Inn, with the intention of doing some work on the boat so that they could take it the rest of the way up the now calmer river, to Sawley Marina. Clive offered to help them. They weren't prepared for the shocking spectacle that confronted them when they arrived at the pub.

'What the hell's happened here?' gasped Jim, a horror-stricken expression on his face as they climbed out of the car and made their way across the grassed area situated between the pub and the still high river.

The boat, which they had left secured to the mooring at the jetty, was laying, badly damaged, on its side some fifty yards up the bank. They were told by the landlord that the river had risen ten feet overnight due to the heavy rain and it had deposited their boat,

Carp, where it was now.

Jim and Clive checked the boat thoroughly. It was plain to see that there was nothing they could do about the damage that had been done to the hull. Luckily Jim had insured it. He got in touch with Sawley Marina and the insurance company. They agreed to retrieve it.

The next day the damaged boat was taken to the marina where it was repaired and eventually, to Betty's relief, sold.

Four days earlier they had set off on the long journey to Sawley Marina. They never in their wildest dreams imagined it would arrive in such a bizarre way.

End

Catch of the Day

A thick fog hung over Boston as Bill Brassett, his flat cap pulled down over his eyes, and his younger companion David Gorton, stealthily approached the jeweller's shop that was situated in the centre of the Lincolnshire town, thick scarves covering the lower half of their faces. Their car was parked on the other side of the road, some thirty yards away. He checked his watch; it showed twelve midnight. Standing in front of the window with its covering of heavy mesh, he paused for a moment; there was a rasping sound as he scratched his unshaven chin, his eyes two slits as he studied the two strong padlocks that secured it. Suddenly he came to a decision. 'Right Dave!' he exclaimed to his partner in crime, keeping his voice low as he reached out with his right hand. 'Hand me the cutters.'

The young man opened a leather bag and pulled out a pair of strong cutters which he passed to the big man. Brassett stood for a few seconds, flexing his brawny arms before placing the jaws of the cutters around the padlock. Taking a deep breath he pressed the long handles together with all his strength. A couple of seconds later there was a sharp crack as the tool cut through the metal lock. The two robbers looked up and down the road to check if anyone had been alerted. All was quiet. Brassett turned his attention to the second padlock, instructing his accomplice, 'Hold the mesh Dave while I cut through the other one.'

The younger man braced himself as he took a firm hold on the mesh. 'Okay Bill I've got it,' he replied, his voice muffled by his scarf, as he prepared to take the weight of the mesh. Brassett gave a grunt as he put pressure on the long handles of the cutter; there was another sharp crack as he cut through the remaining padlock. The heavy mesh suddenly fell away from the window.

'I can't hold it up,' gasped Gorton as the weight of it pressed down on him.

The big man dropped the cutters and went to his aid, grabbing the mesh as it bore his partner to the ground. Manhandling it off him, he carefully placed it to one side. Taking out a sledgehammer from the bag, he flexed his muscles before swinging it at the window and smashing it into small splinters of glass. Reaching inside, the two robbers grabbed all the expensive watches and jewellery that was on display and dropped them into the leather bag with the tools. Suddenly lights started flashing and a loud bleeping sound broke the silence of the night as the burglar alarm was set off.

Brassett and Gorton looked at each other, alarm showing on their faces. Grabbing the large bag the two men dashed across the road to the car. Gorton climbed into the driving seat, quickly turned on the ignition, engaged the gear, and swiftly sped away. A police siren could be heard in the distance as they made their way out of Boston. Gorton gave a quick glance through the rear view mirror. He could just make out the police car about five hundred yards behind them, lights flashing.

'They're on to us Bill!' he exclaimed, a note of panic in his voice as he put his foot down on the accelerator.

Horace Grey got up reluctantly from the comfortable settee that he had been sat on. After stretching his arms out wide and giving a loud yawn he walked across the small lounge and switched off the television. His wife Millie, as usual, had gone to bed much earlier. Horace preferred to stay up longer (to give her time to warm the bed). He checked the time by the old clock on the wooden mantelpiece. It was almost midnight. Massaging the few hairs on the top of his balding head, he switched off the light and tiredly shuffled along the passageway to the bathroom of the flat that was situated over a small shop in the centre of Boston. After a quick wash he undressed and put on his pyjamas, before climbing into bed and snuggling up to his comfortably rounded wife, placing his bony knees into the back of her legs. He was just going off to sleep when there was a loud bang followed by a bleeping noise from outside.

Millie sat up, a scared expression on her face. 'What's that noise Horace?' she gasped, prodding him in the ribs with her elbow.

'How do I know?' he snapped irritably, rolling over and ignoring her.

Again she prodded him.

Shaking his head in annoyance at having to relinquish his comfortable position, he reluctantly climbed out of bed, adjusted his crotch and shuffled across the bedroom to the window. Pushing aside the heavy curtains, he peered, bleary eyed, out into the night. What he saw made his hair stand up. Lights were flashing and a burglar alarm was bleeping incessantly, as two men were filling a leather hold all with items from the jewellery shop across the road. Two or three minutes later he watched them make their way to a car across the road from the shop carrying the large leather bag.

'Two men have broken into a shop across the road,' Horace called out to his wife as he dashed out of the bedroom and picked up the phone that was on a small table in the passageway. Dialling 999 he waited impatiently for an answer.

After a few seconds had gone by a female voice said, 'Can I help you?'

'Th-there's been a robbery,' Horace said hesitantly.

'Now take your time sir,' the voice told him calmly. 'You say there has been a robbery. Can you tell me exactly where this has occurred?'

'It's at the jeweller's, in the centre of Boston. Two

men have stolen all the items that were exhibited in the window,' he told her excitedly. 'The last thing I saw was them getting into a blue Maestro and driving off in the direction of Tattershall.'

'Did you manage to see their faces?' she enquired.

'No, I'm afraid they were too far away and it was too foggy,' replied Horace, shaking his head at the phone.

The woman thanked him before contacting police headquarters and informing them of the robbery. They in turn contacted a police car that was patrolling the area.

Police Constable Rumbleton took the message before addressing the driver, 'Right John, two men driving a blue Maestro, they've taken the Tattershall road.'

Police constable John Belling nodded his head, swung the car round in a U-turn and set off in the direction that the two robbers had taken.

Brassett looked nervously over his shoulder and glanced through the rear window as they left the outskirts of Boston. He could just make out the flashing blue lights of a police car in the distance. 'Put your foot down Dave, they're catching us,' he snapped, as they neared Chapel Hill, a small village about five miles from Tattershall. Ten minutes or so later they approached the main Grantham road. The police car was beginning to close in on them. As it drew nearer Brassett was breaking out in a cold sweat; he turned to his partner, telling him, 'Dave, if we get caught with the stolen goods we've had it.' Being an old lag he had visions of going down for a very long time.

'What are we going to do?' replied the younger man, a perplexed expression on his face.

'Let me think,' rejoined Brassett, pushing his cap forward over his eyes and scratching his balding head. Suddenly he straightened up. 'I've got it!' he snapped, punching the palm of his hand with his fist as he instructed his partner. 'Stop the car when we get to Tattershall Bridge.'

Dave's brow furrowed as he turned to Bill. 'What have you got in mind?'

'Just do as I say and stop the car when we get there.'

A few minutes later they reached the bridge. A thick fog hung over the river Witham, as Bill jumped out of the car, lifted the leather bag from out of the rear seat and carried it to the railings that ran along the length of the bridge. Then, grunting with exertion he heaved the half-open heavy bag over the railings and tossed it out into the deep river, where it quickly sank. Climbing swiftly back in the car, he turned to Dave, a half smile on his face. 'Now get going.'

Dave glanced at him out of the corner of his eye; there was a look of disbelief on his face as he put his foot down on the accelerator. 'Why did you do that?' he enquired.

'They won't have anything on us now,' replied Bill, as the police car closed in, its siren getting louder.

'You idiot, my name and address were on the bag,' declared Dave, a note of exasperation in his voice.

'Don't worry about it Dave; the bag will be at the

bottom of the river by now.'

'That means we've risked all that for nothing!' exclaimed the young man, shaking his head from side to side, frustration showing on his face.

Bill shrugged his shoulders, telling him philosophically,

'You win some Dave and sometimes you have to be prepared to lose some.'

They had just gone through the village of Tattershall, when the police car drew alongside them, one of the officers sticking his arm out of the car window and waving them down, before stopping in front of them.

'What's the problem officer?' enquired an innocent-looking Brassett as the two policemen approached their car.

'Would you please step out of the car?' the well-built Rumbleton requested brusquely, sensing that he was dealing with couple of villains.

The two men climbed out of the car, before the police officers commenced searching the inside of the car thoroughly.

'What are you looking for?' enquired Brassett, a humorous expression on his face, as the policeman walked round to the rear of the car.

'Can you open the boot?' requested a rather annoyed Rumbleton, ignoring his question.

Brassett handed him the keys, telling him cockily, 'You open it.'

Rumbleton, who was obviously the senior of the

two officers, passed the keys to Belling, who in turn, unlocked the car boot and swung it open. After again giving it a thorough search he turned to his colleague. 'Nothing in here,' he told him with a shake of his head as he pushed the boot lid down and handed the keys back to Brassett.

After studying the situation for a few seconds, Rumbleton turned to the rough looking pair.

'What are you doing out at this time of night?' he enquired.

Brassett shrugged his shoulders, 'We've been partying and we are just on our way home,' he lied.

Rumbleton stroked his chin as he weighed up the situation, before turning to Belling, 'Take their names and addresses.'

He stood waiting as the constable took down the two men's details.

'Okay you can go now,' he told them. As they were climbing into the car he added, 'We may want to interview you later.'

Alan Delman reluctantly climbed out of the warm comfortable bed, he checked the alarm clock on the shelf at the head of the bed – it showed six a.m. He stretched his arms out wide and yawned loudly, as he contemplated the day in front of him. He had booked a ticket for one of the local fishing matches. It was to be held on a stretch of the river Witham between Kirkstead Bridge and Tattershall Bridge. He had to get an early start, as the journey from Rawmarsh in Yorkshire to where the match was being held, would take about an hour and a half, he told himself as he ran his fingers through his thinning iron grey hair, before making his way sleepily to the bathroom. Fifteen minutes later he was back in the bedroom getting dressed. His wife Rose sat up in bed, bleary-eyed as he sat on the edge of the bed and pulled on his pants.

'I suppose I'll have to get up and do you some breakfast,' she mumbled, the curlers in her mop of greying hair dangling over her face, as she dragged herself out of bed. She could never understand her husband's obsession for fishing. 'You must be barmy. You go out in all weathers rain, snow or shine and for what?' she had often told him, adding a little sarcastically, 'You never win anything.'

She shook her head from side to side, giving a weary sigh of resignation as she trudged downstairs to the kitchen of the old semi-detached house that was their home.

Alan finished fastening his scuffed shoes, a feeling of excitement going through him at the thought of the day ahead, as he followed his wife down the stairs. Rose opened the curtains and looked through the window. It was just coming light as she observed the heavy clouds and the rain that was beginning to come down heavily.

'Alan, you will catch your death of cold, going out in this weather,' she told him.

'Rose, I've booked a place in the Boston Open. There will be over three hundred anglers besides me there and the weather won't stop them,' he told her, a little irritation in his voice. As he went out of the back door to collect his fishing tackle, he added, 'Anyway you know that I'm not one of these fine weather fishermen.'

Can't argue with that, she told herself, as the smell of bacon frying drifted round the kitchen while she prepared a breakfast of eggs and bacon for him. Alan rubbed his hands together in anticipation as she placed the appetising meal in front of him.

'Just what I want,' he enthused as he picked up his knife and fork before tucking in.

Half an hour later a well-fed Alan picked up his basket and fishing tackle, then, after giving Rose a kiss on her cheek, he went out into the dreary morning, placed his fishing tackle in his old Anglia and climbed in. After a couple of coughs the engine burst into life. With a farewell wave to his wife, he set off on the journey to Kirkstead, where the draw would be made for the match. He shook his head, as his mind went back to when he fished for Boston in the Winter League. He smiled to himself as he recalled having to trudge to his peg through six inches of snow and another occasion when he had to break the ice on the Sibsey Trader. Reaching out, he switched on the air to clear the steamed up windscreen as he continued on the long drive to the match venue, the wipers swishing from side to side as they fought to clear the heavy rain that was lashing down,

'It doesn't bode well for the match conditions,' he muttered out loud as he neared his destination. On arrival at the large communal hut, where the draw was to take place, he parked up and joined the group of diehards (some would say idiots) that were gathered, to find out what peg they would draw. A notice on the wall informed them that there were three hundred entrants.

Suddenly the stentorian voice of one the match organisers who was standing behind a battered old table with a large plastic box on it, called out over the hubbub of the chattering anglers. 'Right lads line up to draw your pegs.'

Alan dutifully joined the queue of hopefuls. A few minutes later he reached into the box drew out a folded slip of paper. Taking a deep breath he unfolded it. His eyes lit up when he saw the peg he had drawn. On the paper was written the number 300. He called out his name and peg number to a man who was holding a book.

'You jammy bugger!' exclaimed a broad Yorkshire voice from behind him, as the official wrote it down.

Alan shrugged his shoulders as he turned to go to his car, telling him, with a half smile on his face, 'It's the luck of the draw mate.'

There was a contented expression on Alan's face as he climbed into his car and drove off, it wasn't often he drew one of the coveted end pegs. The rain was still bucketing down as he approached the spot where he could park his car as near to his peg as possible. It was situated just downstream of Tattershall Bridge. Going over the bridge he pulled off the road and parked his car. Climbing out, he looked up at the grey clouds, the heavy rain hitting his face before donning his water proofs. Gathering up his rods and basket, he made his way, with some difficulty, along the muddy bank to his peg. The first thing he needed to do, was to erect and secure his umbrella; after accomplishing this, he placed his basket under it and sat for a few minutes surveying the fast flowing river Witham, as he contemplated what tactics he would use.

Fishing it the normal way, which was to use the float, to his mind, was definitely out in the fast flowing water, he contemplated as he set up his fishing rod. Finally he came to a decision. The best thing he could do was to use a quiver tip and get on the bottom with a leger. He checked his watch, it was ten fifty, another ten minutes and the whistle would go to start the four-hour match. Reaching out he poured himself a hot cup of coffee from his flask, before gazing out from under his six-foot wide umbrella and grimacing at the heavy rain that hammered down on the river in front of him as he and all the other anglers that lined the river bank waited for the starting signal.

He had just placed his empty cup on the grass beside him when the whistle went. Reaching into a bait tin, he took out a couple of maggots and placed them on the number eighteen hook; getting to his feet he cast out into the strong current, then placing his rod on the rest, he sat back on his basket and waited and waited, his eyes never leaving the quiver tip which was bending to the pull of the strong current. After over a couple of hours had gone by he was beginning to get irritated, he hadn't had as much as a touch. Reeling in, he checked the maggots on the hook, they were still squirming, untouched. Shaking his head in frustration, he took them off; it was obvious, he told himself, maggots were not the flavour of the day. After a few seconds of deliberation he decided to put on a bigger size hook, a size twelve. After the change of hooks, he took out another tin from his basket; plucking out a big fat blood worm, he placed it on the hook. He gave a grunt of satisfaction as he held the wriggling bait out in front of him.

'If they don't take that, then they are not going to take anything,' he muttered to himself as he got to his feet, swung the rod and cast out into the fast flowing river. Placing the rod back on the rest, he watched as the strong current swung the line until it pulled the tip round. Another hour went by of watching carefully the sensitive tip; nothing was happening and Alan was beginning to think that once again he was going to be 'water-licked'. Suddenly the tip slowly pulled round. He coolly lifted the rod and struck; feeling the resistance, he carefully played it as it swung out into the middle of the river. It felt as though he had hit a big eel, he told himself as he gave it more line. A crowd of anglers had gathered on the bank at the back of him, shouting advice as he fought the current.

'Don't give it too much slack kid,' a voice with a Yorkshire accent called out.

Another told him to play it carefully. This went on for over half an hour and he was beginning to tire as he slowly reeled in.

'This is the match winner!' exclaimed one seemingly knowledgeable voice.

Alan reached out for his landing net and placed it in the water under his 'catch' which still hadn't surfaced. Carefully guiding it over the net, he lifted the landing net up and hoisted it out of the water.

There was loud gasp from the onlookers as Alan, a

look of disgust on his face, lifted what looked like an old leather bag covered in weed.

'I thought it wasn't a fish,' declared one 'know-all'.

'I reckon that's the catch of the day,' was another caustic remark.

One or two of them cruelly burst out laughing at Alan's embarrassment, as they went back to their pegs. A couple of minutes later the whistle went, signalling the end of the match. Shaking his head in disbelief, he sat for couple of minutes eyeing the old worn leather bag that was still in the landing net, on the grass, where he had left it. Reaching out he picked it up; there was a rattling of metal as, with some effort, he deposited the heavy bag on the ground in front of him; there was zip that ran along the top of the bag, it was half open. His brow was furrowed as, with an inquiring expression on his face, he drew back the zip and had a quick glance inside it. All he could make out was a short-handled sledgehammer and two pairs of heavy cutters almost buried in mud and weeds.

'Never mind,' he muttered to himself as he zipped the bag up again. 'The tools will probably come in handy.'

Swiftly dismantling his fishing tackle and folding his umbrella, he picked up the bag, then loaded with his basket and tackle on his shoulder and the bag in his hand, he set off, with some difficulty, to go to his vehicle. A few minutes later he arrived at his car, opened the boot and swung the bag and his basket into it. After placing his rods in the back seat, he climbed in the car, started the engine and drove off. The journey home wasn't too bad. The rain had stopped and the afternoon sun was trying its utmost to peep round the heavy clouds as he approached Rotherham on his way to Rawmarsh. He gave a wry smile as he thought of the welcome he was about to receive from Rose as he neared home.

Pulling into the driveway, he wearily clambered out of the car and went into the house, Rose was just putting the kettle on as he walked into the kitchen.

'Another bad day,' she commented, as she observed the miserable expression on her husband's face.

'All right!' he exclaimed. 'Don't rub it in.'

'Well, you never learn,' she countered, with a shake of her head.

'I know I know,' he replied, a note of agreement in his voice as he reached out and picked up the mug of tea that she had placed on the table and took a long drink.

'Didn't you catch anything then?' she asked him.

'No not really!' he exclaimed. He took another drink of his tea before going on to tell her that he hadn't had a bite.

'What do you mean by not really?' she enquired, her brow furrowed.

'Well I did catch something.' There was a humorous smile on his ruddy, unshaven face as he went on to tell her of the leather bag containing the tools that he had hooked.

'What did you do with it?' she enquired her arms folded as if to hold up her ample bosom.

'It's in the boot of the car,' he told her. 'I'll go and fetch it in.'

Finishing off his tea he got to his feet and went out to the car. A few minutes later he came back into the kitchen carrying the bag. 'I'd better put it in the sink,' he told her, explaining that it was half full of mud and weeds.

Rose looked on, a distasteful expression on her face as he hoisted it up and plonked it in her white sink. 'Fancy bringing a filthy thing like that home Alan!' she exclaimed angrily, as the stagnant smell of the bag hit her. 'You should have thrown it back in the river.'

Her husband shook his head as he pulled back the rusty zip. 'I couldn't. It would mean me breaking the law,' he explained, as he opened the bag and looked inside it; he pulled his face as the stagnant smell hit him. Rose, who was standing beside him as he opened it, handed him a pair of her plastic gloves, telling him, 'Here, you'd better use these.'

Nodding his thanks he slipped them on before reaching into the bag. The first thing he pulled out was a weed-covered, short-handled sledgehammer. This was followed by two pairs of heavy cutters, which were covered in thick mud.

'Alan, I think it would be good idea to take the bag outside and empty what's left in it on the garden,' suggested Rose, pulling her face.

He nodded his head in agreement as he picked the bag up again and carried it out of the house and placed it on the small bit of garden. He looked into the bag for a few seconds before bending down, gripping the bottom of it and tipping it up. Rose, who had followed him out, looked down at what looked like a pile of excretia as it splashed on the garden.

'What's that?' she enquired, pointing her finger at something poking out of the mud; Alan reached out and picked the mud covered object up.

'It's a watch,' he muttered, looking at it closely before turning his attention back to the rest of the pile of mud, his curiosity aroused.

He turned to Rose and asked her to get a bucket of water as he cleaned the watch with an old dish cloth before examining it. 'This looks like an expensive watch,' he told her when she arrived with a bucket of water. Taking the bucket from her, he carefully poured it over the muddied heap. His eyes widened in amazement at what was revealed as the water washed the mud away. In front of him was a collection of assorted gold rings, necklaces and half a dozen, what looked like, expensive watches.

'Wow!' he exclaimed excitedly. 'There is a few quid's worth here.'

'What are you going to do with them?' enquired Rose, worriedly.

Alan scratched the back of his head as he mulled over the situation for a few seconds before coming to a decision.

'I'll have to hand them in to the police, luv,' he muttered, saying by way of an explanation, 'It looks to me as if they might have been stolen and deliberately thrown into the river.'

'You'll have to take them to the police station in

the morning Alan,' she rejoined as she gathered up the collection of valuable objects and placed them in a plastic bag.

Her husband nodded his head in agreement as he followed her into the house.

He was up bright and early the next morning; after having his breakfast he picked up the bag of expensive 'baubles' together with the leather bag and tools before setting off for the local police station. On arrival, he approached the rather over weight Police Sergeant Moran, who was seated behind a desk.

'Good morning sir,' said the sergeant, a friendly smile on his fat face. 'How can I help you?'

Alan returned the smile as he placed the carrier bag containing the valuable goods on the desk in front of the officer, before going on to tell him the almost unbelievable tale of how he came by them. Moran listened intently to Alan as he looked inside the bag. 'Leave them with me sir, we'll look into it.'

Alan nodded his head at the sergeant before turning to leave. He had almost reached the door when Moran called after him. 'Can you leave your name and address? We may need to contact you at a later date.'

He turned round and gave the officer his name and address, which he wrote down.

'Thank you, Mr, er, Delman,' he said a little hesitantly, as he glanced momentarily at the name on the paper.

Alan gave a smile and thanked the officer again before leaving the station.

Two weeks had gone by when the phone rang. Rose called out to her husband. 'Answer it, I'm busy.'

Alan who had been stretched out on the settee reading the morning paper, got to his feet and shuffled reluctantly into the hallway; picking up the phone he said a little sharply, 'Hello!'

A voice at the other end enquired, 'Is that Mr Delman?'

'It is,' replied Alan.

'This is Sergeant Moran at the Rotherham police station.'

There was a pause for a few seconds; Alan could hear the rustle of papers being shuffled about, before the sergeant carried on. 'Would it be possible for you to come to the station today?'

Alan's brow furrowed as he thought over the request. 'Yes, I think I can manage that. Would this afternoon be okay?'

'That would be fine. Shall we say two o'clock?'

Alan nodded his head at the phone. 'I'll be there,' he grunted into the mouthpiece.

'Who was it?' asked Rose as she carefully folded one of her husband's shirts that she had just ironed.

'It was the police station,' Alan replied thoughtfully, as he put the receiver back on its cradle and joined her in the kitchen.

'What did they want?' she enquired, a questioning expression on her face as she placed the shirt on a pile of other garments that she had ironed.

He shrugged his shoulders. 'They want me to go to

the police station in Rotherham this afternoon at two o'clock.'

There was a look of alarm on her face as she stopped ironing and looked up at him. 'You're not in trouble are you?'

He shook his head, a look of irritation on his face. 'Of course I'm not in trouble,' he snapped, a little sharply.

'All right!' she exclaimed frostily, 'I was just worried about you that's all.'

He went over to her, put his arm around her shoulders and gave her an affectionate kiss on her cheek before whispering in her ear, 'I know you mean well luv.'

She looked over her shoulder at him, a smile on her face (she liked a little fuss now and then), telling him, with a gentle pat on his bum as he turned away, 'Go on you old softie. Now do something useful. Make a cup of tea.'

He smiled back at her as he went over to the sink and filled the kettle. A few minutes later they were sat in the conservatory enjoying a cup of tea. Alan leaned back in one of the two wicker chairs, his brow furrowed. Rose was sitting in the other one. 'I wonder what they want me for?' he muttered between sips of tea. 'You haven't done any speeding have you?' Rose put to him, knowing what he was like when he was driving on his own. When she was with him, she was always telling him to watch his speed, often to Alan's annoyance.

He shook his head slowly from side to side. 'No,' he rejoined, pausing for a moment to finish off his tea. 'It's nothing like that,' he assured her as he got to his feet and took his empty cup into the kitchen. 'Anyway I'll find out this afternoon.'

The old clock on the stone fireplace gonged; it was one-thirty. Alan had just finished his lunch. Getting to his feet, he stretched his arms out wide. 'I'd better be on my way to Rotherham now luv.'

A few minutes later he was backing his car out of the driveway and on to the road before heading for the police station. It was almost two o'clock when he walked into the station.

He was directed by the sergeant to go in the main office where Chief Inspector Callman was waiting for him. 'Ah Mr Delman,' he gushed, coming from behind his desk, his hand held out.

Alan grasped the proffered hand, a half smile on his face as he nodded his head, acknowledging the greeting. The chief reached into his desk and drew out an envelope, telling him as he did so, 'I've got some good news for you.'

Alan's forehead creased questioningly, as the chief went on, 'It seems that the jewellery that you brought in has been traced back to a jeweller's in Boston.'

He paused for a moment to clear his throat before continuing. 'They have informed us that the value of the items that were stolen was in the region of twelve thousand pounds. The jeweller's insurers informed us that they have a policy of rewarding anyone returning lost or stolen goods with five per cent of the total value.' He coughed into his hand, before handing the envelope to Alan.

'This is for you Mr Denman, with thanks from the

jewellers in question.'

Alan, his eyes wide open in amazement, was almost speechless; thanking the chief of police a little stumblingly as he reached out and took the envelope from him. He was just about to leave when Callman stopped him in his tracks. 'I also wish to inform you that the thieves who threw the bag into the river to escape detection have been apprehended,' he declared. His face broke out in a smile before going on, 'It seems that the bag had the name of its owner on the inside, this led us to the two men involved in the robbery.'

He held out his hand again telling the somewhat flabbergasted man in front of him, 'Well done sir.'

Alan was in a daze as he walked out of the police station and went to his car. Climbing behind the steering wheel he sat back for a few seconds as he gathered himself, the envelope in his hand. He looked down at it momentarily then decided that he would wait until he got home before opening it. Starting the car he drove out of the police car park and made his way back home. He had a serious expression on his face as he walked into the house.

'What was it all about luv?' enquired Rose, seeing the perplexed expression on her husband's face as he placed the envelope on the table, before going on to explain to her what had happened.

He pointed to the envelope. 'You open it,' he told her, not having his glasses handy.

Rose reached out, picked up the envelope and carefully opened it; taking out the letter, she started to read it, her eyes getting wider and wider as she carefully went through it.

'What does it say?' asked a curious Alan.

She just shook her head from side to side in disbelief as she unclipped what looked like a cheque from the one page letter and held it out to him.

Alan went to a drawer in the sideboard and took out his glasses before sitting down again and taking the letter and cheque from her. The letter thanked him for returning the stolen property. It went on to say that they were pleased to present to him with a cheque for six hundred pounds as a reward and commended him for his honesty.

Alan held the cheque out in front of him, a broad smile on his face as he turned to Rose. 'As the man who was on the river bank said, it really was the catch of the day.'

End

A Collection of Poems

By

Ernest Barrett

The Lincolnshire Wolds

I've roamed the lakes and dales,
Seen mountains that reach the skies.
But never has a more beauteous sight,
Been set before my eyes.
Rolling hills and sweeping valleys,
Carpeted with golden corn.
Drifting clouds casting shadows,
On gentle winds are borne.
As I look around, it's a pleasure to behold
The peaceful serenity,
That is the Lincolnshire Wolds.

Gazing upon this tranquil scene,
My heart fills with joy.
The winding brook that drove the mill
When I was but a boy,
Smoothly gliding round gentle bends,
As it wends its way to the placid fens.

Now as the shadows lengthen
And the evening sun turns gold.
I breathe a heartfelt sigh,

At this view of the Lincolnshire Wolds.

The Lincolnshire Fens

I've seen the magic of the Wolds
With its valleys and rolling hills.
Now I meet the fenlands
With its waterways and ancient mills.
Endless fields of corn
Swaying in the breeze from the nearby coast.
What more could I wish for
Than the fenlands as my host.

Now as the sun sinks low in the western sky
A misty shroud falls o'er the fens.
A barn owl glides along the dyke, stops and swiftly descends,
Swooping for its kill.
The heron, unflinching stands,
Sentry like and still.
Bats dart and swerve in the suffused light,
As the fens give way,
To the creatures of the night.

Silver Bird

A single cloud
Opaque and light.
Traversing the blue
That meets the sea,
Choppy, and frothy white.
A sun-kissed silver bird,
A glistening star,
Wends its way to lands afar.

A misty trail hangs,
Long after the bird has flown.
A milky-way that fades and dies,
Leaving the cloud alone.
As I lie, eyes veiled against the sun.
Would that I could sail the heavens,
With the silver bird,
As one.

Now as the golden sun descends,
Taking on its mantle of red.
Ominous rumblings invade my mind,
Clouds gather overhead.
Freshening wind, swelling sea.

Advancing tide reaching out for me.
Reluctantly I turn away,
My fanciful thoughts are done.
Yet I will not rest,
Until my flight with the silver bird
Is won.

Living

Life is what you make it
That's what we're often told.
The problem is,
You don't find out
Until you're very old.

When we're young
We waste our lives,
And care not, for what lies ahead.
We follow a path of life
That adults view with dread.

They can't accept the fact
That we are young and fancy free.
They should remember
They once were,
Just like you and me.

That's Life

When daily chores seem such a burden
And the kids change to rowdy young yobs.
You can't take a rest from it all
Because you're snowed under with jobs.
When your partners unload all their troubles
And you listen to their troubles and strife.
Things can only get better.
Just tell yourself,
That's life.

When you've got to get up in the morning
To earn the proverbial crust.
You've got sleep in your eyes
And you're still yawning.
Turning out in the cold is a must.
When the going gets rough underfoot
And the wind cuts through your clothes like a knife
Take it all in your stride
And tell yourself,
That's life.

Lost Words

Blinding inspiraton
As I lay in my bed.
Poetic words and lines
Are swirling through my head.

I reach out for pen and paper,
Oh no! It isn't there.
The feeling of frustration
Is really hard to bear.

Now I'll need to concentrate,
To impress those words upon my brain.
So that when I wake in the morning
I'll remember them again.

The sun is streaming through the window
My eyes are open wide.
I can't recall those thoughts I had
No matter how I've tried.

Now what were those lines
That last night seemed so clear?
It's futile trying to remember them

They're lost for good I fear.

The Pledge

Marriage is a pledge between lovers
Made on their wedding day.
A vow to help each other
Along life's rocky way.

When things go wrong,
Learn to forgive and forget.
Losing the one you cherish,
Can mean a lifetime of regret.

Don't risk those years of love
On a sudden surge of lust.
Resist that flight of fancy.
Don't break your bond of trust.

On the other side the grass
Always seems a better shade of green.
In truth, the grass is greener
Where you've already been.

Holidays

Dad starts the car, we're on our way,
A journey to the sea.
Seven days on holiday,
We should be there for tea.
Four of us squashed in the rear seat,
Like ferrets in a sack.
Mum's losing her patience:
'Stop fighting in the back!'

'Peace and quiet at last,'
Mum says with a smile.
'Are we nearly there Dad?' asks Steve.
'Don't be silly,
We've only gone ten mile.'
The fields go flashing by.
There's lots and lots to see.
Suddenly young Debbie cries,
'Mum I want to wee!'

'Strewth!' says Dad. 'Whatever next?'
As we pile out of the car,
And make a rush
To the nearest bush.

Which wasn't very far.
'I hope you're settled down now,'
Dad says, as we continue on our way.
'We haven't all that far to go,
I'd like to get us there today.'

At last we saw the Skegness signs,
You could almost smell the sea.
'We'll have to stop again,' said Mum,
'Steve doesn't look well to me.'
Dad groaned, 'I can't stop now.'
'Ooh Mum I'm feeling sick!'
'Use a plastic bag,' says Dad.
'That should do the trick.'
At last we reached our destination.
It was a pleasure to be there.
Dad got out of the car and stretched,
And breathed the refreshing Skeggy air.

Enough

Some ask for the moon and the stars
Whenever the going gets tough.
Others crave boundless riches
When all they need is
Enough.

When loved ones enquire
How deep is your love?
Don't give them a swift rebuff.
Just take them gently in your arms,
And tell them,
Enough.

For that's all we need,
Though life can sometimes get rough.
We ask ourselves,
How much are our needs?
The answer…
Enough is enough.

Help Africa

Every year millions are starving,
They are Africa's living dead.
With their sunken faces and empty eyes,
All they ask for is to be fed.
The affluent look on them with pity,
But that won't ease their pain.
What they need is action,
So that they can lead decent lives again.

The rest of the world should take heed,
And dig deep to help these poor souls.
Easing their unbearable burden,
Should be one of each nation's goals.
Only then will they be self-sufficient,
Giving them the chance to turn the tide,
From poverty to prosperity,
And face the future with pride.

Mum's Mince Pies

At last it's Christmas Eve
My stocking's at the foot of the bed.
I must go to sleep,
So my dad has said.

Santa won't come
If I don't close my eyes.
But I know he'll be here,
He likes my mum's mince pies.

Santa's supposed to come down the chimney.
I can't see him doing that.
From what I've seen,
He's far too big, and fat.

I think he'll climb the stairs,
And come through my bedroom door.
I'll be able to hear him,
When he treads on our creaky floor.

I've met Santa at our local shop,
And told him what I'd like.
But I just want to catch him,

To make sure he's brought my bike.

I think I'll close my eyes,
He won't be here just yet.
I can go to sleep,
After me and Santa's met.

Suddenly I'm being shaken,
'Come on my lad,
We can't have you lying in.'
I ask my dad, 'Where's Santa?'

He points at my bike with a grin.
'He came when you closed your eyes.'
And I know for a fact that's true,
'Cos he's eaten my mum's mince pies.

A Snowman

I stand as the cold winds blow.
A lonely forlorn sight.
Made by laughing children,
From the snow so crisp and white.

My eyes are two buttons;
One is blue, the other red.
They gave me a carrot for a nose,
And placed an old hat upon my head.

They've made me look so jolly,
I must say I don't mind that!
But why did they have to make me,
So big, and round, and fat?

I can see the children through the window.
Sitting round a Christmas tree.
They're opening all their presents;
There's lots and lots to see.

The warming sun is rising
As the children come out to play.
I reckon they've forgotten me

So I'll just melt away.

Departure

Return me to the land
From whence I came,
I wish no sadness when I'm gone.
Smile when you recall my name,
Remember the happy times
When we were one.

Look for me in the morning sun,
Lightening the darkened sky.
Look for me in the dewdrop,
Glistening on a gentle flower.
And as I take my leave,
Don't question why.
It has been ordained,
This is my hour.

End

ABOUT THE AUTHOR

Ernest Barrett was born in Sheffield in 1929.

Spent six and a half years in the RAF.

Moved to Lincolnshire after life changing accident in 1968 at Sheffield Steelworks.

Joined Skegness Writers around 1990 before taking up writing seriously.

13151600R00189

Printed in Great Britain
by Amazon.co.uk, Ltd.,
Marston Gate.